Praise for The Talented Fairy Tales

"The twists and turns come fast and furious in this rapid paced novel... Filled with intrigue and skilled fighting, this fantasy is sure to have hearts pumping and blood racing. The next in this series can't come soon enough!" – *InD'tale Magazine review of Beauty and the Blade*

"Peaky Blinders meets Bridgerton in this lush reimagining of *Beauty and the Beast* with an endearing cast of characters, subtle magic, and a deliciously agonizing slow burn romance. This book was absolutely everything I wanted it to be and more." – *Megan Van Dyke, author of Second Star to the Left*

"Beauty and the Blade by S.C. Grayson entertained me for hours with the perfect combination of fairy-tale and adventure stories." – *Readers' Favorite*

"A fantastic tale with a little magic, fighting, deception, true love, and adventure... this book is incredibly hard to put down with so many laughable lines, and the interactions between Scarlett and Benedict are priceless." – *InD'tale Magazine review of Little Red Shadow*

The Hood and his Thief

S. C. GRAYSON

To Rhys.

The thief of my heart.

Chapter One

Being one of the best pickpockets in London came with certain advantages. For one, Rhosyn was able to easily spot those less practiced at their craft. As her deft eyes swept the street on her normal patrol, they zeroed in on a skinny child bumping into a well-dressed gentleman with a little too much intention. She pulled her standard-issue police baton from her belt and swung it casually in her hand as she veered towards the side of the narrow, cobbled street. Her gaze trained on the urchin darting off toward a shadowed alley, with a prize clutched to his chest.

She intercepted him just before he turned off the main drag, thrusting her baton in his path before he could scamper off into the darkness. He froze in place, gaze trailing up Rhosyn's torso and eyes widening in his dirt-smudged face as he took in the golden buttons and badge emblazoned on her Royal Police uniform.

Before he could turn to run, Rhosyn grabbed him by the kerchief around his neck, not hard enough to jar him, but firmly enough that he couldn't escape. She held out her hand expectantly.

With a degree of wide-eyed innocence that could only be coaxed from a guilty child, he shook his head. "What have I done, ma'am?"

"I'll warrant that watch in your pocket wasn't there when you left home this morning," Rhosyn prodded, propping her free hand on her hip.

With a thick swallow, the urchin reached into his jacket and produced an engraved pocket watch, swinging on a thick golden chain. Rhosyn had half a mind to let him keep the thing, to punish the owner for carrying such an ostentatious accessory through a part of town where every streetcorner was occupied by pickpockets and gangsters, all searching for their next mark.

Instead, she plucked it from his grip and let go. The boy hesitated, clearly wanting to run away, but unsure if it would get him into any more trouble. After all, Rhosyn towered above him, with legs even longer than most of the male police officers, making catching a running youngster all too easy.

"If you look around like you're wondering if you've been spotted, you give yourself away," Rhosyn told the child against her better judgment. "Don't let me catch you again."

He smiled tentatively, the hint of a sparkle in his eyes before turning and disappearing among the shuffle of people in the street. Rhosyn sighed, knowing he was likely to be trouble again, but she didn't have it in her to arrest every person who committed petty theft in the lower city. After all, that would probably be half the populace of the streets she patrolled. She was interested in the more sinister criminals who prowled these blocks, knives up their sleeves and revolvers tucked into their jackets.

A judgmental voice in the back of her mind nagged that she was letting the thieves go because she was one of them. She shoved that voice aside with a practiced hand, and it retreated to the shadowy recesses of her mind with a grumble.

She returned her focus to the task at hand. Rhosyn cut across their street, people giving way for her when they caught sight of her uniform. She stopped before a man smoking a pipe outside of one of the nicer gambling dens in the area.

"I believe you dropped this." She held up the watch, letting it swing on its chain in front of his surprised expression.

Patting his pockets, he found that she was right. "My goodness, I don't know how I could have been so clumsy. Thank you, ma'am."

"Just doing my job." Rhosyn deposited the watch in his outstretched palm. "And keep a wary eye on your purse."

With a brisk nod, she turned and strode up off the street. She swept the area with her gaze constantly as she walked, alert for the trouble that never seemed far away. Many eyes caught hers as she observed, greeting her with a brief nod of familiarity. After several years as a Royal Police officer, the residents of the lower city were familiar with her presence. Many new officers left the lower city beats as soon as they had paid their dues, but Rhosyn had asked Chief Thorne if she could stay on this patrol. As harried as he was in the years since the end of the Inquiries, he hadn't been of a mind to object.

Rhosyn preferred to keep an eye on her old stomping grounds, and if anybody remembered her as the young rascal who ran jobs with the Lions, they had the sense not to say anything. Not to mention, she still felt more at home among the crooked flats and smoky air of the streets here than in the middle city where she now lived. Maybe she always would.

As the sun lowered behind crooked chimneys in the bruised sky, Rhosyn turned her steps uphill, toward the police station at the border of the middle and lower city. The night watch would be heading out and it was time to turn in her report for the day before heading back to her rented room. Her mouth watered at the thought of the scones waiting for her there, carefully wrapped in paper by Gregor and handed to her with a smile when she left the Woodrow's house early that morning.

Before she could contemplate whether she might be able to borrow some jam from the couple she rented from, shouting grabbed her attention. Rhosyn immediately broke into a run, darting into an alley, trying to cut over to the next block where the racket came from.

No sooner had she turned the corner than a solid frame crashed into her, knocking her down with a bone-rattling *thump*. Glaring up, she found a shape dressed in all black, a hood pulled low and obscuring his eyes, another piece of cloth covering his lower face.

"Sorry, ma'am. I'm afraid I have to run," the man said in a light tone, only sounding a little out of breath, despite having been running full tilt just seconds earlier. Before Rhosyn could think to order him to halt, he threw himself at the wall to the right, scaling the uneven bricks with all the ease of a bird taking flight.

Rhosyn sprang to her feet, just in time for two other officers of the Royal Police to materialize at the other end of the alley. Their batons swung in their hands as they huffed and puffed.

"Where'd he go?" one officer wheezed.

"The roof." Rhosyn pointed.

The officers looked up just in time to see the man's coat flaps disappear over the eaves, faces falling in dismay. They turned and retreated back down the alley, apparently planning on pursuing him from the street.

Granted, with how fast the man climbed, the two men would likely lose him faster than a gambler could throw a hand of dice if they tried to follow him across the buildings.

Rhosyn, on the other hand, was far more comfortable among the chimneys and gables of the lower city.

She flung herself up the wall in hot pursuit, using an obliging drainpipe to help her shimmy up the building. She crested the edge, jumping to her feet and looking around. The dark silhouette was already on the next building over, about to leap to a third.

Rhosyn wasted no time in breaking into a sprint. The gap between the first two roofs was narrow enough that she leaped it without having to break her stride. Her long legs carried her swiftly enough that she should gain ground on her quarry.

However, the gap between the next two buildings was larger, almost twice as broad as Rhosyn was tall. The man ran at it full tilt, launching himself into the air and even performing a flip as he arced over the distance, hovering for what seemed to be a moment too long—or maybe that was just the way time stretched in a chase. He landed lightly on the balls of his feet, as if his joints were spring loaded.

Rhosyn didn't have time to gawk as she grit her teeth for her own jump. If she were being judged on style, she certainly would have lost to the pursuant, but she managed to make it over safely, tucking her head in and rolling to absorb the impact as she landed.

Coming to her feet again, she dashed across the slanted rooftop, boots clacking against the chipped shingles. She gained a few meters on the man, but he was deceptively fast for all that he appeared to be a few inches shorter than Rhosyn and much more densely built. Still, he couldn't run forever, and a drop between buildings loomed just ahead.

The hooded man leaped over the edge without hesitation, and without second thought, Rhosyn barreled after him. Her heart stuttered through a moment of free fall before relief restarted it at the top of the adjacent building just a story below.

She landed heavily in a crouch, ready to pounce forward and tackle her target. Instead, her head snapped back, as if somebody grabbed her by her collar.

The hooded man stood a few meters away on the edge of the roof, one arm raised to reveal a small crossbow mounted to his forearm and pointed directly at Rhosyn. He had fired so fast and so sure that she had barely registered the bolt whizzing past her face, piercing through the jacket of her uniform, before embedding in the wood paneling behind her. She yanked on it to no avail, the arrowhead clearly buried deep in the side of the building.

"It's been a while since any of the Royal Police gave me such a good chase, but I'm afraid this is where we part ways." The man lowered his arm.

Rhosyn strained to see under his hood, but he had fastened it well around his face and his features were fully obscured by the shadows of rapidly descending twilight. Instead, she let her eyes rove over his physique, trying to generate as thorough a description of him as she could without seeing his face.

He was clearly athletic, which she could tell from his speed and agility, but the notion was only driven home by his thick, shapely thighs and broad shoulders that tapered to narrower hips. Rhosyn blinked. She would not be writing *shapely thighs* on the report she filed with Chief Thorne under any circumstances.

The hooded man turned away from her as she continued to tug fruitlessly at the bolt pinning her in place. The thin sunlight peaked through the clouds long enough for her to tell that his clothing was actually a dark forest green, instead of the black she had originally thought.

"There's nowhere for you to run," Rhosyn insisted.

Indeed, they had reached the corner of the block, and all the nearest rooftops were far too distant to consider jumping. Crashing and shouting told Rhosyn that the other officers in pursuit had arrived in the street below, blocking him in if he were to climb down.

"Come quietly and I'll put in a good word," Rhosyn offered reasonably, even as she surreptitiously began unbuttoning her jacket under the guise of continuing to struggle. If she could slip out of the garment that kept her trapped, she could tackle the man before he tried to run again.

Instead, he looked over his shoulder, posture casual, as if there were nothing dire about his situation.

"Although this has been fun, I have no interest in being on good terms with the Royal Police."

Pulling free of the jacket, Rhosyn lunged, but her arms closed around open air. The hooded man had leaped into the open space between buildings, arms spread wide as if diving off a cliff into the ocean.

Rhosyn teetered on the ledge, watching in disbelief as he made it a surprising distance into the street, but still nowhere near the building on the far side. As he started to fall, he twisted, grabbing onto a clothesline hung between buildings. With all the skill of an acrobat, he swung around it once, twice—building up momentum before launching himself at the height of his swing. With a light *thunk*, he landed neatly on the far roof.

Rhosyn stared slack-jawed as he had the audacity to look back and offer her a mock salute, before darting off into the rapidly thickening shadows of evening. Jerking herself from her shock, she turned and scrabbled down to the ground as quickly as possible. Dropping from a little too high, her heels hit the cobbles with enough force to rattle her teeth in her skull. Still, she knew the moment she turned to dart across the crowded street that the hooded man would be long gone by the time she managed to scale the next building.

The two officers she had encountered earlier were waiting for her, still staring up at the clothesline above them where moments earlier a man had flown.

"What were you trying to bring him in for?" Rhosyn asked, bringing their attention back to the present. As they lowered their faces to look at her, she cocked her head in curiosity. While their faces were vaguely familiar, she couldn't recall names, and she thought she knew everybody that patrolled the lower city.

"Officer Rhosyn Walsh," she offered.

"Officers Fletcher and Davies," the taller of the two introduced himself and his partner. "Why don't we get back to the station and we can fill you in while you help us file our reports." He looked around pointedly at the crowded streets. Whatever had happened, it wasn't something he wished to be overheard.

Chief Joseph Thorne shuffled through endless stacks of paper, trying to clear enough space on his desk for him to write on and failing. While Rhosyn could tell there was a system to the stacks of reports, the cramped desk in the corner was not nearly large enough to accommodate the amount of work Chief Thorne was burdening it with.

For that matter, Chief Thorne himself didn't seem able to accommodate the amount of work he was trying to complete, if the pallor of his skin and the shadow of a beard that had not been shaved in several days were any indication. Still, he pushed on doggedly, gesturing Rhosyn and the two officers with her to take a seat in the wooden chairs across from him.

The whole setup was rather cramped, shoved into a cordoned-off corner of the Royal Police's headquarters. While there was a perfectly good office down the hall, with more space and a bigger desk, Rhosyn didn't have to wonder why he didn't use it.

The weathered brass plaque on the door to that room still read *Chief Cook,* despite the man's imprisonment years ago. Chief Thorne could easily have his former mentor's name changed out for his own, but Rhosyn got the impression that it was left there as a sort of reminder for all who passed through. After all, the echoes of the corruption bred by Chief Cook's leadership still cropped up every once in a while. The aftereffects of the Inquiries still ruled the city's underworld, and too many of the rich and influential still disagreed with their sudden end, despite the passage of years.

"Officers," Chief Joseph Thorne greeted. "I take it your sitting here means you were unable to apprehend the thief."

"I'm assuming the man you were chasing was the thief?" Rhosyn asked as the other two officers nodded dismally.

"There have been a series of jewel thefts from some of the wealthiest households of the city. We've had shockingly little intel on them, even from our ears in the black market. We finally got an anonymous tip from somebody implicating the man in the hood," Officer Fletcher explained.

"Seems to be causing a lot of trouble for a simple jewel thief. Who is he?" Rhosyn asked. It struck her as odd that such a case would be reported directly to Chief Thorne, but he did have a rather hands-on approach. Rhosyn got the impression he liked to have his fingers in every investigation, to prevent something like the sloppy case that allowed Chief Cook to get away with the murder of his wife.

Chief Thorne scrubbed a hand over his face. "He certainly has picked targets that have made my life difficult. Several of the houses that were broken into belong to those who have sponsored Talented. Given that they have spent a substantial amount of money helping us give the Talented of the lower city another chance, I would prefer not to seem incompetent at catching a petty thief."

"Which is why it is unfortunate that we still don't know who he is. Our informant only gave us a tip on his location," Officer Davies commiserated.

"Perhaps your encounter with him today can help us identify him. With a detailed description, you could use your connections in the lower city to see if anybody has noticed him around," Chief Thorne gestured to Rhosyn, who shook her head.

"He wore a hood and mask over his face. I can give you a general description, but not enough to get a solid identification on him," Rhosyn explained.

The expression on Chief Thorne's face seemed to indicate that he would be banging his head against the solid wooden surface of his desk if it wouldn't be deemed unprofessional. "Well, write up everything you saw and add it to Fletcher and Davies' report. Every little bit of information helps."

"Do you want me to join them in the search?" Rhosyn offered. "I might be able to recognize his voice or movements if we encounter him."

The man had displayed a certain grace in his movements that Rhosyn wasn't sure she would be able to put into words for an official description. She had the distinct impression she would recognize it if she encountered it again, though.

"No." Chief Thorne waved Rhosyn's offer away. "I have a different job I need you to focus on. Fletcher, Davies, go start your report while I finish here with Walsh."

The other officers shuffled from the corner and off to their desks. Rhosyn furrowed her brow at Chief Thorne, wondering what could be so important. To her knowledge, the lower city had been as peaceful as it ever was. Her regular watches kept her fingers on the pulse of the lower city, and she had not noticed the undercurrents of impending trouble. While turf wars between gangs were inevitable, and every so often skirmishes and crooked dealings ignited into full-fledged violence, there had been nothing as sinister as the Wolves' illicit fighting rings in several years.

"I need your help gathering intel on a gang," Chief Thorne admitted. He pulled out a thin stack of papers from a pile and held them out to you. "The Foxes."

"The Foxes?" Rhosyn frowned at the few sheets of paper in front of her, a handful of very sparse reports. "They must be new. Or at least they weren't around when—before I joined the Royal Police."

Rhosyn corrected herself out of habit. Chief Thorne certainly knew Rhosyn had formerly been a member of the Lions, and a key member at that. After all, he had met and recruited her after his best friend married the leader of the Lions and the gang formally dissolved. Rhosyn had jumped on the opportunity for a new purpose, with her role as the Lions' den mother ripped out from under her. Still, Chief Thorne and Rhosyn had an unspoken rule about keeping police business official, and only mentioning the murkier aspects of her past when in the Woodrow's home.

"They've only just started cropping up, but for several weeks there have been skirmishes and thefts that we haven't been able to track back to any known gangs. If they are responsible for even half of those, then they are worryingly active for a new organization," Chief Thorne explained.

"There's not much to go off of," Rhosyn pointed out as she skimmed the reports in her hand. A few overheard conversations from their moles in the Raptors and Rattlesnakes comprised most of the information before her.

"That's why I'm asking you." Chief Thorne lowered his chin, looking at her meaningfully. "The people of the lower city have been oddly quiet about this new group, when normally gossip isn't hard to come by. They trust you though, and you might be able to find something others can't. I trust you can take advantage of...discreet sources."

Rhosyn raised a single brow. That was as close as Chief Thorne came to suggesting Rhosyn use her connections to former Lions to gather information. He must know that he himself could ask Kristoff for help if he ever wanted to do some investigating in a less than official capacity. In this delicate dance, though, he preferred to have a degree of separation—even if Chief Thorne often brushed shoulders with Kristoff with friendly familiarity at the Woodrow's dinner parties.

Paper crinkled as Rhosyn's fingers tightened around the reports. Try as she might to help London in the best way she could think of—protecting the lower city on the right side of the law—Chief Thorne still saw her as the officer to turn to when he needed somebody to brush elbows with residents of London's underbelly.

She forced her grip to relax. This is what she had signed up for, and she had done her job well for years now.

"I'll see what I can do," Rhosyn assured him, tucking the reports into the front of her jacket, retrieved from the roof where it had been pinned before she returned to headquarters. The bolt in the pocket would go with Davies and Fletcher's report to help them track down the hooded jewel thief.

"First, fill out your report and then get some rest. We have a social obligation tomorrow." Chief Thorne made a face of distaste at the reminder.

Rhosyn nearly chuckled at his reaction to the thought of leisure. He was almost as bad as Nate, burning the candle at both ends. Then again, Rhosyn wasn't really in a position to judge.

"You're coming with the Woodrows to the ball at the palace tomorrow?" she asked.

"Unfortunately, making sure the public sees the crown and the Royal Police as a united front is as much a part of the job as actually policing the streets," Chief Thorne sighed. "I guess I'll just have to get as much of tomorrow's work done tonight as I can."

As Rhosyn headed to join Davies and Fletcher, Chief Thorne was already absorbed in reading a paper on his desk, chewing his bottom lip as he frowned at it. She did not envy him.

The creak of Rhosyn's boots on the stairs echoed deafeningly through the quiet house, no matter how lightly she tried to creep. The home in the middle city belonged to two former Lions who had gotten married after the Inquiries, acquiring jobs as a butcher and a seamstress. Not having children of their own yet, they were more than happy to rent a spare room to Rhosyn, having spent their youth running jobs with her.

As Rhosyn passed their bedroom, she paused for a moment, only hearing the deep, measured breathing of people resting peacefully. Sometimes, as she passed them on the stairs in the morning, she considered asking them how they slept so soundly in the quiet, after years of living in crowded safehouses with constant comings and goings—Lions gambling and laughing through all hours of the night.

Shutting the door to her own bedroom, Rhosyn looked around the small space with a sigh. The bed was nicer than any she had slept on in the Lions' Den, the mattress plush and an embroidered quilt to keep her warm even on the coldest of winter nights. As she toed off her boots, she frowned at the empty space.

After years with the Royal Police, she had hoped she'd adjust to the luxuries of a comfortable bed and a room with a door she could lock. Instead, she looked forward to another night of awakening every hour to a phantom cry of a child having a nightmare, only to realize she was no longer responsible for a pack of youngsters. It was still odd to awaken alone in her bed every morning instead of finding a child, usually one freshly rescued from the cruelty of a factory, tucked into her arms, having climbed in to join her as she slept.

As she changed into her sleeping clothes, she chuckled at the irony. For years, she sat on the rooftop of the reclaimed warehouse she and the youngest Lions called home, wondering what it would look like to be free of the responsibility of being a universal big sister to all those Nate and his associates tried to give a better life.

Instead of freedom, the lifting of that burden only made her feel untethered.

Rhosyn splashed water from the bowl on the washstand onto her face, chiding herself for being dramatic. She just wasn't used to the quiet of the middle city at night and was restless after too many weeks of poor sleep.

Maybe she would ask Chief Thorne to let her switch back to nighttime patrols, so she could sleep during the day, soothed by the backdrop of city traffic. After she gathered the information she needed on the Foxes, she would do just that.

Chapter Two

R hosyn grappled with the urge to twirl continuously just to watch her skirts swirl around her. Instead, she settled for a playful sway as she waited, just for the joy of feeling their fullness swish back and forth.

As much as Contessa sometimes grumbled about the impracticality of her wardrobe when trying to get something done, she still held herself elegantly, as if she were born to it. Rhosyn on the other hand, felt rather like she was wearing a costume every time she ventured into polite society, but she let herself enjoy the frivolous novelty.

"You look colorful," Contessa greeted as she walked down the stairs of her home to the front hall where Rhosyn waited.

Rhosyn held up her arms and twisted this way and that, so her friend might fully admire the vivid orchid of her dress. "My hair makes me bright enough anyway, there's no point in trying to blend in."

While Contessa's lady's maid, Julia, had tamed Rhosyn's coppery red hair admirably before scurrying upstairs to help her mistress, it still had an air of wildness about it that could not be smoothed. Julia, thankfully, had practiced doing Rhosyn's hair many times, when she was dreaming of a life as a lady's maid as a young Lion living in the Den. She knew it was better to work with Rhosyn's riotous ringlets, letting the stray curls frame her face instead of pinning them into oblivion and ending up like a rat's nest.

"I have to admit, I like the bright colors better when every available inch isn't covered in frills and bows. The dress suits you well," Contessa complimented as she reached Rhosyn.

She herself was in her customary gunmetal gray silk, and while Rhosyn would have felt silly in something with an air of such understated elegance, it suited Contessa perfectly. Instead of washing her out, the sedate color complimented her pale complexion and silvery hair, the exact opposite of Rhosyn's, as it easily smoothed into a silken twist. Her icy eyes matched the dress nearly perfectly. If Rhosyn hadn't spent several months years ago dumping Contessa on her ass and watching her reddened, sweaty face twist in frustration, she might even find her beauty cold.

Now, Rhosyn grinned wryly, and her friend smiled back.

A familiar stomping interrupted them as Nate marched into the hall. "Ready, ladies?"

"Watch who you're calling a lady," Rhosyn shot back, even as Nate behaved like a perfect gentleman and offered his elbow to his wife, who grasped it delicately with her gloved hand.

Nate shot Rhosyn a look as he donned his top hat, indicating he would ruffle her hair if it wasn't clear how much effort had gone into it, and the trio headed out to the carriage. The Woodrow's manservant, Gregor, already had it out front, waiting to take them to the palace for the night's festivities.

"What about the others?" Rhosyn asked as the carriage began trundling across the cobbled streets, slowly climbing towards the palace at the top of the hill.

"The Pearces are taking their own carriage, and Joseph sent a runner to tell me he would be making his own way to the palace tonight, since he was coming directly from headquarters," Contessa explained.

Rhosyn nodded. Even though the Lions were not what they once were, back when the name and membership in the gang alone was enough to grant you a modicum of protection in the lower city, they existed in a different capacity now. The Woodrows, along with Kristoff, Gregor, and Rhosyn, stayed true to the purpose of helping the Talented in London, albeit in somewhat less illicit capacities. The Pearces, Benedict and Scarlett, had joined their band a few years ago after helping dismantle the underground Talented fighting rings. As much as Chief Thorne—Joseph—was part of their group too, he was unlikely to admit it out loud.

"Well, thank you for bringing me along," Rhosyn said earnestly. "I know this is a bigger imposition than bringing me to the odd party and implying that I'm one of Nate's distant relatives."

"It's not an imposition if you're here on business," Nate pointed out. "Contessa and King Byron want to put a good face on both sponsorships for the Talented and the Royal Police's continued loyalty to the Crown. It's why, on nights like tonight, he has his other security relieve me of my bodyguarding duties, so I can be paraded around like a rehabilitation success story."

Nate's tone held wry amusement, as if the thought of the former Beast being an exemplar of anything for the crown was an amusing joke, but he took it in stride.

When they arrived at the palace, Rhosyn had to focus to keep her mouth from hanging open as she took in the sights. Servants led them into the garden where the soiree was to be held, decorated with enough lanterns to send the Woodrow's sizable house up in flames. It gave the whole thing a dreamlike quality, enhancing the elegance of the socialites already milling about in pools and eddies of luxurious fabrics. The moment they entered the crowd, Contessa and Nate were whisked away into the conniving grasps of those who wished to gain an advantage by ingratiating themselves with the King's bodyguard and trusted advisor.

In a matter of moments, Rhosyn found herself alone at the fringes of the party, spending most of her effort on appearing like she belonged, and most likely only drawing attention to her lack of proper poise in the process.

Rhosyn tugged at her dress, suddenly conscious of the way it hung on her and the tightness where it clung to her waist and dipped low at the neck. As much as she loved it, she almost regretted her bold color choice as she found herself dressed in the most eye-catching shade in the vicinity. She attempted to brush off the thought, squaring her shoulders and not thinking about the way it caused her bodice to pull dangerously low. It always amused Rhosyn that Contessa continued to wear an expression like she was doing something forbidden every time she donned pants when she showed this much of her décolleté on a daily basis.

A playful elbow in her side distracted Rhosyn from her worries about her presence among such elegant company. Rhosyn looked down to see Scarlett Pearce at her side. At this point, it didn't surprise her that the woman could sneak up on her, as Rhosyn was convinced Scarlett was half a shadow herself.

Scarlett looked pointedly at Rhosyn's hands, which were fisted in the fabric of her skirt, sure to leave wrinkles. She uncurled her fingers with effort, intentionally pressing them flat on her lower bodice so they wouldn't misbehave.

"I still feel a little out of place at functions like this, as much as I work with the King these days," Scarlett confided quietly, clearly having sensed Rhosyn's moment of discomfort.

"At least you have a suitable dance partner to make sure you don't end up standing in a corner completely out of place," Rhosyn pointed out, just as the man in question, Scarlett's husband Benedict, stepped up behind them.

"And what a wonderful dancer he is," Benedict joined into the conversation seamlessly. Scarlett smiled up at him fondly, and he smoothed her chin length hair back, as if he would tuck it behind her ear if it weren't on the side where the side of Scarlett's head bore nothing but scar tissue after a run in with a stray bullet.

"If a dance partner is what you need, I might just be able to help," an unfamiliar voice joined the conversation.

Rhosyn turned to find an unknown man, although she didn't know how her eyes hadn't jumped to him the moment she entered the party. After all, how could one consider looking away from someone so ostentatiously dressed, yet disarmingly handsome?

A jade-green waistcoat, nipped in tightly around his waist, accentuated his athletic figure as much as the matching color of his mischievous eyes. A metallic gold vest and cravat, along with canary-yellow pants should have clashed, but the casual pose and crooked smile he wore transformed the look from obnoxious to endearingly eccentric.

Rhosyn blinked. The whole effect was remarkably charming, but it struck her that was exactly what the man was aiming for—like he had modeled himself after a character in one of Contessa's books and not a real person.

"I don't believe we've been introduced," the man prompted, drawing Rhosyn from what she realized had been an embarrassingly long perusal.

"Allow me," Benedict chimed in. "Mr. Ansel Blakely, this is Ms. Rhosyn Walsh. Rhosyn, I had the pleasure of making Mr. Blakely's acquaintance on my unsuccessful quest to fetch my wife some lemonade."

Mr. Blakely inclined his head politely, although his gaze remained trained on Rhosyn's face. The lantern-light flickered over his hair with the movement, revealing a single streak of silver running through his otherwise dark hair near his temple, although he couldn't be much older than her.

Rhosyn gave a small bow in return, before realizing a curtsy would be more appropriate for the occasion and her dress. She smiled ruefully at her new acquaintance and tried not to think about how bending over probably afforded him a view straight down her bodice. To his credit, his polished smile did not slip an inch.

"Well then, Ms. Walsh, I'd be happy to save you from...how did you put it? Ah—standing in the corner completely out of place." Mr. Blakely offered his hand.

Rhosyn took it without hesitation, although she looked over her shoulder as her new partner led her onto the dance floor. Benedict waved her on encouragingly, while Scarlett bit her lips in contained amusement.

Mr. Blakely swept her into his arms as the musicians started a new song, and Rhosyn's hands automatically rose to the appropriate position at his shoulders, thanks to the begrudging afternoons of dance lessons with Contessa on the days when Rhosyn could see that knife fighting practice would frustrate her more than it would help. While Contessa argued that she was not coordinated enough on the dance floor to be a good teacher, those afternoons had led to a surprising amount of giggling as they both attempted to follow, neither familiar with leading. Rhosyn picked up dancing faster than Contessa had picked up fighting, finding that they weren't really that different.

However, afternoons stumbling around the parlor with her friend had not prepared her fully for the intricacies of dancing as a social pursuit. Rhosyn had no idea if she should talk or smile or simply school her expression into one of pleasant vacancy. She didn't have nearly the skill for vapid beauty as those raised in high society, taught to keep their opinions hidden behind bland smiles.

As Mr. Blakely's fingers curled around her waist and the heat of his touch seeped through the delicate material of her gown, Rhosyn decided conversation was a must—something to distract from the unfamiliar fluttering beneath her sternum.

"I have to thank you for saving me from my evening of standing in the corner," she ventured. "My height tends to scare away many men."

"Well, that's foolish. A skilled partner can handle any amount of woman." Mr. Blakely demonstrated the truth of his statement by guiding Rhosyn into a slight dip, despite the top of his head being level with Rhosyn's eyeline.

His hand spread across her lower back as he did so, pressing her to him.

Rhosyn swallowed to combat the sudden dryness in her mouth. "Even if the woman is a woefully inexperienced dancer herself? I must admit, I don't come to these parties often."

"And what could possibly be keeping a lovely lady like yourself at home when there is revelry to be had?" Mr. Blakely asked.

"I'm not really a lady," Rhosyn admitted. "I'm an officer for the Royal Police, but I'm fortunate in my friends."

Something sparked in Mr. Blakely's eyes. It wasn't the disapproval that Rhosyn had come to expect from the admission, but she couldn't place the expression.

"I'm glad you chose to come out tonight, then, because I hear the entertainment is supposed to be incredible." Mr. Blakely's smile was mischievous as he nodded to a stage erected at the far end of the garden. Currently, scarlet drapes hid it from view.

"What is the entertainment?"

Just as Rhosyn asked, the song ended. Mr. Blakely stepped back. "You'll have to wait and see."

The sparkle in his eye as he bowed caught Rhosyn's attention, as the glimmer seemed to come from behind the poreless mask of proper manners. She wondered what else he might keep behind the glass.

Before Rhosyn could think of an argument to persuade him to tell her about the expected show, for she was not known for her patience in waiting for surprises, Mr. Blakely had turned away and melted into the crowd of dispersing dancers. Rhosyn's gaze tracked his receding back, but he was swallowed by the milling partygoers despite the vibrancy of his attire.

Rhosyn blew one of the curls that had fallen into her face aside with a disappointed huff, turning toward the edge of the dance floor where she was sure to wait for the rest of the evening. The three men she knew in attendance who were taller than her were unlikely to take to the floor with her. Benedict liked to dance, but threw propriety to the wind and insisted on stepping out with Scarlett for every single song at most balls. Nate refused to dance on principle and would spend the entire evening hovering over Contessa's shoulder as she constantly elbowed him to stop glaring.

Chief Thorne wouldn't be seen dancing with one of his own officers, determined to keep his professional reputation as spotless as could be. However, Rhosyn had noted with interest that he had taken Benedict's sister, Lottie, for several turns at the last few parties they attended. She hoped he would do so again tonight, as he always seemed a little less exhausted after a dance with the statuesque blonde.

Rhosyn edged her way to the table of lemonade, determined to at least enjoy some refreshments when Joseph intercepted her, apparently not dancing yet, taking her by the elbow.

"I have somebody for you to meet," he said, guiding her away from the lemonade. Rhosyn looked longingly after it as she followed, already sweating in the layers of her dress and her mouth watering at the thought of the cold liquid. Still, she dutifully followed her Chief.

"Who would you have me charm with my less-than-ideal manners?" Rhosyn asked.

"Mr. Gower. He's one of the biggest supporters of the Talented in society at the moment. He's already sponsored about a dozen of them, including Paul and Olivia."

Rhosyn's eyebrows rose in interest. After Scarlett had brought to the crown's attention the difficulties of Talented criminals reintegrating into society, Contessa had the inspired idea to encourage noble households to sponsor them. The socialites would pay the expenses of their pardon with the crown and give them a position in their household where their Talents might be put to use doing honest work.

Very few socialites had taken the bait in the first few years, but after Contessa mentioned that the Woodrow's famously beautiful rose bushes were the result of their gardener, Gregor's Talent, a few wealthy citizens had chanced to sponsor one or two Talented. After all, there was certainly no harm in hiring a coachman who was so uncannily good with the horses it was as if he could talk to them, or a seamstress who could tailor a dress perfectly without even looking at a measuring tape.

It was an imperfect system, leaving out those with more intimidating Talents, like Scarlett, but it was a start. One household sponsoring a dozen Talented was unheard of, though, and a costly proposition.

Joseph stopped in front of a large man with the most impressive mustache Rhosyn had ever laid eyes on. Bowing beside her, Joseph surreptitiously stepped on Rhosyn's toes, startling her into a less-than graceful curtsy of her own. Still, it was with great effort that Rhosyn ripped her eyes away from the silver facial hair, polished and shaped so long that it nearly stuck out past the man's ears.

"Mr. Gower, allow me to introduce Officer Rhosyn Walsh of the Royal Police," Joseph introduced as they both stood up straight once more. "As one of our most experienced officers in the lower city, she sees the benefits of your generosity firsthand."

Rhosyn smiled politely as Mr. Gower's eye swept up and down her form. The smug superiority of his gaze rubbed icily against her skin, and Rhosyn had the sudden urge to point out that it would take more than offering better lives to twelve Talented to undo the harms of the Inquiries to the lower city. She swallowed down the barb, surprised at the sudden ferocity of the thought, and smiled wider instead. After all, Mr. Gower was setting an example, which they hoped more socialites at this ball would follow.

"I hear you've sponsored young Paul and Olivia," Rhosyn said. "They're wonderful children. I doubt you'll regret it."

"You know them well?" Mr. Gower's eyes narrowed and Rhosyn swallowed, sensing it was unwise to admit that they had lived under her care as young Lions at the Den. It was there that Paul's Talent for lulling people into deep sleep with his voice, and Olivia's for lighting fires with a clap of her hands, sprung to life—back when an obvious Talent like that could easily lead to a short drop from the end of a noose.

"I met them when they were quite young," Rhosyn hedged. "I'm glad to hear they are doing well."

Mr. Gower nodded. "Having so many Talented working in one household can be challenging, but I manage to keep them in line. I'm sure my newest additions' abilities will be a valuable asset."

Rhosyn bit her lip to keep from frowning, hiding the expression by looking down and smoothing her skirts—a gesture she had learned from Contessa. She couldn't let the way the man's words rankled show. For him, the Talented sponsorships were an investment—one that the lower city sorely needed.

"I do hope they turn out to be trustworthy," Mr. Gower barreled on, seemingly oblivious to Rhosyn biting the inside of her cheek. "I'm afraid I don't know who to trust in my own household these days."

Joseph made a face that spoke to holding back a long-suffering sigh. "I assure you, Mr. Gower, the Royal Police are doing all we can to apprehend the thief of your wife's jewels and return them to you. It is unlikely to be a member of your staff, considering there have been a rash of these thefts across the upper city."

"You better be right, Chief Thorne." Mr. Gower's mustache bristled. "I'm supporting the Royal Police's efforts by sponsoring these Talented, and it disappoints me to hear that you are still struggling to do your job."

Joseph reddened, and not for the first time, Rhosyn offered silent thanks for being a patrolling officer and not the Chief. After all, it wouldn't be very fitting for the figurehead of the Royal Police to punch an innocent citizen in the gut for being an arrogant prick.

Thankfully, Rhosyn was distracted from the itching in her fists and the strange urge to unearth her trusty brass knuckles by a ripple of excited chattering through the crowd.

"Ladies and gentlemen!" A familiar voice boomed through the garden from the direction of the stage. Rhosyn turned to find a green and gold clad figure standing on the edge of the stage, just in front of the crimson drapes.

"Allow me to introduce myself. I am Mr. Blakely, and it is my absolute privilege to have been invited here alongside my little troupe by His Royal Highness, King Byron, for your entertainment."

A tittering ran through the crowd at the promise in Mr. Blakely's voice, and Rhosyn found herself drifting forward, away from her interrupted conversation, to get a better view of the stage. No wonder her dance partner had been so complimentary of the night's festivities. He had supplied them.

"Tonight, I have the pleasure of introducing the acrobats from Archer's Traveling Circus. Please give a warm welcome to the Merry Men!" With an exaggerated flourish, Mr. Blakely stepped aside as the curtain split in the middle to reveal the scene on the stage.

A gasp escaped Rhosyn at the sight of platforms elevated at a dizzying height above the stage, connected by a series of tightropes and swinging trapeze bars. Six men perched on the elevated platforms, and one of them raised a hand in a confident wave.

Then, he jumped.

Rhosyn's heart hammered in borrowed fear, but he easily caught one of the trapezes, using his momentum to swing, then letting go and performing an elegant flip before grabbing onto the next one.

One by one, each of the men jumped into the fray, weaving between each other in a dizzying choreography of gravity-defying daring. One man levered himself until he was hanging from the swaying bar by his knees and reached downwards so another performer could grab his hands as he flew through the air.

A third stepped onto the tightrope as Rhosyn looked on in awe. Before she could reason that perhaps she, too, might be able to walk on a rope—how different could it be from running across a peaked rooftop?—the acrobat dashed the thought by kicking up into a perfect handstand, still balanced on the rope, but now upside down.

At that point, Rhosyn gave up on making sense of how such a performance was possible and just enjoyed the spectacle. The acrobats flipped and flew, streaks of green swooping across the stage and launching themselves into inconceivable flips. Every time they plummeted towards the earth, Rhosyn's breath caught, sure that this time they would fall, but they caught the next bar in the nick of time.

Rhosyn clapped her hands in delight as they soared higher and higher. One of the performers launched himself off a swinging rope, executing a neat flip before sticking the landing on the elevated platform where he had started. As he did, the vision of the hooded man, whom Fletcher and Davies had dubbed "The Hood", swinging from the clothesline flashed through her mind.

She narrowed her eyes at the performers, but none of them were the right build. Most were long and lithe, slim legs and wiry muscles affording them the mobility to twist quickly in midair. None had the broad shoulders and powerful thighs she remembered all too distinctly on the criminal. Not to mention they were missing...something—the odd hovering in midair before gravity took hold. She shook her head, chiding herself for dramatizing the Hood's skills just because he had managed to slip away.

As the performers landed on their platforms and took a bow, Rhosyn was so busy joining in with the thunderous applause that she almost missed a sudden flurry of movement from the side of the garden. Her hands froze mid clap as her eyes zeroed in on a member of the King's guard pushing through the crowd to where Contessa and Nate mingled. No sooner had he leaned in to whisper something in Nate's ear than the trio began all but sprinting towards the palace.

Rhosyn turned away from the stage and pushed through the crowd, shoulder bumping into Mr. Gower's and making him splash brandy onto his expensive looking waistcoat. He sputtered in indignation, but Rhosyn paid him no mind, hurrying to intercept her friends. If there was trouble afoot, then that's where Rhosyn belonged.

She reached them as they entered the palace, turning to head into the bowels where the walls were adorned with less decoration and the corridors seemed slightly narrower. Rhosyn quickly overtook Contessa, who made slower progress with her shorter legs, to jog alongside Nate.

Before she could ask what had happened, Nate and the other King's guard turned abruptly off the main hall. They stopped suddenly in a doorway, faced with the carnage of what appeared to be an office. Papers lay strewn everywhere, drawers pulled from the desk and cast on the floor, cabinets on the walls left hanging open as if somebody dug through them unceremoniously and emptied their contents on the ground.

A sharp gasp behind Rhosyn signaled Contessa's arrival.

"My office!"

Contessa pushed between the trio standing motionless in the entry, but Nate's hand shot out to grab her wrist before Contessa could make it to the desk. She looked up at him and furrowed her brow at her husband, but she shook her head gently.

"We're not in any danger," she assured.

At this, Nate nodded and let go of her wrist. Her skirts puddled around her as she crouched to the ground to look at the papers littering the floor, gathering them up into a stack.

Rhosyn stepped further into the room, eyes darting around to carefully catalogue anything that might be evidence of how somebody had gotten into the office of the King's advisor, and who it might have been. However, she breathed easier at Contessa's assurance that they weren't in danger, and if Nate agreed with her, then it must be true.

After all, Contessa's Talent for sensing peril had only become more precise over the years, and with Nate's Talent being so attuned to Contessa's feelings, he would know if his wife's mental alarm bells were ringing in the slightest.

As Contessa continued to shuffle through papers, Nate grumbled orders to Rhosyn and the King's guard to watch over her before hurrying out the door. While he technically wasn't on duty bodyguarding the King tonight, the office might not be the only target if somebody broke into the palace.

Rhosyn nodded, reaching into the front of her dress to produce a short, but still quite sharp, knife. The King's Guard frowned at it, clearly concerned that a guest had been able to bring such a weapon to a celebration when His Royal Highness was in attendance. Rhosyn resisted the urge to roll her eyes. She knew as well as anybody that one didn't need a weapon if they were intent on doing some serious damage.

"It's fine, I'm an officer of the Royal Police," Rhosyn offered by way of explanation instead, which seemed to placate the guard. "Contessa, keep track of anything you think might be missing."

Contessa nodded, eyes already narrowed in on each report she rifled through, her steel trap of a mind likely cataloging each and every one. Stepping around the desk, Rhosyn headed toward the window on the far wall to inspect it for any sign of forced entry. Before she could reach it, she paused with a frown. While all the cabinets lining the walls of the office hung open, contents in some degree of disarray, the one in the far corner remained tightly closed, seemingly untouched. Rhosyn edged closer to it, seeing that no lock kept the handles closed.

She looked back at Contessa as she approached it, but the woman remained on the ground, seemingly unperturbed by any mental signs of danger. The King's Guard had stationed himself in the doorway.

Tightening her grip on her knife, Rhosyn reached for the handle of the closed cabinet, curious why this one had escaped the intruder's ire.

The door nearly smacked Rhosyn in the face as it smashed open, a slight figure springing forth from the enclosed space. In her effort to avoid having her nose broken by the swinging wood panel, Rhosyn jumped aside, giving the hidden occupant just enough room to slip past her.

With a crash, the thief leaped through the window, shards of glass exploding outward as they avoided the guard in the doorway. Shouting erupted behind Rhosyn, but she had already leaped into pursuit. She threw her arms up to protect her face from any errant glass as she followed her quarry out the window.

A tearing sound and a tug at her waist told Rhosyn her skirts had caught at the jagged edges clinging to the window frame, but she paid them no mind as she pounded through the courtyard. The shadowed figure had gained the slightest lead in Rhosyn's moment of frozen surprise. Now, they turned out toward the gardens and the surrounding buildings.

Rhosyn's long strides ate up the ground between them, but her legs tangled up in her now tattered skirts. With a huff of annoyance, she hoisted them out of her way as much as she could without slowing her pace.

In the moment it took her to slow, the thief turned abruptly, crashing through the doors to one of the outbuildings. Rhosyn hurtled through after them and nearly pulled up short at the cacophony of color that greeted her within.

"Stop them!" Rhosyn shouted into the crowded room, the words nearly swallowed by the hubbub.

The thief was already bobbing and weaving between brightly dressed figures in all manner of curious ensembles. Rhosyn tried to follow, but found herself slowed considerably by trunks and boxes, as well as the crowded nature of the room. She frowned at the people around her as glimpses of her quarry in the distance became less frequent.

Finally, breaking free of the crowd, she dashed out the back exit the thief must have taken, only to barrel headfirst into a familiar figure.

"Rhosyn," Chief Thorne exclaimed as he righted himself.

"Did you see where they went?" Rhosyn panted without preamble.

He frowned at her. "Nobody came out this door. I was just coming in to sweep the outbuildings after Nate told me what happened."

Rhosyn spun on her heel, staring back into the crowded room and blinking in confusion at the sight that greeted her. Now that she wasn't running, she recognized the strange outfits as costumes of performers. A nearby woman in a short, frilled skirt held the type of clubs used for juggling while a man wore the outfit she remembered on the acrobats, what seemed like hours ago.

This was where the circus was preparing for their performances.

"I was chasing the thief. They disappeared when I followed them in here," Rhosyn explained.

"Then we better start searching," Joseph ordered grimly.

Together, they swept through the open space, Rhosyn keeping a keen eye out for anybody in plain, dark clothing. To her dismay, everywhere she looked was a performer dressed more flamboyantly than the last. They all moved aside easily, letting her search, even opening the larger trunks for her, in case the burglar had attempted to hide again.

A few King's Guards joined them after several minutes, but by then Rhosyn knew the trail was lost. The thief must have doubled back and slipped out the front entrance when she ran into Joseph. She asked the circus performers if they had seen where they went, but they all shook their heads earnestly, citing that it had all happened so fast.

The guards moved on to continue sweeping the area, but the thief would likely be long gone by now. Rhosyn trudged back to Contessa's office, this time with Joseph, failure weighing heavy on her heart.

"I could have caught them if not for this damn dress," she grumbled, only for it to turn into a grimace as she looked down at the now ruined garment. With the way the skirts were torn, she was showing a near indecent amount of ankle and calf, but Joseph had the civility not to comment on that.

"You weren't expecting to be in a chase tonight," Joseph offered, his tone clearly attempting to be reassuring, but coming out more tired than anything.

Rhosyn's upper lip curled in a snarl of frustration. This was the second criminal in as many days she had failed to apprehend, this one caught sneaking around the palace, no less. Some credit to the Royal Police she was.

They entered Contessa's office to find her deep in muttered conversation with Nate. They both looked up hopefully when Rhosyn and Joseph entered, only to frown at their clear expressions of disappointment.

"Do you know what they took?" Joseph asked.

"From what I can tell, there is just one stack of papers missing," Contessa admitted with a grim look. "I can't seem to find any of my records on the sponsored Talented."

A muscle in Joseph's jaw ticked and he scrubbed a hand over his face. "Why would somebody want those?"

"I don't know, but I doubt it will be good," Nate grumbled.

"Will the King's Guard need help investigating?" Rhosyn asked. "I could—"

"You already have a case that I need you to focus on," Joseph reminded her sharply but not unkindly. "You can just give me your description of the thief and then rejoin the festivities."

Rhosyn sighed, looking down at the wrinkled tatters of her dress. She wasn't likely to get the good kind of attention dressed like this, and certainly wouldn't be putting forth a good face for the Royal Police.

It was too bad, really. She would have enjoyed seeing the rest of the Circus's performance. She wouldn't have minded another dance with Mr. Blakely either.

Chapter Three

Rhosyn was never more grateful for pants than when she had spent the prior night traipsing around in a skirt. She bounced down the cobblestone street of the lower city feeling herself again and ready for a more successful day. The Foxes wouldn't escape her like her last two targets.

The warm, spiced scent of roast meat filled the air and Rhosyn paused, nose turned up. Looking around, she located the source of the smell as Mrs. Landon's cart, selling meat pies just across the street. Rhosyn bobbed among the busy traffic to reach it, hand already digging into her purse, her mouth watering at the prospect of a heartier breakfast than the sip of tea and stolen bit of toast she had grabbed from the kitchen as she ran out the door.

Mrs. Landon's pies were a fixture of the lower city and a favorite of Rhosyn's, although when she was younger, she could only stare at them longingly. Instead, she had pinched her pennies, saving every spare coin for secondhand clothing and toys for the young Lions in her charge.

Now, very occasionally, she would treat herself to a Cornish pasty when she passed by. Today, she had an extra incentive to part with the small amount of coins she carried with her.

Once Mrs. Landon had deposited two pies into Rhosyn's waiting hands, she turned and strolled towards the street where Granny's haunt was located. Given that Granny's was a safe haven for many lower city children, she was sure to find what she was looking for there.

Warmth seeped through the paper wrappings to Rhosyn's hands as she walked, and she resisted ripping into it to get the meal beneath. Finally, she found what she was looking for. Outside of one of the dingy shops on the street stood a familiar urchin, sweeping the front stoop with a ragged broom. She didn't know his name, but she walked these streets often enough to recognize his round face and the too long bangs that fell into his eyes.

Rhosyn approached slowly, twisting her baton to the back of her belt so she didn't approach the child weapon first. He looked up as she approached, but when he started to draw back into the shop, Rhosyn gave her friendliest smile—the one she had reserved for the most skittish of Lion cubs in her care.

He paused.

"What are you up to?" she asked.

"Not stealing," the boy answered automatically.

Rhosyn chuckled easily. "I wouldn't think so, unless you're stealing that broom."

That coaxed a smile from the boy.

"I've seen you around here before haven't I...."

"Bruce," he offered.

"Bruce," Rhosyn repeated with a genuine smile.

"You might've," Bruce admitted. "I help Mr. Corvey at his shop for some extra coin." He jerked his head towards the shop behind him.

"You look like you're working hard," Rhosyn observed. "You must be hungry. Mrs. Landon gave me an extra meat pie. Do you want to sit with me for a minute and eat it?"

Bruce's gaze darted back and forth from the brown paper packets in Rhosyn's hands to the shop door, clearly fighting a losing battle between hunger and responsibility.

"I won't let Mr. Corvey get you in trouble," Rhosyn assured. "It'll just be a minute."

As soon as they were both seated on the stoop, Bruce tore into the offered pasty, biting into it with the ferocity of a rabid dog. Rhosyn set to hers at a more restrained pace, but not by much.

Rhosyn swallowed as Bruce chewed a particularly large mouthful. She used the opportunity to ask, "So I hear there's a new big gang in town?"

Bruce's gaze narrowed in suspicion, but Rhosyn just took another bite of her pasty. She used the back of her hand to wipe the flaky bits of pastry from her lips, making a point not to use her better manners.

Bruce shrugged. "Maybe, but I don't know much."

"Really?" Rhosyn snorted. "Even I've heard about the Foxes. The others at Granny's must be talking."

"I don't know any runners for them or anything, honest." Bruce talked around a large mouthful of spiced meat. "But some of my friends did just get work with Mr. Barrett. Seems he's got more to sell these days."

Rhosyn nodded to herself. Mr. Barrett was a well-known fence in the lower city. If the Foxes were supplying him, then he would be able to give her more intel. He would be a tough nut to crack, as his reputation in the gangs as a safe merchant to sell to kept him in business. Mr. Barrett had given Rhosyn reliable information on a few occasions when the situation was serious. She would just have to convince him that this was one of those situations and assure him nobody would ever find out he turned nose.

"Thanks, Bruce." Rhosyn rewrapped the remaining half of her pie and handed it to him. He snatched it up eagerly despite not having finished his own yet.

"Thanks, ma'am."

Rhosyn stood and turned back down the street, pleased with herself even as her heart sunk. It pained her how easy it was to get the children of the lower city talking just by distracting them with the promise of a full belly. She could only hope more Talented children secured a place in a home with regular meals through a sponsorship.

The walk to Mr. Barrett's shop took her across the lower city, right to the border between the poorest neighborhoods populated by the gangs and the neater but still cramped houses of the middle city. Here, Mr. Barrett could still be easily accessed by his "suppliers" while catering to a slightly wealthier clientele.

The light tinkle of a bell on the door signaled Rhosyn's entrance, causing Mr. Barrett to look up and instantly scowl at her uniform. Then again, Rhosyn got the feeling that Mr. Barrett scowled at everybody.

"I don't have time for you to be breathing down my neck today." He turned his back to her and stomped away to the far end of the counter.

"Is that any way to treat an old friend?" Rhosyn's tone was easy as she walked further into the shop. She stopped casually before the counter, pausing for a moment as if to peruse the cases filled with the more valuable trinkets.

Mr. Barrett folded his arms, lines around his eyes and mouth deepening. "Ain't friends with no Royal Police officers."

It was Rhosyn's turn to frown. "What are friends if not people who help each other out once in a while?"

Mr. Barrett glanced around his shop as if to make sure they were alone. Only the two of them stood among the shelves of odds and ends.

"What are you looking for?" he asked, tone furtive.

"The Foxes...have you heard anything about them?" Rhosyn leaned over the counter as she spoke, keeping her voice low in case any prying ears paused at the doorway or open windows.

It also gave her the advantage of being able to closely observe Mr. Barrett's body language—the way his knuckles whitened where they gripped the edge of the counter and the slight irregularity in his breathing as the name of the Foxes left her lips.

"Haven't heard of them." Mr. Barrett shrugged. "Are you sure your intel is good?"

Rhsoyn's eyes narrowed. "Come now, if I've heard the whispers of a new gang in town, you must have too."

Mr. Barrett turned away to fuss with some merchandise, as if he needed to do something with his hands. "Listen, if you want to waste your time investigating a gang that doesn't exist, then be my guest."

Rhosyn sighed internally. She had worked with Mr. Barrett enough times to know that he wouldn't change his mind if it was made up, and badgering him would only make him less inclined to cooperate on her next case.

"Maybe it's just people telling tales," she suggested, also turning away. As she did, the thin sunlight flashed on something silver in the glass case below the counter. She hesitated, leaning in to get a closer look.

The sparkle that had caught her attention came from a dramatic hat pin, the ornamental end wrought in the shape of a silver flower with a large green gemstone in the middle. She didn't spend much time around people who would wear such a decoration, but something about it rung familiar.

"Where'd you get this?"

"You don't strike me as the type for such a shiny thing," Mr. Barrett deflected. "Although the green might look good with your hair."

"How long have you had it?" Rhosyn ignored his comments. She did enjoy wearing green, but no matter how much she pinned it, a hat never sat nicely on her unruly hair.

Mr. Barrett shrugged. "Quite a while. It's hard to sell such a pricey piece."

Rhosyn nodded; it would be expensive. Likely stolen by one of his suppliers from a wealthy family.

She grinned in triumph as it hit her. The stolen jewels.

When helping Officers Fletcher and Davies fill out their report on the hooded man, she had flipped through the description of the stolen jewels, including one jeweled hat pin. She might not be making progress on her own investigation, but she had made a discovery on another by happy accident.

"That's interesting," Rhosyn said with feigned casualness. "You can't have had it that long, because it was just stolen a few weeks ago."

Mr. Barrett looked at her with tired eyes, but Rhosyn couldn't help the wolfish grin that crossed her face.

Chapter Four

"Your second high society event in a week. Contessa might turn you into a proper lady yet," Joseph mused as their carriage trundled up the hill to the wide streets where the wealthiest residents of London lived.

"If I'm proper, then Contessa is meek and demure," Rhosyn scoffed.

Joseph laughed and the smile made him look younger, softening the constant creases of consternation he wore from frowning at paperwork so often.

"I hope you can at least put on the act for another night," Joseph commented. "Mr. Gower specifically requested that I bring the officer responsible for the return of his jewels, so he could thank them personally."

At this, Rhosyn frowned. "We still haven't caught the Hood yet though."

Indeed, when Fletcher and Davies showed up to retrieve the stolen jewels and question Mr. Barrett on who sold them to him, he had described the same man Rhosyn had chased across the rooftops earlier: a piece of fabric hiding his lower face with a hood pulled low over his eyes. They had gained no further hints to his identity, and so could still only refer to him as the Hood.

"That might be true," Joseph admitted, "but hopefully he won't try to steal the same jewels twice. As long as Mr. Gower is happy and will keep sponsoring Talented, then it will at least take that worry off my plate."

Rhosyn didn't respond, playing through her chase with the Hood in her mind again. She told herself she was searching for some hidden clue in her memories she had overlooked earlier. In reality, the picture of him performing a perfect flip in the air, quads flexing as he landed and threatening to split the seams of his pants, came to her mind at all sorts of odd times. When she was taking a pause to eat lunch. When she was lying in her bed at night waiting for sleep to come.

Rhosyn was infuriated that he had gotten away.

She was also curious.

The cease of rumbling around her drew her from her musings, and she realized the carriage had come to a halt. They had arrived at the Gowers'.

Joseph helped her down from the carriage as Rhosyn suppressed the odd urge to giggle as she lifted her canary-yellow skirts out of the way of her satin slippers. The whole production felt similar to the first time she played dress up with Contessa's gowns years ago.

Still, she did her best to seem like she belonged there as she took Joseph's elbow and let him lead her into the grand house. The crystal chandelier and ornate wood railings on the sweeping staircase did nothing to make her feel more at ease.

However, the sight that greeted her just inside the parlor lifted her heart. A familiar young man hovered in the corner, a tray of crudites balanced in his white-gloved hands.

"Paul." Rhosyn made a beeline across the room to her former charge, although she knew she should probably greet the more distinguished guests first. He must not have heard her the first time, not reacting at all. "Paul!"

When Rhosyn stepped in front of him, he blinked several times as if not processing what he was seeing. It was probably since Rhosyn was dressed far more formally than she ever had been while minding the young Lions in the den. She took his moment of recognition to look him over.

It struck her immediately that he was still so young, barely more than just a boy. It seemed impossible that he could already have a job in a fine house. Then again, Rhosyn had been the same age when she put herself in charge of all the Lion's rescued children.

"Rhosyn?" Paul said slowly.

"I'm so glad to see you here," Rhosyn gushed. "I was so happy to hear that Mr. Gower sponsored you, but I wanted to check on you."

Paul's lips turned up in a smile, but something in his eyes seemed vacant, a strange flatness Rhosyn hadn't remembered in his expression. "I was glad to be sponsored, too."

"Are you feeling alright?" Rhosyn resisted the urge to press the back of her hand to his forehead and check for a fever. He seemed glassy-eyed, and taking care of him was a habit that died hard.

"Yes," Paul assured. "Just tired from learning how to be a proper footman."

"They're not working you too hard, are they?"

Paul shook his head. "I mostly use my Talent to help Mrs. Gower sleep—she suffers from insomnia—and lend a hand at parties like this."

Rhosyn opened her mouth to tell Paul to reach out to her if he was mistreated, but a hand on her elbow interrupted her.

"I think some of the other guests might be offended you prefer the footman's company over theirs," Joseph murmured in her ear.

The heat of annoyance flared in Rhosyn's chest, but she knew Joseph was right, and her irritation was further soothed by the apologetic look Joseph gave Paul. As Rhosyn let Joseph guide her into the thick of the party, Paul resumed his initial posture against the wall, looking like a decorative statue.

They picked their way through the assembled guests, looking for their host, the only person Rhosyn expected to recognize in there. The thick aroma of expensive perfumes mixing in the air threatened to overwhelm Rhosyn more than the cacophony of smells down at the ports ever did. Some women had already congregated near the piano where a lady much more well-bred than herself was picking out a cheerful melody. Rhosyn couldn't help but think that Scarlett played much better.

Joseph spotted Mr. Gower in a knot of gentlemen at the far end of the room and jerked his chin, indicating they should head in that direction. Just as they stepped into the circle surrounding Mr. Gower, a familiar voice sounded from Rhosyn's right.

"Why, if it isn't Ms. Walsh."

Rhosyn's eyebrows rose at the sight of Mr. Blakely, this time dressed in eggplant purple silk, a silver cane with some sort of animal head at the top balanced loosely in his hand.

"I see you are familiar with my guests of honor, Officer Walsh and Police Chief Thorne." Mr. Gower puffed up as he spoke, as if having such a collection of people in his drawing room was a momentous accomplishment. "I invited them after they returned some of my wife's most valuable jewels to her."

"Did they now?" Mr. Blakely asked, his tone impressed even as something inscrutable passed over his face.

"They did, although I wish they would apprehend the scoundrel that stole them in the first place."

Joseph stiffened beside Rhosyn, but Mr. Gower plowed ahead as if oblivious to the sore spot he obviously struck.

"And after the ball at the palace, I simply had to have Mr. Blakely to one of our soirees. Mrs. Gower was so taken with his contortionists that she insisted I invite him over at once."

"I'm afraid I missed the contortionists," Rhosyn admitted to Mr. Gower, although her eyes kept darting to Mr. Blakely.

"I heard you were drawn away by a commotion," Mr. Blakely commented. "It's a shame, I would have liked another dance."

Rhosyn usually tried to avoid blushing at all costs, as the flush clashed terribly with her flame-red hair, but she felt heat climbing up her chest to her neck. For the first time, she understood ladies' urges to carry a fan.

"I'm afraid there won't be any dancing tonight to remedy the situation," Mr. Gower said apologetically, "but maybe a game of cards would suffice?"

"I certainly wouldn't mind a hand of Whist," Rhosyn offered, a sly smile inching across her face. "Chief Thorne and I will be a team."

"Then, Mr. Blakely and I will play against you," Mr. Gower offered as he ushered them over towards one of the tables set up around the edges of the room for just such a purpose.

As they walked, Joseph grumbled in Rhosyn's ear, "You know I'm terrible at Whist."

Indeed, every time a deck of cards came out at the Woodrow's occasional dinner party, it became a tight race between Rhosyn and Benedict to see who would win the most hands, with Joseph losing trick after trick.

"It doesn't matter, I'm good enough for the both of us," Rhosyn murmured back.

"I don't think fine society takes kindly to cheating." Joseph spoke low enough that only Rhosyn could hear.

She grinned.

"Then they won't find out."

And so, Rhosyn found herself seated at a small square table with Joseph directly across from her and Mr. Gower and Mr. Blakely to her left and right. Before anybody could offer, Rhosyn snapped up the deck of cards and began shuffling.

Out of habit, she showed off a bit, making the cards flutter down in a perfect bridge before tossing them back and forth from hand to hand. Joseph cleared his throat and Rhosyn looked up, finding Mr. Gower glaring at her with undisguised disapproval. She might have expected as much, as the ladies of breeding he was used to would not have spent their youths among sharps in gambling dens.

More disappointing, though, was the scowl Mr. Blakely shot towards her hands as her fingers deftly controlled the cards through their acrobatics. Rhosyn resisted the urge to duck her head and dealt four even hands. After all, who was Mr. Blakely to judge her for knowing her way around a deck of cards, when he owned a circus?

The match began with Mr. Gower, as he sat to Rhosyn's right, and Mr. Blakely promptly took the trick with the queen of spades. Joseph lost the next trick by playing the ten of diamonds, but it was worth it to find out that Mr. Gower did not have any of the correct suit. On the next trick, Mr. Gower played the queen of hearts, already confidently reaching out to sweep the cards onto his side of the table when Rhosyn stopped him by slapping down the ace of hearts.

"Don't get too confident," she teased as she swept the cards away, using Mr. Gower's moment of consternation to flick a card up her sleeve. Now the queen of hearts replaced the three of spades in her hand.

Honestly, maybe she should have worn gowns with these wide, lacy sleeves in the gambling dens of the lower city. They made it incredibly easy to palm a card.

"Maybe you're the one that's too confident," Mr. Blakely quipped. "What if we made this more interesting?"

"I wouldn't have taken you for a gambling man," Rhosyn shot back.

"Well, I'm certainly not," Joseph grumbled.

"Me neither," Mr. Gower agreed.

"Then what about a bet between just me and Ms. Walsh," Mr. Blakely suggested. His voice took on a low timbre that made Rhosyn sit up straighter in her chair.

"And what would we be betting?" she asked.

"If I win, you have to be a special guest at one of my circus's performances," Mr. Blakely said firmly.

"That hardly seems like an imposition," Rhosyn pointed out.

"Imposing isn't my goal. And what would you like if you win?"

Rhosyn narrowed her eyes at him thoughtfully. "I want you to tell me what act you performed in the circus."

Mr. Blakely's eyes flashed. "How do you know I ever performed? Maybe I just run the shows."

Rhosyn snorted, nodding to his outfit. "I know a showman when I see one."

"Alright, if you win, I'll tell you about my act in the circus, if I performed at all."

They reached across the table to shake on it. As Mr. Blakely's hand grasped hers, rough calluses at the base of his fingers scraped her palm. She raised her eyebrows. Maybe he was a juggler.

Then they returned to the game. They went around the table playing the first card, both teams being evenly matched. Coming into the last trick, both teams were tied, and Mr. Blakely smiled at Rhosyn triumphantly.

"I'm afraid you'll never know my hidden performance skills," he said in mock disappointment.

It was Rhosyn's turn to set down the opening card—her last one—and she grinned. "You're so confident you can best the queen of hearts?"

Mr. Blakely blinked down at the red silhouette staring up at him from the table. Slowly, he laid down his own card, the jack of clubs.

"Oh ho!" Mr. Gower clapped his hands in delight, even though his team had lost. "Now, Mr. Blakely, you must tell us of your hidden talent."

Mr. Blakely stiffened.

"Oh, I didn't mean Talent as in..." Mr. Gower hurried to rectify himself.

"Of course not," Mr. Blakely waved a hand of dismissal, as if Rhosyn hadn't felt the air quiver as the muscles in his body went rigid a moment earlier. "But maybe a demonstration of my skills would be a better explanation."

"Some entertainment!" Mr. Gower exclaimed, clearly pleased to have a similar show to the King at his party.

"I'll need a few things though," Mr. Blakely said, "A knife, an apple, and of course a lovely volunteer."

"I think you have your volunteer right here," Joseph chimed in, gesturing to Rhosyn.

"As long as you promise not to be scared," Mr. Blakely said, something hard and challenging in his gaze.

"Oh, so this is going to be dangerous? I'm growing more excited by the second," Rhosyn quipped.

"I'll see if I can't get a servant to fetch the other things." Mr. Gower pushed to his feet, meandering off to find one of the footmen doing their best to blend into the walls.

An anticipatory silence fell over the table, broken by Joseph. "So how does a young man like yourself come to be running a circus?"

"It belonged to my father." Mr. Blakely folded his hands carefully on the table in front of him. "When he passed five years ago, I knew he would want me to keep it running."

"Ah, a family business," Joseph nodded. "I'm sorry to hear of your father, though."

A crash sounded from above them before Mr. Blakely could speak. Rhosyn's gaze snapped to the ceiling above her, the chandelier quivering with the force of the noise. A hush fell over the assembled partygoers. Another crash, this time accompanied by the sound of shattering glass, and Rhosyn was on her feet.

Joseph was hot on her heels, as she darted through the crowded parlor towards the grand stairs in the entrance, cards forgotten on the table behind them. Hindered as she was by her dress, Joseph overtook her as they bounded up the stairs. They turned right at the top, in the direction of the noise.

Mr. Gower stood red-faced with a stricken expression on his face, the carnage of what appeared to have been a library around him. "There—When I... I came in and there was somebody here... They tried to attack me!"

"Which way did they go?" Joseph demanded, his commanding officer persona surfacing in the moment of chaos.

Mr. Gower pointed to the hallway behind them. As one, they turned and looked down the series of doors on the upper level.

"We didn't pass them on the way up the stairs, so they must still be here," Joseph thought out loud.

"I'll sweep the rooms on the right, you get the ones on the left," Rhosyn suggested. She took two steps down the hallway, before Joseph's hand on her arm stopped her.

She turned and found him holding out a knife, handle first. She took it, observing it to be the flat kind that Nate wore no fewer than nine of beneath his clothes.

Rhosyn raised her brows at Joseph.

"I've picked up a thing or two," he grumbled.

With that, they set off down the hallway. Rhosyn peeked into every darkened room she passed, looking for any wardrobes that could hide a thief or open windows that could serve as an escape route. The hilt of the knife was smooth and heavy in her palm as she held it in a reverse grip.

Looking into the third room, a guest bedroom by the looks of it, she was glad for the weapon in her grasp, although part of her itched for her trusty brass knuckles. She wasn't as good with a knife as Nate, and it had been too long since she wielded anything but her police baton.

Every room Rhosyn glanced in appeared completely undisturbed, although the amount and opulence made Rhosyn's head spin. All the children who had crammed into narrow bunks in the Lion's Den could nearly have their own bedrooms here.

When she reached the last door on the right side, she paused. The modest-sized sitting room appeared deserted, but something about the stillness of the air drew Rhosyn further into the room. Her eye caught on a large fireplace along the far wall and her brow furrowed.

Scarlett had relayed a horrifying story about escaping up a chimney one time, and it flickered through Rhosyn's mind now.

Maybe—

The open door slammed into Rhosyn, catching her in the temple and nearly knocking her to the ground. As she took a step to regain her balance, she tripped over her skirt and had to grab onto a nearby settee with her free hand to remain upright.

Her assailant took the moment to jump out from behind the door where he had been hiding. As he stepped into the beam of light coming in from the hallway, Rhosyn gasped.

"You!"

Standing in Mr. Gower's sitting room was the Hood, complete with fabric covering nearly all of his face and a miniature crossbow strapped to his forearm. He pressed the advantage in Rhosyn's moment of surprise, lashing out with a madcap right hook.

Rhosyn ducked, the blow barely missing her and wind from it ruffling her rapidly deteriorating hairstyle. As she sidestepped, she threw out an elbow, catching the Hood square in his stomach.

He let out a soft *oomph* but was not deterred, taking advantage of Rhosyn's proximity to throw an upper cut. Rhosyn tried to dodge, but her skirts caught on the table behind her, and she couldn't get completely out of the way in time. The blow glanced off her cheekbone, skittering across her temple.

A familiar ringing filled her ears from the impact. Rhosyn's lips pulled back in an expression halfway between a grin and a snarl. She leaped forward as best she could, given the constraints of her current attire. Her fists flew in a series of rapid blows to Hood's face and torso.

He blocked most of them with his forearms, but Rhosyn was too vicious a brawler and pummeled through his defenses, landing a solid blow to his shoulder.

The Hood staggered back, the grace with which he had scampered over rooftops disappearing in the face of Rhosyn's assault. She prepared to leap, hoping to pin him to the ground and rip the covering from his face.

Before she could act, Joseph burst through the still open door, clearly drawn by the commotion. His appearance distracted Rhosyn just enough that she didn't notice the Hood fish his hand into his pocket until it was too late.

Glass shattered as Hood threw a small vial to the ground, and immediately a thick smoke with an odd bluish tint filled the air. It nearly blocked the silhouettes of the two men from view as it billowed up from the ground.

Rhosyn jumped forward into it with an annoyed growl. She was not going to lose her mark a second time, letting him disappear in a puff of smoke like some half-rate magician.

As she stepped into the fumes, they filled her nose and she coughed around the strangely sweet scent. The smoke swam around her. Or maybe it was her vision. Rhosyn continued to push forward, but her equilibrium was nowhere to be found. Her silky slippers, so different from the thick soled boots of her uniform, caught on the carpet.

Her knees hit the ground before she knew she was falling, the world continuing to spin around her. The Hood emerged from the smoke, looking down at her with his head cocked. Rhosyn tried to curse at him but her tongue was too large and thick against her teeth.

Instead of responding, the Hood bent down. An odd shiver ran up Rhosyn's spine as he appeared to reach for her, only to pick up something on the ground at her side.

He held up a playing card—the three of spades, Rhosyn knew—that must have fallen out of her sleeve during their altercation. Without a word he tucked it into his pocket, offered a tiny, mocking bow, and disappeared.

Rarely had Rhosyn been so happy to collapse onto the too-soft bed in her too-quiet bedroom. She flopped onto her coverlet, burying her face in the pillows. Lying perfectly still, she hoped sleep would take the last of her wooziness away.

Whatever had been in the smoke bomb the Hood had used hadn't ever knocked her completely unconscious, but it had left her and Joseph disoriented enough to do nothing but lay on the ground while he made an escape. The cloth across Hood's face, likely combined with him knowing to hold his breath, had given him a chance to slip away into the night.

By the time Mr. Gower came and opened a window to let the fresh air in, their culprit was nowhere to be found. Unfortunately, the night had not ended there.

While the rest of the party guests had left quickly, scared off by the commotion and threat of an intruder, Rhosyn and Joseph stayed as Mr. Gower went through his documents and valuables to ascertain if anything was taken.

As their host did, Rhosyn ventured through the house looking for signs of forced entry. By the time Mr. Gower announced that nothing had been taken, she had found no signs of how the Hood may have entered, although with so many comings and goings for the evening's revelries, and not knowing what he looked like under the mask, it was possible he may have slipped in unnoticed without even picking a lock.

Rhosyn and Joseph had shared a carriage back to the middle city, Joseph resting his face in his hands.

"Why would they try to rob him after we just managed to return his wife's jewels to him?" he asked in a tone of utmost despair.

Rarely one for quiet, Rhosyn had just shaken her head and looked out the window. In two weeks, she had gone to two parties that ended in ruined dresses and failed chases. Even before she was an officer of the Royal Police, Rhosyn had tasked herself with protecting the people of London in whatever way she could. Recently, she had failed at every turn.

Now she rolled onto her back with a sigh, closing her eyes and letting her mind drift. Despite the unusual heaviness of her limbs from the remnant of the drugs in her system, Rhosyn's blood rushed through her body with unnerving speed. She would not be able to sleep soon. It had been too long since she had been in a proper brawl, and even just the taste of a fight with the Hood today had been enough to reactivate old instincts. Hell, the last time she had been able to let her reflexes take over like that was when she fought Scarlett in the Wolves' fighting pits. She missed it—the adrenaline and freedom that came from throwing herself at a problem with everything she had.

Rhosyn rubbed a hand over her eyes. She was now an officer for the Royal Police, and that was the best way for her to protect the city she had called home all her life—where she had chosen to stay to be with her adoptive family even when adventure and the sea had tugged at her blood. It didn't do to dwell on such things, though, and she forced her mind to focus on something else.

The memory of trading blows with the Hood morphed into exchanging easy jabs with Mr. Blakely over cards. Disappointment flooded her that he, along with the rest of the guests, had been gone by the time she and Joseph recovered from the drugged smoke. It was probably for the best though. As much as she enjoyed Mr. Blakely's charms, it was clear she should keep him at arm's length.

With the way he had stiffened when Mr. Gower spoke of being Talented, and how determined he seemed to be to climb the social ladder by brushing elbows with the elite and wealthy, she doubted Mr. Blakely's casual flirtations would continue if he were to find out about her checkered past.

Still, if she wasn't going to be able to sleep anyways, it didn't hurt to imagine. She and Mr. Blakely might meet again, but instead of leading her towards a dance floor, they would break out into a shadowed corner of the garden—perhaps an ostentatious hedge maze like the Worthingtons had.

But then what would he do? Mr. Blakely was a gentleman, but Rhosyn was far from a lady. She knew how things would go in the darkened alley of the lower city, but proper romantic trysts were not in her repertoire.

In line with these thoughts, the vision morphed, so it wasn't Mr. Blakely she pressed herself against in some darkened corner, but a masked figure with a hood pulled low over his face. With those powerful thighs and broad shoulders, Rhosyn didn't doubt that the Hood could easily hoist her in his arms.

She shook herself, snapping her eyes open and tracing her gaze over the spiderweb cracks in the plaster ceiling. She really wasn't fit for society if her mind preferred to ponder romantic entanglements with the man who had just punched her before leaving her fighting for consciousness on the floor. Maybe she just hadn't been in a proper brawl in too long.

Rhosyn's fingers drifted up to her face, tracing over her battered cheekbone, the ache of something deeper bothering her more than the pain of the bruise. She missed running with the Lions.

Joseph intercepted Rhosyn the moment she walked in the door, pouncing on her as if he had been waiting. She blinked at him groggily, having tossed and turned most of the night. The deep furrow between his brows chased the sleepiness from her mind though.

"Mr. Gower sent a message early this morning." Joseph began without preamble. "He found that something was missing."

"What?"

"His household staff, the Talented ones," Joseph admitted grimly.

They had been walking through the mess of desks towards Joseph's station in the corner, but Rhosyn froze.

"Paul..."

"He and Olivia are missing," Joseph explained.

Rhosyn turned on her heel, ready to storm out and march through the city until she found her former charges, but Joseph's hand on her shoulder stopped her. Her head snapped toward him and at the very last second she schooled her face out of the snarl that threatened the corners of her mouth.

It wasn't Joseph's fault.

"I already have Davies and Fletcher on it. They've been investigating the Hood for months now."

"And do they have any leads?" Rhosyn snapped.

"I need you in the lower city," Joseph side stepped the question, giving her all the answers she needed.

Rhosyn pulled her arm from his grip, but his beseeching expression kept her from storming away.

"There was another turf war in the lower city last night, by the train yards," Joseph admitted in a low tone. "They dispersed by the time we got there, but my gut tells me it was the Foxes. This is escalating too quickly. With so much happening with the Hood in the upper city, I need to know I have somebody I can trust keeping an eye on things."

The heaviness in Joseph's eyes said the words he left unspoken. He knew she would take care of the lower city, because those were her people. While many of the Royal Police were from the middle city, with the higher-ranking officers consorting with those in the upper city like

Chief Cook had, the dirty back alleys and dice houses were Rhosyn's London.

"Alright," she acquiesced. "But don't keep me in the dark."

Or I may not be able to stop myself from performing my own investigation.

"That's why I told you. I'm not a Chief that keeps secrets."

"I know," Rhosyn nodded. In that moment, she was sure he was comparing himself to his former mentor.

And so, Rhosyn found herself walking a familiar beat among her usual streets, eyes darting around for signs of violence. She had roamed these neighborhoods on many days where furtive glances and a certain tenor in the voices of those out and about had made the city seem like a powder keg about to blow—usually when turf wars and skirmishes reached a peak.

Today wasn't one of those days. The sun was strong enough to pierce the perpetual smog, and voices echoed loudly off the cobblestones as people shouted their greetings and went about their business. Rhosyn frowned. Perhaps this area was too far from the rail yards to be affected by last night's bloodshed.

She directed her steps away from the shops and factories and in the direction of the mess of intersecting rails where goods from the factories and those received from the port would begin their journey to the rest of the country. It wasn't an area she spent much time in as a youth, being firmly ensconced in Scorpion territory, but she knew it was a prime area for violence and crooked deals. The rail workers cleared out at night, and there were plenty of heavy shadows and abandoned train cars where people could conduct business best done in the dark.

So, as she stepped out from behind a spare train car languishing on the track, she started in surprise at the brightly colored sight that greeted her. Workers scurried about, loading bundles and boxes into carts that then trundled out to the surrounding streets. At the epicenter of the activity stood a train, brightly colored in green and yellow, a far cry from the dark steam engines that dominated the area.

Rhosyn drifted closer, gaze catching on words printed on the side of one car in dramatic, curling script.

Archer's Circus

No sooner had her brain fired in recognition, than a familiar voice greeted her.

"You certainly don't take any time off."

Rhosyn spun on her heel, little pebbles crunching underfoot as she turned to see Mr. Blakely. Today, the trappings of a man trying to wheedle his way into society were gone, replaced with a workman's garb. A light shirt was tucked into plain trousers, his sleeves rolled up to nearly his elbows. A sheen of sweat made his hair cling to forehead, dark aside from the contrasting streak of silver at his right temple.

"Neither do you, it seems," Rhosyn said, trying to keep her gaze from lingering on his bare forearms. Perhaps there was something to exposed ankles being indecent, if such an innocuous thing could be so thoroughly distracting.

"Ah, but I didn't end up working last night," he responded, crossing his arms across a surprisingly broad chest for one of his stature.

"I'm afraid I might become an unpopular party guest, if every event I attend continues to end in a police investigation," she griped.

Mr. Blakely's eyes twinkled. "Or maybe it will just give you an air of mystique."

"That doesn't get you as far in law enforcement as it might in the circus," Rhosyn pointed out.

Mr. Blakely laughed, the sound light and easy. Rhosyn had found him charming in all his finery, but she found her smile coming more freely with him like this.

"And what brings you down to the railyard the morning after such an eventful celebration, Mr. Blakely?" Rhosyn prodded.

He waved a dismissive hand. "Call me Ansel, please. Nobody else in this traveling pack of fools calls me Mr. Blakely, so I save the airs for when I'm trying to impress."

"Well, Ansel," Rhosyn started, a strange amount of bite working its way into her tone as she processed that she was not somebody he was intent on impressing—although she had presumed as much in the quiet of her bedroom the night before. "What brings you to such a part of town?"

"The rest of my show has arrived," he explained, gesturing to the train behind her. "I came to London a few weeks ago with just a handful of my best acts, trying to drum up interest. After performing at the King's party, the Merry Men have gained enough notoriety for me to bring my entire circus for an extended stay. They just arrived."

Rhosyn's eyes narrowed. "Did your train have any trouble upon arriving?"

"No," Mr. Blakely—Ansel—cocked his head. "Other than the ungodly early hour it arrived this morning."

Rhosyn considered him. Her mental hackles rose at the thought that he might be lying. His train had arrived at the spot of a dangerous turf war just hours after it occurred. What's more, he had been at the last two events that had ended in thefts or kidnapping. Then again, so had she.

Ansel observed her as she thought, expression guileless.

"I guess it's for the best that yesterday's festivities ended early then, if you had to be up before the sun," Rhosyn commented.

Ansel shrugged. "Despite the fact that I lost our bet, I found myself disappointed that I didn't get to show off my skills for you. After all, your slight of hand was very good, and I don't like to be upstaged."

A fire in Rhosyn's chest sparked at his accusation—despite the fact that she had cheated—but settled into the heat of a challenge, instead of rage, when he saw that his expression was more amused than angry.

"Only a sore loser confuses luck for cheating," she quipped.

"Oh, I'm no stranger to luck," Ansel answered cryptically, "but I do have a knack for remembering what cards have been played. I'm pretty sure you played the Queen of Hearts twice."

"Well, there's no proof of that."

Ansel's eyes flashed, green catching in the sun like the emerald at the center of Mr. Gower's stolen hat pin. "Then I guess I still owe you a demonstration."

"Technically, you only have to tell me about your circus act."

"And deny a performer a chance for dramatic effect?" Ansel asked. It struck Rhosyn as an odd comment somehow, in the broad daylight where he seemed to be just another man working to unload a train of its cargo, in plainclothes with a smudge of something like grease along his jaw. Last night, in all his finery, he had certainly seemed the consummate showman, but now it seemed as if he was missing something. It left Rhosyn unbalanced, wondering which man was the real one—the suave Mr. Blakely she played cards with last night, or Ansel who she bantered with in a trainyard.

"Maybe we can still find time for you to show off," Rhosyn suggested.

"My circus will be performing its opening show next weekend. Why don't you come and see for yourself. Front row seats are hard to come by, but I know the owner," Ansel joked.

"Now you're just cashing in your side of the bet."

"I have very little incentive to play fair against you." He grinned, expression sly.

Rhosyn's rational mind told her to refuse his offer—steer clear of a social climber who likely wouldn't take kindly to her background. After all, she had a thief to catch, the Foxes to bring down, and missing Talented to find.

But Ansel wore his smile like a challenge, and Rhosyn never backed down.

"I expect tickets on opening night."

"So it shall be." Ansel opened his mouth as if to say something more, but his gaze caught on something over her shoulder. "Careful with the trapezes! You'll get them all tangled doing that."

In a second, he strode away, commanding the workers who were loading bundles of ropes into a wheelbarrow. Rhosyn stood watching for a moment in the middle of the mayhem, a rock in the center of a hive of worker bees. Then she turned from the Archer's Circus train and began weaving her way through the much bleaker and less lively engines.

She wasn't sure what she expected to find. The gangs of the lower city were skilled at hit and run tactics, striking each other swiftly and melting back into the shadows before the authorities arrived. Such guerrilla tactics were how the Lions had thrived for nearly a decade.

It was doubtful the Foxes left any more evidence around than boot prints in gravel, already worn away by the stomping of the rail workers this morning. Maybe the trains themselves would give her a clue as to what they might be smuggling that was worth spilling blood over.

A quick perusal of the manifest in the small office at the side of the rail office showed nothing of note, besides the arrival of the Archer's Circus train, which she already knew about. The only things coming in and out yesterday and today were steel and coal, as well as a large shipment of textiles. The last would be very valuable—prices had been driven up enormously since Contessa advised the King to enact a policy demanding fair wages for the factory workers—but not something any gang would try to steal.

Rhosyn left the rail yard behind her with lead in her usually bouncy gate. Perhaps Chief Thorne's faith in her was misplaced, thinking she could protect the lower city from whatever trouble was brewing.

A comforting weight like a blanket settled over Rhosyn's shoulders as she opened the sky-blue front door of the Woodrow's house. The only thing that would make it feel more like coming home would be climbing up from the secret passage beneath Nate's desk in the study. However, it had been filled with stones and boarded up after the Royal Police were alerted to the secret passageways' presence a few years ago. Nate was unwilling to give those that might want revenge such easy access to his home—and his wife—now that the secret of tunnels was no longer owned only by the Lions.

Still, Rhosyn was no more inclined to knock on the front door than she was when entering through a trap door, and she strode into the foyer and past the sweeping staircase casually. Nate and Contessa wouldn't mind. After all, two of their most frequent visitors were Kristoff and Scarlett, who Rhosyn knew through experience preferred windows to doors.

Rhosyn meandered through the parlor, listening for signs that the Woodrows were home. It looked much the same as it had since Nate first moved into the mansion, elegant but plain furniture and nondescript still-life paintings adorning the walls. The most prominent sign of life was the overflowing vases on every surface, immaculate flowers kept blooming by Gregor's presence. As much as Rhosyn had hoped the place would be more lively after Contessa moved in, she had proved disinterested in decorating, most of her time spent either helping the King or working with the Lions on projects of more questionable legality.

Still, certain details spoke of the home's inhabitants. An ornate marble chessboard sat prominently on the table in the middle of the room, a birthday present for Contessa that Nate had agonized over several years back. Dozens of books, a mix of poetry, fairy tales, and politics, lay stacked on the surfaces not occupied by flowers. On top of one of the teetering piles, a silvery blade gleamed, apparently unable to have been packed onto Nate's relatively well armed form.

It appeared they weren't home.

Rhosyn sighed, turning towards the rear of the house where the kitchens would be, along with the possibility of hot tea and Gregor's round smile. She should probably go try to get a good night's sleep, but she wasn't willing to leave just yet. This house brought her more of a feeling of home than the barren bedroom in the middle city.

Hand reaching for the doorknob that would lead her into the kitchen, Rhosyn froze, ears pricked at a sudden noise. It had sounded like a groan, and Rhosyn hesitated to burst into the kitchen. While it wouldn't be the first time she had accidentally barged in on the Woodrows in a compromising position, Contessa was still enough of a lady to be mortified every time.

It came again—a breathy moan in a voice Rhosyn recognized. She smiled and grabbed the doorknob.

"Kristoff, stop defiling Gregor," she shouted.

From the other side of the door came a scuffling and a deep chuckle, along with a quieter, more embarrassed-sounding groan, then the door sprung open.

"How do you know *he* wasn't defiling *me*?" Kristoff asked by way of greeting.

Rhosyn raised a brow as she stepped past him into the kitchen.

"Maybe nobody was defiling anybody," Gregor remarked in a deceptively even tone from where he stood at the wooden table, chopping potatoes as if he had always been doing so, but a blooming bruise just below his ear gave him away.

"Sorry to interrupt," Rhosyn teased, bumping Gregor with her hip on her way past him.

"Would you like some tea?" he deflected.

Rhosyn nodded as she perched on the wide windowsill at the back of the room swinging her legs. "Thank you. I'd be glad to have the walk over not be for nothing, since it appears Contessa and Nate aren't home."

"I'm afraid they haven't made it home for dinner yet this week," Gregor admitted as he lifted the kettle onto the stove. "If you need something though, I can give them a message."

Rhosyn shook her head. "I don't need to worry them if they're already that busy. The Royal Police are working on it after all."

"But?" Kristoff folded his arms as he leaned one hip against the table in the center of the room, his deep blue eyes sharp.

Rhosyn cocked her head. "But, what?"

"But obviously you're still worried if you came."

Rhosyn's boot heels thumped against the wall behind her as she considered Kristoff. His dark hair managed to look perfectly disheveled from Gregor's hands, and whirls of black ink covered his forearms where he had pushed his shirtsleeves up. Every inch of him still screamed rogue, despite the fact that most of the jobs he ran these days were on behalf of the crown. After all, Nate and Contessa worried about the specifics of how Kristoff executed his missions, while King Byron remained glad to benefit from having an inside source in the underbelly of the city.

A lick of envy flared in Rhosyn's heart, and she moved to quash it quickly.

When the Lions had ceased to be a street gang and Rhosyn had considered her future, Kristoff had been the first to encourage her to train for the Royal Police. He knew she craved a purpose and action, and he convinced her this was her chance to go straight—to live the life she might have had if not for the Inquiries. When she asked him why he didn't join the Police too, he ruffled her already messy hair and told her he was far too much of a troublemaker to ever wear a uniform.

Now she wondered if the same couldn't be said about her.

"It's Paul and Olivia," Rhosyn admitted. "They're missing."

"And you're investigating it with the Royal Police?"

Rhosyn shook her head. "There are officers on it, and Joseph wants me to stay in on a case in the lower city. But..."

"But Lions protect their pack." It was Gregor who finished for Rhosyn in a decisive tone.

"I just worry about doing off-the-books investigating when Joseph is trying so hard to keep the Royal Police spotless," Rhosyn pointed out.

"Isn't blindly following orders what got the force into such a mess in the first place?" Kristoff asked.

Rhosyn folded her arms. "Only because the Chief was the one doing illegal things."

"Still, I think that's enough evidence that the spirit of the law is more important than the letter of it."

"I'm not sure it would be above board for a Royal Police officer to concede that point." Rhosyn frowned.

"And yet you came to some of the most notorious criminals in London for advice."

Rhosyn resisted the very immature urge to stick her tongue out at Kristoff for verbally backing her into a corner. He had a way of pulling argumentative urges out of her like Rhosyn imagined a sibling would, if she had been lucky enough to have one.

"You have good instincts," Gregor chimed in more gently. "Chief Thorne knows it, I'm sure."

Rhosyn jumped as the teakettle started whistling, and Gregor turned away to remove it from the heat. Kristoff kept observing Rhosyn pensively, the corner of his usual devilish smirk slipping slightly.

"I'll keep my ear to the ground for any news about Paul and Olivia," he promised quietly, "But I don't think you should be hard on yourself for wanting to make sure they're safe."

Rhosyn nodded her thanks as Gregor bustled over with a cup of tea. Like a brother, Kristoff had a way of knowing what she needed to hear, just like he knew how best to tease her.

"Maybe you just need a man in your life to distract you," Kristoff prodded. "Contessa said something about you dancing with a gentleman at the King's ball."

"I hardly see how who I dance with has anything to do with my job as a police officer," Rhosyn shot back.

Gregor grinned. "He's just trying to play matchmaker with everybody since he's tired of waiting for Contessa and Nate to have a baby he can slowly corrupt to his villainous ways."

"They say they're trying, but I hardly see how that's happening when they spend every night working into the small hours of the morning." Kristoff threw his hands up in defeat.

Rhosyn snorted into her tea. "Well, I'm sorry but I don't think I'll be supplying you with a child to dote on any time soon, either. I'm more concerned, at the moment, with finding the ones who have gone missing."

Rhosyn jumped up and down, wiggling inelegantly to pull the too small pants over her hips and thighs. Finally, she managed to button them, blowing a stray curl off her sweaty forehead. For years, she had worn only the navy uniform and gold buttons of the Royal Police, or an occasional gown gifted to her by Contessa and altered to fit, but tonight's task required discretion. So, she had dug to the very bottom of her small chest of clothes and fished out the black shirt and trousers she used to wear when the Lion's went on liberation missions.

Fortunately, Rhosyn had filled in since the lanky days of her teenage years, but she had failed to update her espionage wardrobe. She would just have to deal with tight pants during tonight's creeping about, and avoid thinking about how Contessa would blush at the way the trousers showed every curve of her ass and thighs.

Rhosyn wasn't exactly a lady, after all.

Shoving a black scarf into her shirt, to conceal her hair once she reached her destination, Rhosyn slipped out of her middle city residence and turned her steps uphill. Where Rhosyn normally strode confidently down the middle of the street where all could see her uniform, tonight, she stuck to the edges where the shadows of buildings might obscure her face. As the houses changed from wood to stone, becoming more widely spaced with blooming flowerbeds out front, a thrill ran up Rhosyn's spine.

Something wild in her lifted its head in interest at this new development, as if it had missed illicit midnight missions. She mentally wagged a finger at it. This was a one-time thing, to make sure Paul and Olivia were found. Still, she shivered as she paused to pull out her scarf and wrap it around her hair and lower face.

Soon, the silhouette of Mr. Gower's house shadowed the cobblestones in front of Rhosyn. Surveying the front of the house, the windows remained dark and impenetrable, concealing anything that might be happening within. No matter. Rhosyn was more interested in the back of the house where the servants' quarters resided.

She darted between shadows, creeping around towards the back of the mansion. Her brows drew together as the rear windows remained darkened, but the flickering of a lantern off to the side caught her eye. She crept towards it, finding the light seeping out the cracks around a large door, leading to what must be the carriage house and stables.

Rhosyn inched forward, pressing her palms to the wooden panels and aligning her eye with the seam between the double doors. With her narrow frame of vision, she could just make out a sleek black coach occupying the center of the stable, backlit in shadowy lighting that appeared to be spilling from one of the stalls.

She stiffened as voices drifted through the still night air. Straining forward, nearly pressing her nose into the door, she tried to distinguish words, but only succeeded in making out a faint murmur.

Perhaps it was only the groom, indulging in a little late night...conversation. But nobody knew more about the goings on in a great house than the help, so often treated as invisible but carrying secrets that could ruin many socialites if they so chose. Mr. Gower's household staff may have some inkling of what happened to Paul and Olivia.

As slowly as she could muster, Rhosyn unlatched the stable doors—still unlocked as if the groom hadn't yet closed up for the night—and pressed the door open. She sent up a silent thank you for the wealth that kept Mr. Gower's stable hinges well-oiled, as the wood silently swung forward just wide enough for her to slip inside and ease it shut behind her.

She placed her feet gingerly on the hay-strewn floor, soft boots padding gently as she inched towards the source of the voices. The voices became clearer, and she paused next to the coach, which took up the majority of the open space, crouching partially behind it near one of the large, spoked wheels to listen.

"—need them back as soon as possible."

Rhosyn frowned at the familiar voice. She hadn't expected to hear—

"They might still come back of their own accord, Mr. Gower."

She inhaled sharply through her nose, air full of the warm smell of hay and sleepy horses. What would Mr. Gower himself be doing in the stable in the middle of the night?

"If they wanted to come back, they wouldn't have left, Hamish." The voice was definitely Mr. Gower's, but gone was polish of civility that coated his tone in ballrooms and parties. He sounded frustrated.

"We don't know that. The Royal Police might still bring them back."

"The Royal Police wouldn't know a lead if it bit them on the nose."

Rhosyn bristled and tried not to think about how she herself was working outside of the Police's jurisdiction at the moment.

"I expect them back soon." Mr. Gower spoke again. "I refuse to change my plans."

"They weren't here for long enough for me to—"

"I don't take kindly to excuses, especially from you, Hamish." Mr. Gower interrupted the groom's attempts to explain. "Remember what will happen if you fail to help me."

A rustling came from the stall where the two men spoke, and Rhosyn's heart leapt into her throat as she realized Mr. Gower was about to step around the corner, with her only partially obscured by the shadow of his carriage. She had been so preoccupied by his conversation that she had failed to devise her plan of escape.

She sprang from her crouch, preparing to make a break for it, hoping she wouldn't be recognized even if she was seen. Before she could run, the door of the coach at her back slid open and an arm wrapped around her neck. She tipped backwards into the interior of the coach, another hand clamping over her mouth, muffling the instinctual scream that threatened to break free.

The carriage door closed before her with quiet *snick* as she squirmed in her assailant's hold, one arm firm across her chest as they hunched over her on the lushly upholstered seat.

"Quiet," a male voice hissed in her ear. "I don't want to get caught any more than you do."

Rhosyn froze, still but for the frantic pounding of her heart and the rushing beneath her skin. She knew that voice. Her eyes darted down, and sure enough, a wrist bow decorated the forearm banded across her heaving chest.

The pair stilled, listening for any sounds indicating their scuffle had been noticed. A shadowed silhouette drifted past the small glass window set into the door, but it didn't pause or give any indication they had been found.

Still, they didn't move yet, the only sound in the space their carefully schooled breathing. If Rhosyn's was a bit ragged, it was from the sudden jolt of adrenaline. It certainly wasn't the sudden wash of awareness coursing through her body as she strained to remain perfectly still, despite the press of the Hood against her back, his muscular thighs bracketing hers. His chest against her was certainly as solid as the width of his shoulders suggested it might be.

Rhosyn opened her mouth, quickly deciding to bite the Hood's palm. She needed him to let go of her, and certainly the immediate danger had passed. Before her teeth could close around the meat of his hand, he snatched it out of the way, as if he had sensed her intentions. Her teeth snapped on thin air.

"That wasn't very nice, considering how I just helped you." The Hood didn't release her, his fingers instead drifting up to where a coppery curl had slipped out of her scarf. He plucked at it gently, rubbing it between his thumb and pointer finger. The red of her hair was stark against the dark gloves he wore. Rhosyn swallowed.

"Ah, I thought I recognized you," the Hood murmured as if to himself. "I shouldn't have expected you to play fair."

"I'm not the one who has to drug my opponents to escape," Rhosyn hissed.

He huffed in what might have been a chuckle, the breath filtering through his mask warm and ticklish on her neck. Rhosyn squirmed.

The Hood tightened his grip. Rhosyn prepared to throw her head back and break his nose, but she hesitated. Even if it seemed they were now alone in the stables, she wasn't willing to risk a full-on brawl on the Gower's property—especially when she wasn't supposed to be there.

As if reading her thoughts, the Hood spoke. "And I'm not the Royal Police officer who appears to make a hobby of breaking and entering."

Rhosyn flushed, seriously considering breaking his nose anyways just for the satisfying crunch. "You were here the night of the party," she deflected. "What do you know?"

Maybe he was the one responsible for Olivia and Paul's disappearance. Perhaps an associate stole them away while the Hood distracted Rhosyn and Joseph. After all, Mr. Gower's description of his attacker didn't match the Hood...but then why would he be here now?

"Are you here to steal more Talented from their new lives?" she hissed accusingly.

The Hood's arm stiffened around her, but he didn't answer her question. "I'm going to let you go, and you're not going to tell anybody you saw me here, or you'll have to explain why you were here too."

"I'm investigating a crime scene. There's nothing hard to explain about that." Rhosyn hoped her words would distract him as she shifted surreptitiously in his grasp, searching for a way to slip free without things descending into a full out brawl. Then again, maybe throwing a few punches would clear her head.

"Something about the way you slipped in under cover of darkness makes me think that you don't exactly have a warrant."

He was right, but Rhosyn wasn't inclined to confirm that. Instead, she hooked her foot around his calf where she kneeled between his legs. She simultaneously threw her weight sideways, grabbing at the arm around her neck and grappling with her leg to take him down with her. The pair rolled on the floor of the carriage, the Hood falling on his back with a heavy *ooph* as Rhosyn landed on top of him.

The momentum of the fall from the seat was more than Rhosyn expected, and her shoulder crashed into the carriage door with a bone-rattling thump, slamming it open. She tipped out of the black box and hurtled to the ground below. The Hood held fast to her shoulders, following her down.

Rhosyn flung out her arms and bent her knees, trying to tuck into a roll that would bring her to her feet. A ripping sound filled the still air of the stable as Rhosyn failed to break her fall. Her forehead smacked the straw strewn floor, and her ears rang.

When awareness of her body beyond the sharp pain in her head returned, the Hood's weight was no longer on top of her, and the strange sensation of a cool breeze caressed her ass.

"I thought those pants might be a little tight for crime fighting," a familiar voice chuckled just above her. "If you were trying to distract me, it very nearly worked."

Then light, quick footsteps began retreating.

Rhosyn regained control of her limbs a second after realizing Hood was escaping. Hastily, she scrambled to her feet, grateful that the stable now appeared to be empty of both Mr. Gower and the groom, Hamish. She raced to the door, left slightly ajar, just in time to see a dark silhouette leap from the top of the garden fence, performing a flip in the air before landing lightly on his feet and darting off into the night.

With a sigh, Rhosyn let him go. The Hood seemed to be made of smoke, and the harder she tried to grasp him, the more he slipped through her fingers with surprising agility. She couldn't risk being caught chasing him through the streets at night and being forced to explain herself to Chief Thorne.

Rhosyn twisted and looked over her shoulder to assess the damage to her pants, finding the entire back middle seam torn open and amended her thoughts. She definitely couldn't be caught racing through the streets at night with her entire *bahookie* on display.

She slipped back into the stable and made sure to set the carriage to rights before exiting and shutting the door behind her. Once she had snuck back around to the front of the grand house and onto the street, she unwrapped the black scarf from her head and used it to tie around her waist. It would be enough to keep her halfway decent on the walk home, if any late-night drinkers were still wandering the streets.

Not that it seemed to matter too terribly much anymore. Hood had quite literally caught her with her pants down tonight before slipping away, and she still didn't know where to find Paul and Olivia.

Chapter Five

The flags at the zenith of each large tent flapped lazily in the thin breeze that gained energy this short distance from the concentrated buildings of the city. Rhosyn craned her neck to look up at the green banners emblazoned with the golden bow and arrow of Archer's Circus.

She picked her way through the main thoroughfare, boots sinking gently into the well-trodden ground of mud and hay. Even though the Circus had only been open for a day, word seemed to have spread quickly. What appeared to be half of London had turned out at the end of the workday to see the spectacle.

The air swirled with excitement and the rich, buttery aroma of popcorn, working to dispel the frustration that clung to Rhosyn's consciousness throughout her day patrolling the lower city. Even now, Mr. Gower's whispered conversation with Hamish replayed in her head as she tried to make sense of it and decide where she might look for Paul and Olivia next. Maybe she should turn around and spend the night scouring the rooftops for the Hood.

Instead, she trekked towards the tallest tent, standing proudly at the center of the festivities. That was where Ansel had indicated he would be when he sent her ticket with a messenger, and Rhosyn could certainly do with the distraction of some entertainment right now.

As she walked, she peeked through the entrances of some of the surrounding structures, revealing small stages occupied by brightly dressed jugglers or gaudily painted contortionists. At one point she jumped at the roar of a mighty beast somewhere nearby. She had seen posters for a lion tamer, and she hoped he was skilled enough to keep the animal in check.

Finally, she reached the grandest of the quickly erected structures, marveling that such a cathedral of green and white striped canvas could be constructed overnight. This tent seemed to be drawing the bulk of the crowds, and Rhosyn let herself drift inside with the milling tide.

The setup looked familiar: tightropes and trapezes towered above the stands, already filling with spectators. It seemed the acrobats were considered the crowning jewel of Archer's Circus—the Merry Men, as Ansel had introduced them.

As if summoned by her thoughts, a touch at her elbow drew Rhosyn from her thoughts, where she gaped at the network of ropes above her.

"I was hoping you'd come," Ansel said by way of greeting. He smiled magnanimously, just the barest peek of the silver stripe in his hair visible below the silk top hat he wore.

"Why wouldn't I?" Rhosyn followed in the direction he nudged her elbow, out of the thickest of the entering crowds.

"I know you're busy." Ansel shrugged. "Clearly you've been working."

Rhosyn glanced down at her pressed, navy-blue uniform, looking dusty after a full day's wear, and inwardly shrank. She might have changed, but she wasn't inclined to ruin one of the dresses Contessa gifted her in the muck of the grounds, and it had become clear last night that her older clothes were no longer a safe option.

"Crime never sleeps," Rhosyn grumbled.

And neither do I, she added silently.

"Then we'll have to make the most of your time off. I saved the best seat in the house for you." Ansel led them through the spectators, milling this way and that as they found their seats, and back behind a flap that appeared to separate the backstage area.

He turned right up a narrow set of wooden stairs, only slightly too deep to be called a ladder. Rhosyn took her first step upward only to find this angle gave her an extremely close view of Ansel's backside. Immediately, she paused, letting him get a few extra steps in front of her and looking determinedly at her feet as she followed. She should be behaving professionally, especially while in uniform, Rhosyn reminded herself, not gawking crassly like the lower city street urchin she was.

Such thoughts were forgotten when Ansel pulled back the curtain at the top of the steps and revealed a small box overlooking the stage from above. From this height, she was nearly level with some of the tightropes. As Ansel beckoned her into the space, she approached the edge and looked over the railing at the other spectators below.

What would it be like to be one of the acrobats, to dangle from this height with only your balance and wits to protect you? Even as the idea made her dizzy, a thrill ran up her spine.

"I take it you like the accommodations?" Ansel asked, a brow raised.

"I think a private box might be a little grand for just me," Rhosyn said, turning to the small number of comfortable-looking chairs crowded into the tight space.

"You did best me," Ansel argued.

"Don't think this will get you out of showing me your circus act." Rhosyn jabbed a finger into his chest. It was surprisingly firm, indicating more muscle than his size would suggest. "Were you an acrobat? The strong man?"

"You don't have much patience, do you?" Ansel deflected. "Even when you're given entertainment fit for a king to occupy you while you wait."

"Why is patience always the virtue people espouse?" Rhosyn grumbled. "Why can't getting things done be the virtue?"

Ansel chuckled. "I guarantee I'll give you the promised demonstration. For now, I must leave you to your own devices to go and get the show started."

With a small bow, he backed out of the space, leaving Rhosyn to take her seat. She didn't have to wait very long until Ansel appeared on the stage below, raising his arms. The voices of the spectators fell to hushed whispers, the air practically quivering with the barely contained tension of anticipation. It captured Rhosyn in its threads, pulling her to perch on the edge of her seat, leaning forward so she wouldn't miss anything.

As Ansel spoke, thanking the audience for coming and welcoming them to Archer's Circus, the Merry Men slipped quietly onto the platforms across from her, from which they would leap. They wore the same green outfits as before, and Rhosyn's heart rate accelerated in excitement. Sitting level with them, imagining diving off the edge in a freefall before catching the trapeze at the last moment, added a thrill she hadn't anticipated.

The crowd erupted in applause as Ansel finished his introduction, gesturing upwards to direct the rest of the audience's attention to the acrobats, moments before they began the dizzying dance of falling and flying.

Seeing the Merry Men for the second time did nothing to lessen the heart-pounding effect. Gravity seemed to have lifted its spell temporarily, letting the performers achieve feats that Rhosyn wouldn't have even dreamed of attempting.

As one of the men flipped off a platform before easily grabbing a swinging trapeze at the peak of its arc, the image of the Hood performing a perfect front flip from the fence last night flickered through her mind. She had entertained the thought he was one of the circus performers before, but dismissed it when she didn't spot anybody fitting his build at the King's ball. Maybe he hadn't been performing that night though. Or perhaps she had missed something.

Rhosyn's eyes narrowed as she began consuming the performance with a clinical eye. One by one, she appraised the men flying through the air. A good number of them she ruled out quickly for being too tall. A few were too thin, while several were bulkier than the wiry strength of the arm banded across her chest last night would suggest.

What's more, something in their posture was off. As awe inspiring as the Merry Men were, none of them quite carried themselves with the effortless confidence she remembered on the Hood as he repetitively slipped from her grasp.

Rhosyn shook herself. She was just exaggerating the Hood's prowess for being the most challenging and intriguing criminal she had encountered in years. These men were her best suspects. After all, she had encountered the Hood for the first time just the day before they performed at the King's ball.

She just needed evidence.

Rhosyn tore her attention from the spectacle before her, instead inspecting the rest of her surroundings. For now, she was unattended, and everybody in the vicinity was preoccupied with the performance. If there was any evidence to be found backstage, now was the time for an unapproved investigation.

With one last look to confirm Ansel's position at the corner of the stage, eyes darting between the forms flipping above him, Rhosyn slipped from the private booth. She descended the ladder to the ground level quickly and quietly. When she turned and looked around the backstage area, she found it deserted, as she had hoped.

Finding what she was looking for, though, might be another challenge entirely. The area wasn't exactly organized—or if it was, it was sensible only to the people who had done it. Cracked open crates with swathes of colored fabric spilling out the top dotted the area. Rhosyn had to slip past a large spinning wheel and a stack of painted wood slats as she perused the area.

Finally, in the back, against a wall that had green curtains hung against it, folded over as if for storage, lay a series of bundles. They looked like discarded clothes and personal effects—likely where the performers kept their things after changing into their less practical costumes.

Rhosyn knelt and began rifling through the bags and bundles with deft fingers. As she went, she carefully catalogued exactly how clothes were draped and packs stacked. It was a habit from years of lifting little trinkets and emptying purses to feed her young charges—and thankfully one that returned quickly when she wanted to investigate without giving herself away.

As she reached the third pile of belongings, she asked herself exactly what she was looking for. Maybe the familiar hood itself, or the wrist bow that the Hood seemed to favor, although he might not carry those everywhere. She had already uncovered several small blades, but carrying a knife didn't necessarily mean one was a criminal. For those who walked alone at night, Rhosyn would nearly consider it reckless not too.

Although, as the fourth bundle revealed yet another set of knives—clearly well cared for and stored in sheathes that could easily be strapped to ankles or forearms—she did have to wonder at how well armed this performing troupe was.

So focused was Rhosyn on looking through the remaining contents of the satchel, intent on sussing out any hidden pockets that could contain incriminating evidence, that she didn't hear the footsteps coming up behind her. A hand reached over her shoulder and deftly pulled free one of the knives, forgotten in her hand as she continued her search.

She spun in place, already swinging her leg out in her crouch to catch her potential attacker in the ankles. Rhosyn stopped her kick just short, as she found Ansel staring down at her with a bemused expression.

He tossed the knife up, where it flipped twice before he plucked it out of the air easily by the handle. Rhosyn blinked, nearly forgetting that he had caught her looking through his performers' belongings. He hadn't even been looking at the knife as he tossed it. The only person who she had ever seen handle a blade so confidently before was Nate.

"You don't seem concerned with waiting for a warrant," he commented. He twirled the knife absent-mindedly and Rhosyn suddenly became all too aware of her position kneeling at his feet. She shot upright and scowled.

"What's that supposed to mean?" she demanded.

"An officer of the Royal Police rifling through my circus unattended? One would think you suspected us of something," he shrugged. His tone was casual, but his eyes were sharp.

"Maybe it was personal curiosity," Rhosyn deflected, knowing it was a weak argument.

"I thought you made it clear this wasn't personal when you showed up for a night of revelry in uniform," Ansel said, and although his tone remained teasing, for some reason the observation rang of sadness to Rhosyn.

She shrugged. "Well, it hardly matters, because I didn't find what I was looking for anyways."

"Oh, and what was that?"

"Clues to what your circus act was, since you seem intent on keeping that information under wraps." Rhosyn knew Ansel was too sharp to let her meddling drop, but was surprised when he rose to the bait, eyes twinkling as a smirk curled his lips.

"Oh, but you did." Ansel tossed the knife in the air again, and Rhosyn's gaze tracked the swirling silver as it rose and fell.

She raised her brows in question.

"Call a target," Ansel instructed, gesturing to the empty backstage.

Rhosyn's eyes swept over the cluttered area and landed on the stairs up to the box she had occupied before her ill-fated exploration.

She pointed. "The steps. Fourth one up, dead center."

Without windup or preamble, Ansel's arm whipped past Rhosyn's face, wrist snapping forward a moment before the knife embedded itself in the wooden stair with a solid *thwack*—exactly where Rhosyn had specified.

She blinked in surprise, but quickly schooled her features.

"*Psh.* That's hardly worth selling tickets to see. I could do that."

On a good day, with a healthy amount of practice, she amended in her head. She had once been proficient with throwing knives, but they hadn't been in her repertoire for a while now.

"You're a tough sell." Ansel reached for Rhosyn's hand and pulled the second knife out of the sheath, which dangled forgotten at her side. "How about something a little tougher then."

He bent and rustled through the packs at their feet, making no effort to leave them looking undisturbed, as Rhosyn had. He emerged with an apple and handed it to Rhosyn.

"I'm not really in the mood for a snack," she commented drily.

Ansel fixed her with an impatient look. "Go on. Throw it."

Rhosyn gave him a look of question. When his expression remained sincere, she shrugged and gave the fruit a solid toss. It arced through the air away from them.

At the zenith of its flight, Ansel threw the second knife. It embedded itself in the far wall a moment before the apple fell to the ground, split neatly in two.

Now, Rhosyn didn't hide her surprise. Comparing knife tricks was a classic pastime among the gangs, but she had never seen somebody perform such a feat.

"I'll admit, I don't have any tricks quite that good."

"Come now, I'm sure we could find a place for you in the circus if you got tired of police work. Maybe some sleight of hand?"

Rhosyn sighed dramatically. "Well, I do know one trick." She turned to face Ansel and stepped close. He blinked at her sudden proximity. Rhosyn took advantage of the moment, leaning in and widening her eyes at him pleadingly. "It's silly though, so you have to promise not to laugh."

Ansel swallowed thickly and nodded, clearly so thrown by her sudden invasion of his space that he paid little attention to anything besides her face, inches from his. It was far closer than people tended to get in proper society, but she wasn't above using her lack of her propriety to her advantage.

A smile split Rhosyn's face and she stepped back. As Ansel frowned, Rhosyn lifted her hand, which had subtly slid into his pocket as he was distracted.

"I'm quite a good pickpocket. Let's see what we have here."

Ansel lunged forward as if to steal her prize from her grasp, but Rhosyn danced back to examine what had felt like a slip of paper. Perhaps it was a secret note or an embarrassing letter.

To her confusion, upon examination, it seemed to be a single playing card. She turned it over in her fingers, wondering why he might be carrying such a thing in his pocket. The three of spades stared up at her and her eyebrows knit together.

An image flashed in her head—the Hood, hunching over her and picking up a fallen playing card from the ground as she gasped for air. He had tucked it into his jacket before slipping away into the poisoned smoke.

Rhosyn had swapped this card for the queen of hearts in her hand the night of the Gower's party.

Her head snapped up to stare at Ansel, but he had already realized his mistake by the time her mind fit the pieces together.

His fist flew towards her face, but she had just enough time to turn away. The blow brushed past her nose by the breadth of a hair.

Rhosyn let the momentum of her dodge carry her into a full spin. As she came back around, she threw her elbow out. It caught Ansel square in the chest and he stumbled back. With him on the back foot, she advanced.

She lashed out with fists and feet, her standard issue police baton remaining forgotten at her belt. Sure, she was attempting to apprehend a criminal, but the Hood's crimes remained in the back of her mind.

This brawl was personal.

Ansel had flirted with her and tricked her—he had been right under her nose the whole time, smiling and dancing. He would answer to her fists. Rhosyn was a daughter of the Lions, after all.

With a kick to his knee, Rhosyn sent Ansel sprawling to the packed dirt ground. She fell on top of him, pinning his torso to the ground beneath her thighs. As frighteningly competent as he was with a knife, both blades were now on the opposite side of the room, and he was no match for Rhosyn in an all-out brawl. She was used to inelegant fights and had the crooked nose to prove it.

However, even as Rhosyn bore Ansel into the ground, his hands remained free. He managed to get one on Rhosyn's face, shoving it to the side. This time, she didn't refrain from biting him, closing her teeth savagely around his finger.

His howl of pain split the air as Rhosyn tasted copper. His shout was loud enough to risk being heard in the main tent, even over the roar of the still-cheering crowd.

He wrenched his hand away, trying to hook Rhosyn's legs to flip them over. Rhosyn countered by grabbing his wrist, trying to pin him to the ground. She nearly lost focus as pounding footsteps sounded behind her. Ansel's shout must have drawn an audience to their tussle.

"You. Are under...arrest." Rhosyn grunted as she continued to wrestle Ansel into the ground despite his struggles. She was suddenly glad she was wearing her uniform.

"John," Ansel gasped. "John!"

Rhosyn only had a moment to frown before thick arms wrapped around her torso, hauling her up and back. She kicked and hissed but it was no use.

The form behind her was easily twice as broad as Ansel. Her efforts to dislodge his grip were as fruitless as attempting to push a steam engine by hand. Still, Rhosyn kicked out, nearly catching Ansel in the head as he pushed to his feet. She bared her teeth, prepared to call him a set of creative names, but a cloth pressed over her nose and mouth just as she inhaled.

It smelled and tasted just like the smoke from Hood's bomb, but so concentrated it made her eyes water and throat burn. She coughed as her lungs tried to reject the vapors, but it was too late. Her vision began to swim, her efforts to escape weakening quickly.

Ansel's mouth moved as if he was saying something, but his voice reached her muffled and quiet, as if she were listening to him from under water. Just before the darkness at the edges of her vision closed in, Rhosyn met Ansel's eyes, but instead of triumph, she could have sworn they held regret.

Chapter Six

R hosyn sank luxuriously into the mattress beneath her. Even though it was lumpy and thin, she couldn't bring herself to open her eyes. She couldn't remember the last time she felt so relaxed. Usually, she jerked awake before dawn out of habit, ready to don her uniform and head out on patrol. Even now, she often shot up, imagining she heard a child's cry, even though she hadn't had any in her charge for several years.

Today, though, she lounged, embracing the heaviness in her limbs that seemed to keep her bound to the bed. It was that feeling of immobilization in her limbs that planted a seed of doubt in Rhosyn's mind. Questions slowly wormed themselves into her sluggish brain: what time was it? Where was she? Why wasn't she jumping up to prepare for a day of work?

Voices, somewhat muffled as if passing through a door, interrupted her thoughts.

"—can't keep her here. Somebody is sure to come looking."

"You know I wouldn't consider the alternative."

Rhosyn's eyes snapped open at that voice. Ansel—the Hood—the tone belonged to both of them, yet neither of them. It didn't have the flirting cadence of Mr. Blakely and wasn't pitched quite as low as the

Hood's. Instead, Ansel sounded resigned, but his voice brought memories rushing back all the same.

Rhosyn's gaze focused on an unfamiliar ceiling, after a few slow blinks to clear the blurriness from her vision. Battered gray slats, looking weathered enough Rhosyn was surprised she couldn't see the room above, told her she was no longer in the tent where she had been knocked unconscious.

She made to sit up, only to find that the heaviness of her limbs was not just from her exhaustion, but from a set of ropes binding her wrists and ankles to the bedposts. With a grunt, she struggled against them and succeeded only in rattling the rickety bedframe.

"*Shhh.*" Ansel's voice filtered through the door again. "I think she's awake."

Rhosyn exhaled heavily through her nose in frustration. In her anxiousness to get free, she had given up any chance to inspect her surroundings unnoticed. She stilled, listening for any snippets of the conversation outside that could give her an idea where she was, or how to escape.

"Well...what are you going to do?" the unfamiliar voice asked, low but still just audible.

Silence stretched.

"You can't just leave her in there," it pressed.

"I'm going to...talk to her."

Ansel's companion responded with a snort. "Oh, she definitely seemed like she would respond well to a reasonable conversation."

"I can hear you, you know!" Rhosyn shouted at the ceiling, losing patience. She may as well make something happen if her captors were intent on waffling in the hall.

After a moment of extended stillness, a creak indicated the opening of a door. Rhosyn lifted her head, the crane of her neck an uncomfortable strain with her arms stretched above her. Ansel stood in the doorway, an unmistakable combination of the two men who had haunted her life of late. He was dressed like the Hood, in dark green, practical gear that contrasted greatly with the pageantry of his circus-owner garb. He had forgone the hood though, leaving his expression visible. Although his green eyes and the silver streak in his hair were familiar, his welcoming smile was replaced by a hard look. He stared at Rhosyn like she was a problem he couldn't solve. From his frown, she would have thought he was the one who had woken up tied to a bed.

After a moment of staring, Rhosyn raised her brows in silent question.

"I didn't mean for this to happen," Ansel started.

"Funny, these knots seem rather intentional." Rhosyn tugged on her wrists for emphasis.

A furrow formed between Ansel's brows. "You know that isn't what I meant."

"I wouldn't have thought you would need to resort to drugging and kidnapping to lure a woman into your bed." The words popped out before Rhosyn could think better of them or realize that she wasn't in the best situation to be taunting her captor.

Ansel pursed his lips. "It's not my bed."

"Well, if this isn't a social call, would you care to enlighten me on where I am?"

"You know who I am," Ansel pointed out. "You were going to arrest me."

Rhosyn huffed. "Assaulting and kidnapping an officer of the Royal Police is a criminal offense too, in case you didn't know."

With a tired sigh, Ansel took a few steps further into the room, coming up next to the bed. At this angle, Rhosyn could finally relax her neck against the pillow and just turn her head to keep him in her line of sight.

"I am aware, but I couldn't let you stop me. I have some important things to take care of." Ansel didn't meet Rhosyn's eyes, instead reaching out to run a finger along the rope binding her. She watched as he slid one finger between the loop and her wrist, as if testing to see how tight it was. The callused pad of his finger rasped against the sensitive skin of her inner wrist. She thought of the dexterous way he twirled a knife and swallowed thickly.

"If you keep me for more than a few hours, people will realize I'm missing." Rhosyn commented to distract herself from Ansel's touch as he repeated the same movement on the other wrist. She tried to curl her fingers to claw at the back of his hand, but he withdrew quickly. "Chief Thorne will notice if I don't show up for my patrol in the morning."

"I'm afraid that ship has left the harbor." Ansel grimaced.

Rhosyn furrowed her brow. "What do you mean? How long have I been here?"

"You've been out for almost twenty-four hours. I was afraid Little John accidentally killed you, although I shouldn't be surprised that you needed the sleep—"

"It's been a whole *day?*" Rhosyn cut off his conjecture and began squirming anew.

"Honestly, it seems like you should be thanking me for helping you catch up on your rest." Ansel snorted. "With you patrolling the streets during the day and prowling on your own by dark, it's no wonder you haven't been sleeping."

Rhosyn drew back her lips in a snarl at the mention of her private investigations. She certainly wasn't going to be able to find Paul and Olivia while tied up goodness-knows where.

Ansel cocked his head at her. "You clearly don't trust the Police's methods if you are doing your own investigations off the books. I had hoped we would be able to come to some sort of...understanding."

An audible growl worked its way up from the back of Rhosyn's throat. "Don't you *dare* think I'm a thief and a kidnapper like you. I am a good officer of the Royal Police, because I care about this city, and I will do whatever it takes to protect it from people like you."

Ansel's boots *thunked* heavily against the floor, a juxtaposition to his normally graceful gait, as he stumbled back like Rhosyn's words hard been physical blows.

Rhosyn settled back on her pillows, partially satisfied that she had managed to verbally wound Ansel. Under the thin layer of vindication lay a hollowness, though. The city's criminals looked at her and saw not somebody who was there to protect her home, but an ally. Sure, she had started life on the wrong side of the law, back when the Royal Police were rife with corruption, but now things were different. Still, a thief—and potentially a kidnapper—looked at her and saw somebody who could be corrupted.

Her glare hardened further and Ansel's expression turned stricken.

"I see you aren't ready to talk. Maybe you'll change your mind after another day or two." With that he backed out of the room. Part of Rhosyn wanted to scream and snarl and tear apart her bonds through strength of will, but she remained quiet as he left the room, not trusting her words. Her lack of judgment had gotten her into this situation, and now she needed to think.

The door thudded closed, signaling that Rhosyn was alone once more. Murmured voices told Rhosyn that Ansel's friend had been waiting for him, but the conversation drifted away before she could catch any more words.

She turned her attention to her bonds and anything in the room that might help her, but came up blank. The grayish wooden slats of the walls stared back at her bleakly, looking like every room for rent in the lower city, and giving her no indication where she might be. Straining her ears, she thought she heard some boisterous laughter and the sounds of general merriment from the floors below.

Perhaps the ground floor held a tavern. It almost reminded her of the sounds one would hear in one of the Lion's communal safehouses, above their gambling parlors—the ones where young Lions who outgrew the Den lived, while Rhosyn lingered behind to keep the next wave safe and fed.

It seemed counterintuitive that Ansel and his partners in crime would want to keep her in a tavern though, where it would be difficult to keep her presence a secret. Rhosyn's brain sparked. Perhaps she *was* in a gang hideout, and the Hood had already made some dodgy friends who were willing to hold her hostage in exchange for a cut of whatever plot he was undertaking.

She winced as the rough ropes of her bonds chafed her skin, pulling tight in her struggles, even after Ansel had checked that they wouldn't do her permanent harm.

Escaping would be no easy task. If she had been in shackles, she might have been able to use some of her Contessa's lockpicking tricks, but they wouldn't be any use on the expertly tied knots. She wished for

Scarlett's shadowy Talent to help her slip free, but she remained Talent-less—something she had fervently thanked luck for during the Inquiries.

Rhosyn was left only with herself and her unfortunate tendency to punch first and ask questions after.

She tried to ask herself what Nate or Kristoff would do, but her brain unhelpfully refused to offer anything outside of an amusing image of Kristoff trying to flirt his way out of his predicament. It might not have been such a bad idea if Rhosyn hadn't just spat a slew of insults at her captor.

Despite her best efforts, Rhosyn's attention soon drifted to the soft pillow under her head. It sucked her in with unusual gravity, lulling her into abandoning her plans of escape for the time being. Sleep sang its siren song, more alluring than ever, even after a full day of unconsciousness.

Maybe the drugs Ansel's ally had used on her were inordinately strong. Or maybe, tied down with nobody to punch and no fight to pick, Rhosyn gave into rest.

A door slamming jerked Rhosyn awake hard enough that she nearly gave herself whiplash trying to jump to her feet, before remembering her bonds. As it was, her head snapped forward to see the figure who had made the sudden noise.

A man, so wide and muscular Rhosyn was surprised he fit through the door, stood at the foot of the bed frowning at her. Every thought she had of clever things to say to her captors flew from her mind as she took in the sheer mass of him.

"Where'd the H—Ansel—dig up a lower city bruiser like you?" The words tumbled out of her mouth without a thought.

The man's wide-set features crumpled into a frown. "I'm not from London."

Rhosyn blinked, but her visitor didn't offer any more information. She looked him up and down curiously once more, when her gaze snagged on a cup of water, dwarfed in his meaty paws. Automatically, she tried to swallow around the incredible dryness in her throat, after so much rest and nothing to drink. The sight of water drew unavoidable awareness to the feeling in her mouth of having swallowed a fistful of sand.

"Is that for me?" Rhosyn asked, trying and failing to nod at the water with her neck crooked at such a tight angle.

The man nodded, but stepped forward hesitantly, as if Rhosyn were the one that looked like she crushed boulders with her biceps to pass the time.

Impatient, Rhosyn snapped, "I don't bite."

"The teeth marks on Ansel's hand say otherwise."

Rhosyn grimaced. "I try not to bite the hands that feed me," she corrected.

He resumed his approach, still slowly, and Rhosyn watched him carefully. While the bulk of his frame was clearly composed of muscle, he didn't carry himself with the grace of a fighter. Not to mention, size wasn't everything in a scrap. The hardest fight Rhosyn had ever had was against Scarlett, who didn't even make it to her chin.

Maybe Rhosyn shouldn't try to emulate Contessa or Scarlett's skills to escape.

Maybe she should just be Rhosyn, and let the chips fall where they may.

She kept her eyes trained on the liquid sloshing in the cup as her captor leaned in, trying to appear completely distracted by her thirst. He put his hand behind her head to help her tip forward to drink, the move so polite that Rhosyn nearly felt bad for what she was about to do.

The moment he bent over to tip the water into her mouth, she snapped forward, slamming her forehead into his nose.

The world went white as the man let out a loud curse. A shattering crash split the air as the cup of water fell to the floor, but Rhosyn couldn't feel any satisfaction at landing a solid blow. She was too busy blinking stars from her vision and wondering if it was possible to scramble your brains in your skull.

As her sight cleared, she was incredulous to find that the man looked relatively unfazed, thick fingers wiping the tiniest dribble of blood from his nose and upper lip. Rhosyn had used her face as a weapon more than was strictly advisable in her life, and in her experience that should have shattered her opponent's nose. Instead, she was left reeling, while he only seemed mildly annoyed.

She would have to stop teasing Contessa about breaking her own nose in an ill-advised headbutt after this.

Before Rhosyn or her visitor could do more than take a quick stock of her injuries, the door slammed open once more.

"I see you've taken the liberty of introducing yourself to Little John, Rhosyn," Ansel observed as he took in the chaotic scene before him.

"... don't know why you're insisting on keeping her," the man, who must be Little John, grumbled under his breath.

Ansel ignored his comment and Rhosyn tried to wrap her head around him referring to this giant as "little".

"Go wash your face. I'll handle this," Ansel instructed. A few heavy footsteps and a creak of the door on its hinges, and they were alone in the room.

Rhosyn tried to scowl but was pretty sure she ruined it with eyes still crossed from the blow to her head. She didn't regret it though. If Ansel insisted on holding an officer of the Royal Police captive, she wasn't inclined to make it easy for him.

"I was trying to convince Little John that we could at least untie your feet, but you seem determined to undermine me at every turn." He crossed his arms over his chest as he stared down at her with the look of a man assessing the broken wheel on his carriage.

"Being tied down doesn't induce me to act quiet and polite," Rhosyn countered.

Ansel snorted. "You would have more of a point if you hadn't been asleep for the better part of a day."

"Which is concerning for you, because the longer you hold me here, the worse it will be for you when Chief Throne tracks you down."

"He won't be finding you here."

Ansel's tone held so much surety that a thrill ran up Rhosyn's spine. Maybe she was trapped here, immobilized at the mercy of a man who had become a notorious criminal nearly as fast as Nate had been dubbed "the Beast". Perhaps she should have been more concerned by her predicament, but an oddly familiar fire burned in her gut, the threat of danger igniting in her blood.

"I wouldn't be so sure," Rhosyn threatened with a too-wide grin.

Ansel's brows rose at the challenge in her words. "Oh, because your Royal Police were doing so well at tracking us down before now. And the one officer who came close to discovering us is no longer on the board." Ansel inclined his head towards her. "If they can't track down the missing Talented, they won't be able to find you."

Rhosyn jerked, the excitement in her veins sizzling into anger at Ansel's implication. He didn't just know what had happened to Olivia and Paul—he had them.

"Where are they? Where are Olivia and Paul?" The words came out a hiss between her gritted teeth.

Ansel's posture straightened, as if he wanted to back up a step against the force of Rhosyn's anger, but had trained himself too well to retreat in the face of danger. "I'll tell you, but I need you to show me that I can trust you first."

"And why would I do that?" Rhosyn asked, voice like stone.

"Because I have a feeling you might see things my way, but I need to know you're not going to ruin our plans before I tell you anything."

Her curiosity piqued, but her hands still involuntarily curled into fists, tight enough that nails she had bitten down to the quick still dug into her palms. "If you've hurt one hair on Paul's and Olivia's heads, you'll have more to worry about then spending the rest of your life rotting away in prison."

Ansel's solemn nod indicated that he took her threat seriously. Rhosyn wasn't wholly satisfied, but her inner Lion purred in pride.

"I'm going to untie your legs. If you can prove to me that you won't immediately try to break all my associates' noses, I'll let you see Paul and Olivia."

After a moment's hesitation, Rhosyn nodded. Ansel bent over to untie her feet, although he watched her warily, as if he half expected her to kick him in the face. She didn't blame him, but remained relaxed against the mattress.

As the bonds immobilizing her lower body went slack, Rhosyn flexed her legs and circled her ankles, grimacing at the stiffness in her hips after staying in one position for so long.

To her surprise, Ansel put a hand on her calf, rubbing it to restore any lost circulation. Once again, she noted calluses rasping gently on the sensitive skin just below the inside of her ankle bone. It almost tickled, and Rhosyn had a sudden urge to squirm, despite his touch being focused on such an innocuous area—no, she would not admit to Contessa that there was anything remotely scandalous about ankles, thank you very much. Instead, she thought about the roughness of Ansel's palm, which made more sense now that she had seen his practiced ability with a knife. She snorted quietly at the thought.

Ansel looked at her curiously.

"When I felt your hand the first time, I guessed you were a juggler because of the calluses. I don't know how I didn't recognize the hands of a knife-fighter," she explained. In fact, Ansel's hands felt similarly rough to her own, although missing the hardened skin across the fingers that came from Rhosyn's brass knuckles.

"Who says I can't juggle knives?" Ansel asked, a hint of the charismatic circus performer leaking into his voice. Now though, it didn't seem as exaggerated, less the purposeful airs of a performer than a teasing twinkle in his eyes. Rhosyn wondered if it was genuine.

Realizing his hand had stilled on her calf, Rhosyn yanked it out of his grip. He had dazzled her into overlooking his guilt before, and it wouldn't happen again.

Ignoring the weight of Ansel's gaze, she twisted her legs this way and that to relieve any stiffness. She stretched her spine too, frowning. She felt...great. Certainly not how she would expect to feel after being knocked unconscious and kidnapped.

Her muscles felt pliant but strong, responding quickly to her commands, a far cry from the sluggishness she often battled against at the end of her patrols. She was still thirsty though, and her stomach grumbled in hunger. Although she had ruined her chance at a glass of water a few minutes earlier, she couldn't completely bring herself to regret it.

She continued to work out her stiffness, surreptitiously testing the bonds on her wrists. They remained immovable, clearly expertly tied—perhaps assembling the trapezes and tightropes that held the weight of multiple performers every night conferred you with impressive knot tying skills—but the rickety bedframe creaked with her movements.

Rhosyn smiled sheepishly at Ansel, trying with difficulty to summon the more docile side of her nature. "If I promise not to break your nose, can we try again with a glass of water."

Ansel nodded. "If it's any consolation, I doubt you did any permanent damage to Little John's nose."

"It makes it sound even crueler when you call him 'Little'," Rhosyn grumped.

"When he was younger, his friends thought it was a clever name for the circus's strong man. They realized it wasn't, but the name had already stuck." Ansel smiled wryly.

Rhosyn blinked at the realization that Ansel hadn't hired John from a gang for intimidation. He was actually a member of the circus.

Ansel took a few steps back in her silence. "I'll be back with water."

As the door hinges creaked, Rhosyn lay still, waiting for the click of the lock to tell her she was alone. The moment Ansel was gone, Rhosyn heaved with her abs, folding her body in half.

She wasn't as flexible as she once was, when she spent so many hours teaching youngsters self-defense and how to stay limber, but she still managed to swing her legs over her head until her feet planted on the wall above the headboard.

Her face twisted into a combination of a grimace and a chuckle, thinking how she had only ever found herself in this position in very different circumstances. Ansel would be greeted by a remarkable view of her ass if he were to open the door at that moment, but she needed the leverage.

She pushed against the wall, thighs straining next to her ears. The ropes around her wrists creaked at the pressure but showed no sign of breaking. Rhosyn paid them no mind—it wasn't them she was trying to break.

As she had hoped, the bed, which had already been squeaky and rickety, gave an almighty groan. Rhosyn gritted her teeth and redoubled her efforts, veins beginning to pop in her neck. Splintering gave way to cracking as the bedframe surrendered to her strength.

The entire headboard ripped free so suddenly that Rhosyn almost hit herself on the head with the heavy plank of wood. Before the bed could collapse completely, she rolled sideways, letting her legs fall so she could land on her feet.

Her boots hit the floor so hard the entire downstairs would have heard, but secrecy had flown out the window with the earsplitting groan of wood giving way. She straightened, head whipping back and forth as she absorbed her predicament. Her hands were still bound to the heavy board she had ripped free, but it would be useful as a makeshift club to use against those who would resist her escape.

The hazy light of the lower city filtered in through one grimy window. Rhosyn hurried over to it and grimaced when she saw a several story drop. Scarlett might have made the jump, but Rhosyn didn't have shadows to break her fall. She wouldn't be able to climb down with her hands hindered.

No matter. Fighting her way out the front door was more her style anyway.

Feet pounded on the stairs outside and Rhosyn turned towards the entrance, ready for the onslaught. The door swung open, but Rhosyn was already charging, lowering her shoulder to bowl over anyone in her way. Ansel jumped out of the way, but Rhosyn barreled past, straight into an unfamiliar man behind him.

They teetered for a moment before tumbling down a narrow flight of stairs. Lightning lanced up Rhosyn's limbs as she banged knees and elbows against the walls and steps. She shoved the sensations aside as they rolled to a stop on a landing, springing to her feet.

The man who fell with her tried to do the same, but a kick from Rhosyn left him howling in pain. She spun, finding the next flight of stairs and bounding down them two at a time.

"Rhosyn!" Ansel shouted behind her, but Rhosyn didn't hesitate.

She leaped down the last few stairs and skidded around a corner, only to be brought up short by the sight before her. A crowded room, filled with young men and women sitting around tables scattered with dice and tankards, stood between her and the exit.

Grimacing, she had the fleeting thought that she regretted being right about being kept in a gang hideout. She didn't have time to consider what gang it might be before the sound of Ansel pounding down the stairs behind her told her she was out of time.

In the few feet of open space between her and the nearest cluster of people, she took a running start before leaping. She landed on the surface of the first table in a crouch. Shouting broke out as she stood, traversing the length of the table in a few long strides.

She jumped to the next table as people leaped into action. A burly man tried to reach for her ankle, but she kicked a tankard as she passed. It caught him full in the face, and he reared back, spluttering.

By the time her long legs carried her to the next table, a hardened-looking woman stood in her path, fists raised in challenge. Her opponent swung, and Rhosyn lifted her arms, headboard still bound between them. She caught the blow on the wood like a shield, and the woman swore as her knuckles met a surface far more solid than flesh.

Rhosyn pressed the advantage, driving her knee up into the woman's lower stomach. She doubled over with a gasp as the breath was punched from her. Rhosyn rolled over her back, kicking out as she did so at another grasping hand.

Another jump and she was just a few tables from the door. Her balance slipped as the sole of her boot landed on a deck of cards. She threw her hands out, but the unfamiliar weight of the headboard overbalanced her.

Her knees hit the tabletop with an eye-watering crack. Another man wasted no time jumping on her. She lashed out, smacking him in the face with her plank of wood. He grunted, but the blow had been off center, and he continued to try to pin her down.

With a cry, Rhosyn raised her hands before bringing the board down over the crown of his head so hard, the already-splintered wood cracked in two. At this, the man stilled, dazed from the impact.

"Rhosyn, wait!" Ansel's voice cut through the crowd, but the blood pounded too intensely in Rhosyn's ears for her to make sense of his words.

Rhosyn wrapped her calf around her opponent's, flipping them over and continuing the roll until she landed with her knee at his neck. She pressed down with enough weight to keep him subdued without strangling him.

Her head whipped left and right, hair falling in sweaty tendrils across her face as she looked for her next opponent—her snarl dared them to approach.

"Rhosyn." Another familiar voice cut through the cacophony of the hideout, but it wasn't Ansel.

"You have to let him go, Rhosyn."

She searched the faces around her for the source of the voice, the fury of the fight rushing from her as if somebody had thrown a bucket of cold water over her. The anxious expressions of those surrounding her swam, blurring together until she found him near the entrance—a child that had somehow grown into a man without her noticing.

"Paul?" Rhosyn asked, her chokehold on the man beneath her slackening. "Paul, I have to..."

She had to save him and Olivia. She had to protect her Lion cubs as she always had, even though they had left the Den.

"Just let him go and we can work it all out," Paul soothed. Rhosyn recognized the rhythmic cadence in his voice that always emerged when he used his Talent. While it had been a godsend when other children in the Den suffered from nightmares, Rhosyn bristled at the realization of what he was doing.

She shook herself, renewing her pressure on her opponent's neck.

"No, please. It's alright." Paul insisted, the Talent overtaking his voice entirely. Try as she might to ignore him, his voice wormed into her skull and laid a warm blanket over her thoughts.

Even as her eyelids grew heavy and she couldn't make out what Paul was saying, only the lulling cadence of his words, she tried to make sense of what was happening.

Paul must be working with Ansel. Maybe he had left his sponsored position with the Gower's for a life of crime after all.

The sting of betrayal cut through the exhaustion now weighing down every limb. She fought against it, trying to blink rapidly and shake her head. A wave of anger rolled over her as her sluggish brain processed the thoughts, almost breaking her free of Paul's mental grasp.

She had given her youth to protecting the Lions and fighting the Inquiries, so children like Paul and Olivia could have the life she had given up by choosing to stay with Nate and Kristoff. All that sacrifice, and here Paul was, throwing in with a criminal despite it all. Maybe being a lower-city urchin wasn't something you could outgrow, no matter how much Rhosyn fought.

With that thought, despair washed away the tide of Rhosyn's rage, leaving her empty and vulnerable to Paul's Talent. The thug beneath her slipped out of her slackening grip, leaving her off balance. She tipped forward, too tired to even put out her hands to break her fall.

Before she could pitch off the table and slam face first into the parquet floor, arms closed around her. Her face pressed into a well-sculpted chest, as the one who had caught her pulled her to him. Rhosyn's nose filled with a smell that was both sweet and spicy, like burnt sugar, undercut with a musk of masculinity.

She was too tired to muster up frustration at Ansel having the audacity to smell so good while ripping her life to shreds. Instead, she used the magically-induced exhaustion as an excuse to take a deep lung-full as she fell into a dreamless sleep.

Chapter Seven

R hosyn's position this time she woke from an artificially induced slumber was much less comfortable. The wooden slats of a chair dug into her arms, wrenched back and tied firmly behind her. Still, her eyes opened sluggishly, despite the sharpness of the discomfort dragging her towards consciousness.

As she blinked away the bleariness in her vision, the reason for her placidity became apparent. Paul sat in a chair across from her, expression wary as he muttered soothing nonsense. It left her too tired to struggle against her bonds, but he wasn't keeping her fully asleep.

Instead of trying to tug free, she took inventory of her situation, looking down to find her ankles and calves roped to the legs of the chair.

"I see my accommodations have been downgraded." Her voice came out more drowsy than scathing, but Paul still grimaced when she looked back at him.

"It was the one piece of furniture around here we thought you might not be able to break," he admitted.

"You're stronger than you look, but we already knew that," a female voice chimed in.

Rhosyn turned her head, the movement feeling slow, as if she were underwater, and was greeted by a familiar round face.

"Olivia!" A mix of relief and disappointment washed over her. She was glad to see the girl safe, even if she had hoped Paul's sister hadn't also fallen in with Ansel.

"I would say it was good to see you again but..." Olivia twisted her hands fitfully in the apron she wore.

"Tying me to the chair wasn't the greeting I had hoped for. And after I had been so worried about you!" Rhosyn's words came out with more bite now that Paul was no longer talking, his Talent only working with his voice.

"I couldn't let you hurt any more people," Paul admitted ruefully, his tone devoid of any persuasive hypnotism.

"You can't blame me for roughing up the people who I thought had kidnapped you," Rhosyn argued.

"But now you know we're not here against our will—" Olivia started.

"Which doesn't make me any less inclined to punch something," Rhosyn shot before biting her tongue. Olivia's eyes widened and Rhosyn shoved down the guilt she felt at causing such an expression. Even though that doe-eyed look made her look like the child who had been plagued by nightmares until her brother's Talent awoke, she was a teenager now, and old enough to know wrong from right.

"Nate and Contessa, they—we have fought too hard to give you the chance for a life where you don't have to run from the law. And then you throw it all away...for what?" Rhosyn fumed. "You've thrown in with thieves. After all we've gone through."

Rhosyn swallowed thickly, the acid taste of hurt clawing up her throat. How could Paul and Olivia be siding against her? Not when they had been in that group of children captured by Caleb and the Rattlesnakes, who Contessa and Nate had risked life and limb to get back.

But the real bitterness came from the fact that a small part of her understood. After all, hadn't she just slipped into the haze of a street brawler so easily when faced with a challenge? Her police training had flown out the window in a mere second, leaving her throwing punches in a gambling den like she had never left.

"It's not like that," Paul chimed in softly. "You've—I'd hoped you'd understand, if you'd just give us a chance to explain."

Olivia's wide eyes continued to fix her with a beseeching stare. Rhosyn slumped, the awkward angle pulling at her shoulders as they bent around the chair behind her.

"You have until my arms go numb to convince me that I wouldn't be a corrupt police officer for not arresting you alongside Ansel."

The siblings exchanged a glance before both started speaking at once.

"We couldn't stay at the Gower's—"

"We heard the Foxes—"

They both cut off until Olivia nodded at Paul to continue. He took a deep breath, before beginning again more calmly.

"When we were first offered the positions with the Gowers, we thought it was the best thing we could ever hope for. A chance that we only ever dreamed of as Talented children." Paul shifted in his seat. "We barely read the sponsorship papers and jumped in. But after years in the factories as children, it didn't take us long to after we started to realize what it actually was—indentured servitude."

Rhosyn frowned. Contessa wouldn't support something like that—not after fighting so hard to free so many orphans from the horrendous working conditions in the factories—and sponsorships had been her idea. She opened her mouth to chime in before snapping it shut.

Chief Thorne had impressed upon her, with great difficulty, that interrupting witnesses was not a good way to go about gathering information.

"In the factories, they paid us, but they forced us to live in their rooms and charged us more than we made. After a few weeks, we were in such deep debt that they basically owned us, while acting like they were saints for taking in children who lost parents to the Inquiries." Paul's face twisted at the memory, the movement pulling on the scar in his forehead and hairline. It had healed to a shiny white, not nearly as gruesome as Nate's, but Rhosyn still remembered how he got it. He had arrived into her care, head wrapped in bandages after being injured in his escape from factory service.

"The Gower's house was the same. After he paid our pardons, took us in, and dressed us for his house, we owed him so much that it would take decades of work to ever be free of him," Paul explained.

"Did he mistreat you?" This time, Rhosyn couldn't stop herself from interrupting.

Paul hesitated.

"The whole time we were there is such a blur," Olivia chimed in. "We were so busy, I could barely keep up with my work and think straight at the same time."

Rhosyn had to take a deep breath in and out through her nose to stay composed. Olivia's voice was so small, still so terribly young. Her childhood had been stolen from her by the textile factory she worked in, and the job that was supposed to be her salvation had apparently worked her so hard that her mind became addled from lack of sleep.

"Why didn't you come to me?" Rhosyn asked, her voice low. Only through an effort of will did she restrain the growl that threatened to creep in, both in anger that Mr. Gower would treat them so badly they felt the need to run away and that they would choose a random thug to help them over her.

"I...I don't know." Paul seemed genuinely baffled as he tried to dig up an answer. "I just—I went on an errand for the Gowers, and at the market I heard a rumor that a new gang was helping Talented people leave London. It felt like the first time my head had been clear in months when I heard that. So, I followed the man who had been gossiping.

"I had to use some of the...skills...you taught me," Paul looked sheepish, "but I eventually tracked the rumors back here. I met Ansel and the Foxes, and they told me he could help. He would even steal our sponsorship papers from the palace so they couldn't hunt us down and force us back. And then...well, I guess you can fill in the rest."

For a moment, Rhosyn thought Paul was infusing his words with his Talent again, as her mind couldn't seem to keep up with what he was saying. In the long pause when he finished, staring at her with a mix of expectancy and apprehension, her mind hummed with all the force of the factories in the industrial district.

"The Foxes?" she asked, her police brain homing in on that detail first. Her investigation into Foxes left her thinking that they were more myth than reality, and Paul had stumbled on them by accident.

"That would be us." Ansel stood in the doorframe, leaning casually against it with his arms folded, one leg crossed in front of the other. It would have been a relaxed pose, but something in his posture told Rhosyn he was ready to jump into action in a moment's notice. To be fair, she hadn't given him a reason to believe that any given conversation with her wouldn't end in a fight. He must have appeared there sometime during their talk, with his uncanny knack for stealth.

"You?" Rhosyn echoed. She had surmised Ansel had gang help, but he seemed to be suggesting that he led the gang.

"Well, my associates and I," he clarified with a shrug.

"…The circus?" Rhosyn asked.

"We are a group of many skills," Ansel said, the hint of a wry smile tugging at his lips, even though the rest of his expression remained serious. Rhosyn stared for a second, taking in the lines creasing his forehead that seemed too deep for his age and the hollows under his eyes. They looked like hers.

"I wouldn't have thought clowning and crime had much overlap," Rhosyn admitted.

"Little John is our strong man, and he seems to do just fine at standing in as the muscle."

Rhosyn blinked dumbly. "So, Archer's Circus…is the Foxes?"

Ansel bowed his head in affirmation.

With this admission, more pieces of the puzzle started falling into place. Contessa's office had been robbed of the sponsorship papers the night Archer's Circus had performed there, and the thief had disappeared into the hubbub of the dressing room. The supposed turf fight with the Foxes had occurred in the rail yard the night the circus train had arrived. And the gang had supposedly sprung into life out of thin air a few weeks before, when Ansel and his advance guard of performers arrived in London.

Rhosyn slumped. She swung her head to look at Paul and Olivia again. Grown as they were now, something in their expression still made them look like children waiting to be scolded for some mischief or another—although truth be told, they were some of the less devious children she had minded at the Den over the years.

"So, you were just trying to run away, and the Foxes were your way out." It wasn't exactly a question, but the siblings nodded in affirmation. A few pieces of the puzzle were still missing though.

"Why are you stealing Talented away from their sponsorships?" She directed the question at Ansel.

He signed heavily and pushed off the doorframe, taking a few steps further into the room. "That is a question with a lot of history behind it."

Rhosyn looked pointedly down at her ankles where they were bound to the chair. "It doesn't look like I'm going anywhere."

Paul, Olivia, and Ansel all grimaced in unison.

"Sorry," Paul mumbled under his breath.

"I would prefer not to have you bound at all times," Ansel admitted. "But your fists have already cost me my juggler for tonight's show. If my performers keep getting mysteriously injured, people might start asking questions."

"I suppose promising to be on my best behavior doesn't mean much at this point." Rhosyn tried to look contrite, but it wasn't an expression that came to her naturally.

Ansel shook his head. "How do I know you won't run off and tell your Chief all you just learned about our little operation?"

Rhosyn chewed her lip to keep herself from spitting back that he didn't. After all, she should do just as he said. The Foxes had done more than break the Talented siblings free. They had broken into the palace—Contessa's own office—and stolen a small fortune in jewelry from several upper city families.

A good police officer wouldn't hesitate to put the entirety of Archer's Circus behind bars. But the fear that Rhosyn had pushed aside for too long reared its head and couldn't be pushed down this time.

Maybe she wasn't a good police officer.

She desperately wanted to be—wanted to claim that she lived fully on the right side of the law and had reclaimed the life she might have had if she hadn't chosen to throw her lot in with the Lion's after she aged out of the Den. After all, Chief Thorne worked tirelessly to turn the police around and make them the protectors they were always meant to be. Rhosyn had never wanted to do anything but help the people of London, and joining his new force had seemed like the best way.

But the dirt of the lower city had rubbed its way under her skin.

Rhosyn closed her eyes, steeling herself. She picked her next words carefully. "If I'm being held hostage, I can't very well tell the Royal Police where Olivia and Paul were. It would be a shame if I weren't to escape until after they had left London. Then, they'd be outside our jurisdiction and the Royal Police would be unable to see that they were returned home safely."

Ansel cocked his head, his green eyes inscrutable. Paul and Olivia, on the other hand, slumped in relief.

"Thank you," Olivia breathed emphatically.

Their gratitude twisted her gut with guilt even as it lightened her heart. *The Lions protected their own.*

A knife sprang into Ansel's hand, having been hidden somewhere beneath his sleeves. The thin lamplight in the small room reflected off a blade sharp enough to make Nate proud. Ansel knelt before Rhosyn's chair and gave her a long look.

Her throat felt tight as she swallowed with difficulty and nodded. She would not run. She told herself that this was a compromise—a necessary evil. Rhosyn hadn't promised Ansel that she wouldn't get the Foxes arrested for their crimes. She had only suggested that she wouldn't be doing so until after Paul and Olivia were far away.

A dull *snick* and the ropes around Rhosyn's calves loosened, sliced cleanly through by Ansel's blade. She flexed her legs and rolled her ankles as he stood and rounded her chair.

The heat from his body soaked through her uniform as he bent over her to cut away the binds on her arms. As he leaned in, his breath disturbed the curls at the nape of her neck, long since escaped from the knot she tied them in for patrol. She tried not to focus on the goosebumps it raised as her wrists sprang free and she was able to move her arms into a more comfortable position.

As she stretched, pulling her arms alternately across her chest to regain her mobility, Ansel rounded the chair and looked at her appraisingly.

"If you're going to be the Foxes' guest, you'll need something else to wear. Olivia, Paul, can you see if you can dig your friend up some clothes?"

Rhosyn looked down at her uniform and grimaced. It was rumpled and dusty after three days of wear, a stain on one thigh from a spilled drink as she jumped over tables. She had even managed to lose one of the golden buttons that dotted the navy fabric. Not to mention, it wouldn't do to have her walking freely in a gang hideout wearing the outfit of an officer of the law.

Paul nodded. "Something of mine might work, even if the pants are a little short."

With that, he and Olivia scurried off to do Ansel's bidding. The door banged against the frame as they left, and they found themselves alone. Ansel stood before Rhosyn, close enough his thighs nearly brushed her knees. She tilted her head up to look at him.

"So, what now?" he asked.

She stared at him, lifting a quizzical brow. "Aren't you the one in charge here? You don't seem to have mastered the art of holding someone hostage."

"And you have?"

Rhosyn shrugged, "Maybe not holding a hostage. But I have put lots of people behind bars, and I'm certainly better at conducting interrogations."

"This wasn't an interrogation." Ansel let out a frustrated huff through his nose. "It was a...persuasion."

"Well, now that I've been *persuaded,* I'd like to stretch my legs if you're leaving the plan up to me." Rhosyn stood, forcing Ansel to take a step back.

He immediately stepped forward again as Rhosyn's knees buckled, an odd mix of wobbly and stiff after being tied for so long. Ansel caught her with one arm under hers and the other around her waist. Rhosyn threw her arms around his neck on reflex.

They stood like that, perfectly still. Rhosyn's nose was a few inches from Ansel's, close enough that she could make out the shimmering lamplight reflected in his eyes. The way they held each other, it was almost like the time they first met, dancing at the King's ball. But that wasn't the first time they had met—that had been a chase over steep roofs, ending in Rhosyn's humiliation.

That thought gave Rhosyn the impetus she needed to wrench away, legs much more prepared to hold her weight this time. The man who had flirted with her—who had made her hope she had successfully left her past behind her, while making her wonder if she were broken for wanting to shatter the layer of veneer that coated his manner—that man was a lie.

This man was the Hood. More a representation of the past that she was trying to leave behind than her present. And while the Hood's manner was also naturally flirtatious, she chafed at the way she had jumped to his challenges.

"I did untie you, but I'm not sure giving you a tour of the premises is wise," Ansel admitted, drawing Rhosyn from her thoughts, apparently completely unfazed by their recent proximity.

She jutted out one hip and rested a fist on it. "You have your insurance for my cooperation."

For now, she added silently.

Ansel bit the inside of his cheek as if considering. It was a more human gesture, speaking of indecision and doubt, than Rhosyn had ever seen on him as Mr. Blakely. She found herself softening her posture.

"You don't even have to let me see where we are, just let me walk the hallways," she compromised. After all, she could learn plenty about the Foxes from inside their hole, even if she didn't know its precise location.

"Alright," Ansel conceded. "But I'm not letting you wander anywhere alone."

"Of course not. You need to tell me the story of how you found yourself stealing Talented away from their jobs."

Ansel gave her a long-suffering look as he led her from the small room into a narrow hallway. It was dingy and cramped, with doors lining it all the way down. He didn't speak as he led the way down past the doorways, some stood open to reveal tiny bedrooms and others closed, voices coming from within. It looked so much like the safehouses where her friends in the Lions lived that if she closed her eyes, she could pretend she was seventeen again, visiting the teenagers who had aged out of the Den and her care.

"It started when Mr. Archer still owned the circus actually," Ansel started without any preamble as they turned the corner at the end of the corridor towards the stairs.

"Mr. Archer?"

"The one whom the circus is named after. He was my...mentor."

Rhosyn considered the back of Ansel's head as he led them down the stairs. He didn't elaborate for a minute as they squeezed past others, many of whom nodded courteously at Ansel before catching sight of her and paling. Their shock at seeing her walking free told her that most of them witnessed the scene in the common room earlier. She grinned.

Finally, they arrived on what Rhosyn surmised was the ground floor, where a familiar room full of tables and chairs greeted them.

"Will, get our friend here something to eat and drink. She'll be staying for a while." Ansel shouted toward a group of men gathered around a table with their heads bent together. One of them looked up, staring for a moment before hurrying to do Ansel's bidding.

Rhosyn watched him go, wondering why he seemed familiar until it hit her. "Your acrobats."

Ansel nodded as he took a seat at an uninhabited table, gesturing for Rhosyn to take another. "The Merry Men. The act that made the circus famous."

"I originally thought that one of them was the Hood," Rhosyn admitted.

"The Hood?"

Rhosyn cleared her suddenly stuck throat. "It's what I—we—the police started calling you, since we didn't know who you were. You always wore a hood though."

"I don't know if I should be flattered that I'm notorious enough to have a nickname with law enforcement." Ansel grimaced.

"The best criminals do." People still called Nate "the Beast" behind his back, but nobody would do it where the king or his intimidating bodyguard might overhear.

"If I were good at doing my job, I wouldn't be drawing enough attention to be infamous," Ansel admitted.

"Your acrobatics aren't exactly subtle." Rhosyn shot Ansel a meaningful look. "Now that I know who you are, I'm honestly surprised your act in the circus was knife throwing."

Ansel reclined, leaning the chair he was sitting in back on two legs and balancing there. "It wasn't at first. When Mr. Archer took me in, when I was just a boy, I was one of the first Merry Men."

"Then why did you take up knife throwing?" Rhosyn asked, as Will put a plate of bread and drippings in front of her and scurried away. She didn't hesitate digging in, saying around a mouth full of bread, "You clearly didn't leave acrobatics for a lack of skill."

"That's just it. I was too good at it."

Rhosyn wanted to say something scathing in response but was too busy chewing, so she settled for rolling her eyes, only to freeze when Ansel continued.

"Mr. Archer was afraid I was going to give away my Talent."

She forced her mouthful down her throat with difficulty. "You're Talented?"

Ansel smiled, the expression simultaneously mischievous and wistful. "You asked me how I started stealing the Talented away from the sponsorships, but in truth, it isn't anything new. It's what we've always done, since long before I was in charge.

"That's the beauty of the circus, you see. People come to see things that shouldn't be possible—things that are extraordinary. The spectators expect things to be inexplicably magical. So, when a lion seems to truly understand what his tamer is telling him, or a fire breather can shape flames like a sculptor...well, that's just the magic of show business."

Rhosyn stared. "You're *all* Talented?"

"Not all." Ansel shook his head. The silver strand of hair that Rhosyn had only seen neatly coiffed into his pushed back hairstyle, fell forward with the motion. "It was...a passion of Mr. Archer's. You see, he had a son who was Talented. Had a way of predicting the weather down to the second that was almost scary—as if he controlled the rain. They hid it easily when they lived in the country, but when Mr. Archer started the circus, he moved them to London for the bigger crowds.

"They learned too late that the cramped quarters of the city, combined with the bloodthirstiness of the Royal Police, made it nearly impossible to conceal a Talent for long."

Rhosyn's stomach dropped to the soles of her boots, the bread she had hastily swallowed turning leaden. "He..." She trailed off, not wanting to ask the question and fearing she already knew the answer.

Ansel nodded solemnly. "I think that Mr. Archer thought that if he could just smuggle enough Talented out of London, it would wash away the guilt he felt for his son's death. And so, he sent out word through whispers in the lower city that he was searching for incredible acts to go on tour. People were skeptical at first, but when they realized it wasn't a trap, the Talented flocked to him with all sorts of interesting displays, which he played off as clever tricks and sleight of hand. Then, he bought the train and headed out to the country.

"Acts would drop off at every remote stop where we put on a show, and Mr. Archer never said a word. Just gave them their coin and let them set out to start a new life. Every year, we would come back to London and fill up with a fresh set of performers."

A question built in the back of Rhosyn's mind and spilled off her tongue when he paused. "But you, you never left to start a life in the country where you could hide your Talent?"

Ansel let his chair fall back onto four legs and rested his elbows on the table. "Some of us—I—fell in love with performing. After being petrified to use my Talent for so long, it was liberating. It felt like cheating the system to flex that muscle in front of unsuspecting audiences and be praised for it, even if they never knew. After a while, the circus train became more of a home for some of us than London ever had been. So, a group of us stayed for the long haul."

Rhosyn looked around the room they were in, with plenty of young men and women both milling about and sitting at tables with drinks or dice. The sight, the warmth of casual laughter, even the smell of cheap alcohol and tobacco—it would be enough to make Rhosyn nostalgic if not for the feeling that she was watching the scene through a pane of glass. These weren't the Lions, and the wary glances and wide berths everybody but Ansel gave her told her they still noticed her uniform, however rumpled. After so long trying to cover the blemish of her history with a spotless police record, she should have been proud that Ansel's compatriots saw her as the enemy. Instead, bitterness rose up in her throat to choke her.

"So, once you inherited the circus from Mr. Archer, you turned it into a band of thieves and kidnappers?"

A splintering thud, and the tip of a dagger buried itself in the table millimeters from where Rhosyn's hand rested. To her credit, she didn't flinch away, but the suddenly hard look in Ansel's eyes made her wish she had.

"Mr. Archer died for this circus, and those of us who stayed honor him by continuing what he started." Ansel's voice carried a flinty edge that gave Rhosyn pause. So far, as both the Hood and Mr. Blakely, she had delighted in teasing him, rising to the challenge of a suave attitude that promised to never take itself too seriously. The steel in his green gaze now, though, was something else.

It flashed away as quickly as it had come when Ansel pulled the knife from the table and leaned back in his chair. He tossed the blade with one hand and flipped it, catching it by the handle without looking, in an action that was as much soothing habit as it was intimidation tactic. It was the same way Rhosyn used to twirl her brass knuckles around her index finger.

"The Foxes were born out of necessity, but we're still Archer's Circus at heart."

Rhosyn sat back in her own seat, taking a deep breath to keep up with Ansel's changing posture as he slipped back into his curated demeanor. "The Inquiries are over. I wouldn't think you'd have much business smuggling them out of the city anymore."

"Do you have the life you would have if the Inquiries never happened?"

The question hit Rhosyn like a slap to the face. The dreams of being a sailor like her father—of visiting distant lands and never staying in one place for too long—had dissipated like smog from a smokestack the day she had decided to stay with the Lions. She knew she would never forgive herself if she turned away when she could give the children living in the Den a better childhood than she had. But the Lions had slipped away too, like so much smoke at the end of the Inquiries, and Rhosyn had grasped at the straws of yet another life, helping people in the best way she knew how.

"I have the life I need," Rhosyn bit out.

"Not everybody was so lucky," Ansel observed. "It seems to me that the Talented have two choices: continue to make a living as a criminal or sell themselves into a lifetime of servitude with a sponsorship. The Foxes wanted to give them another choice. A fresh start."

"And so, you steal them away from their sponsors."

Ansel inclined his head in his acknowledgment.

Rhosyn cracked her knuckles to distract herself from the desire to argue further. She wanted to tell Ansel that robbing the residents of the upper city who were trying to use their power to aid the Talented wasn't a long-term solution. But wasn't that what she and the Lions had done, stealing orphans away from brutal factory jobs?

It wasn't news to her that the law and what was right were not always aligned, but things were supposed to be different now. Chief Thorne was a good man. Contessa and King Byron worked tirelessly to right the injustices of the past.

Rhosyn was saved from having to answer by the appearance of Paul, a small bundle of fabric carried in his arms.

"These will have to do, although you might have to show an indecent amount of ankle," he admitted, putting the stack of clothes on the table.

"It would hardly be the first time somebody accused me of indecency."

"I doubt it will be the last," Ansel added, seemingly under his breath but still loud enough that Rhosyn shot him an exasperated look.

She pushed back from the table, picking up the pile of fabric. Maybe once she got changed, the Foxes would be more comfortable with her, and she would be able to glean more specifics of their activities to report back to Chief Thorne. And maybe she wouldn't feel like such a traitor to the uniform for walking freely among thieves.

Either way, it was time to live with the Foxes.

Chapter Eight

"**Y**ou can't be serious."

"Why not?" Ansel asked.

Rhosyn stared suspiciously at the single, rickety bedframe before her. "Aren't you worried about your reputation?"

"I'm a young man who is apparently wanted by the Royal Police and owns a circus. I wouldn't think I had much of a reputation to maintain." Ansel shrugged, sitting down on the bed and beginning to pull off his boots as if the matter had been decided. "Besides, aren't you worried about *your* reputation?"

"That ship has left the harbor," Rhosyn admitted. "But why can't you just tie me to the bed again?"

"You've already proven that isn't enough to hold you, unless we immobilize you completely, and that hardly seems humane. Besides, we only had one free bed, and you have left it unfit to sleep in," Ansel pointed out.

Rhosyn grimaced.

"There are no more beds, and besides, wouldn't you be more comfortable if I only had to bind one hand? I'm a light sleeper, so if you try to escape, I'll wake. None of my performers will have to lose a full night's sleep keeping an eye on you and need the next day off," Ansel explained.

"You sharing a bed with me should be the most agreeable solution for everybody."

"I slept just fine when I was tied down," Rhosyn grumbled.

Ansel moved on to removing his waistcoat and unbuttoning his vest. "I noticed, and honestly, I'm mildly concerned. But if you could sleep like that, then certainly my presence shouldn't bother you. I'm told I don't even snore."

Rhosyn swallowed. Truth be told, it shouldn't be an imposition to sleep in the same bed as Ansel. These days, she so rarely got an opportunity to shut her eyes for multiple hours together, and any offer of sleep wasn't one she should turn her nose up at. After years of multiple small, squirmy orphans pushing their way onto her narrow cot with her, she could likely share a bed with the circus's lion without issue.

It was the fact that the bedmate in question was Ansel that gave her pause. He had already wormed his way past her defenses as Mr. Blakely, and Rhosyn had paid the price for her lapse in vigilance. Now, letting her guard down around him, even in the unconsciousness of sleep, seemed unwise.

For the rest of the afternoon, as she spoke with Paul and Olivia under Little John's always watchful eye, Ansel's tale had seeped into her brain. He made it sound so sympathetic—so like something Nate and the Lion's would have done. As the Foxes joked and conversed around her, she had to remind herself on occasion that these were criminals, wanted by the Royal Police, who were no longer corrupt.

She would wait until Olivia and Paul were safely away. Then she would do her duty as an officer of the Royal Police, escape, and turn in Ansel and his whole operation. A few nights in the same bed wouldn't change that.

With determined steps, she walked to the opposite side of the bed and sat.

"That's a shame for you," Rhosyn commented, "as I snore terribly."

She pulled her own boots off, keeping her back to Ansel but still hyper aware of the sounds of rustling cloth as he undressed. Her shoes hit the ground with a startling thump as she dropped them, and Rhosyn paused in the resulting stillness, staring down at her clothes. She would normally undress further for bed, but that level of familiarity seemed ill-advised.

When she and Mr. Blakely had danced, blood had rushed to her cheeks—and much less ladylike places—at the firm grip of his fingers on her waist, despite having engaged in more than polite dancing in her life. In the moments Rhosyn had spent with him as the Hood, his hard chest pressed tightly against her back as they hid in the confines of a carriage, her heart had pounded with a cocktail of adrenaline and something wild, which awakened at the feel of his hand muffling her mouth.

Now, she was about to let her guard down almost completely around Ansel, who was the amalgamation of two men who had led her thoughts down the path of impropriety. Staying anything but fully clothed seemed almost comically unwise.

"It's nothing I haven't seen before, you know."

Ansel's voice came from close behind her, startling Rhosyn out of her thoughts where she had been staring at her boots, haphazardly toppled on the floor. They were filthy, she noticed dispassionately.

"Excuse me?" Rhosyn asked as the meaning of his words hit her.

"If you keep yourself under the blankets, I'll see far less than I did that night in the Gower's stables."

Rhosyn turned to glare over her shoulder, finding Ansel staring at her with a single brow arched. The expression, casual as it was, hit her like a challenge.

Rhosyn didn't back down from a challenge. Not from a rival gang in her youth—as evidenced by the slight bend in her nose and her callused knuckles—or from a difficult case facing her as a police officer.

Her fingers drifted towards the button of her pants, slowly but deliberately. Refusing to undress now, when Ansel had already reminded her of her former indecent exposure, would be admitting that she had something to be embarrassed about.

To his credit, Ansel didn't watch her undress, the rustling of the bedding indicating that he was busy sliding under the covers as Rhosyn slid her pants down her legs, kicking them off on top of her boots. The shirt Paul had dug up for her was long enough to cover her hips and the very top of her thighs, but plenty of skin was still on display.

She made a point not to hurry her movements as she turned to slide her bare legs beneath the sheets, despite the goosebumps rising on her thighs. Rhosyn hoped Ansel couldn't see them.

When she settled beneath the covers, she chanced a glance at him, finding him determinedly staring at his own fingernails. Part of her relaxed at the thought of him not trying to disarm her further with his proximity. Another smaller and more rebellious part in the back of her mind—the part of Rhosyn she had been determined to shove into a tiny drawer since she left the Lions—was disappointed that he hadn't looked. After all, how could you win the challenge if your opponent didn't show up to the fight?

The rough sheets rubbed against her bare skin as she slid down, pulling the blankets up to her chest. She tried to focus on getting comfortable, and not the warmth radiating from beside her, when a sudden shift made her freeze.

Rhosyn's breath stole from her lungs and Ansel rolled towards her, propping up on one elbow to lean over her. His unlaced shirt gaped open, giving her an unobstructed view of a broad chest dusted with dark hair, just inches from her nose.

"Wrist," Ansel prompted expectantly.

Rhosyn didn't move, her suddenly addled brain struggling to catch up with his request. When she simply stared, Ansel dangled a looped rope before her face, snapping her back to reality.

She resumed breathing and rolled her eyes all at once.

"You lock me in a room with you and still insist on tying me to the bed? One might think you expect me to cause trouble." Still, she held out her arm.

The scrape of rope against the soft skin of her inner wrist was enough to keep her cognizant of why it was imperative to keep her guard up around Ansel. Sympathetic as his story might be, he was a criminal, and she was a police officer.

Besides, resuming breathing meant being engulfed by his sweet and sharp burnt sugar scent again, and the sooner he leaned away, the sooner she could get back to building a mental wall between them.

When the knot was tied to his satisfaction, he rolled back to his side of the bed, and Rhosyn looked up to survey his handiwork. Once again, the knot was expertly tied, but not so tight as to be dangerous. The other end was affixed to the headboard.

"Aren't you concerned I'll untie myself?" she asked against her better judgment.

"I'd be more concerned with you picking a lock if I had cuffed you, but my trapeze artists' lives depend on me being able to tie a knot that can't be undone with just one hand. And I should wake up if you try to rip another bed in half."

Rhosyn slumped back against her pillow. It wasn't like she would run anyways—not with Paul and Olivia still at risk of being returned to the servitude they ran from so fervently.

"Good night, Rhosyn." Ansel snuffed out the lantern at the side of the bed, and they were plunged into darkness.

As his breathing slowed to a deep, even rhythm, Rhosyn urged herself to stay alert. Tied in the bed of a wanted criminal, she should be a sleepless mess, especially after so much rest in the preceding day. Maybe if she tossed and turned enough, she could keep Ansel awake too, and he would slip up in his resulting exhaustion.

She stared at the ceiling, trying to run over the events of the day with an analytical mind—to find a weakness of Ansel's she could exploit without putting Olivia and Paul in harm's way.

Her bedmate shifted in his sleep, reducing the distance between them to mere inches, the warmth of him seeping through the sheets and the minimal layers of clothing between them. Even now, the faintest burnt sugar scent still permeated her brain, likely worn into the pillow beneath her head.

Her eyelids grew impossibly heavy, and as she closed her eyes, she tried to justify to herself that there wasn't much to be done right now anyway. The last thought that flickered through her brain before sleep took her was that escaping might not be the issue—maybe it would be remembering that she was a hostage at all.

The sheets chilled Rhosyn's bare skin as she woke. She moved to pull the blankets more closely around her and tugged at the forgotten bind around her wrist. The chafe of rope snapped her back to reality and her eyes sprang open. But when she turned her head, the pillow beside her was empty, barely a dent left where Ansel's head had been, making it seem as if she had imagined his presence. It might have been a comforting thought, given how well rested she felt, when she should have spent a sleepless night in the bed of her enemy.

A clearing of a throat drew her attention and her eyes snapped to the corner the noise came from. Scrunched onto a small stool sat Little John, knees nearly coming to his chest as he folded himself onto furniture clearly not built for someone of his stature.

"Do you make a habit of watching people sleep?" she grumbled, voice scratchy.

"I do when Ansel tells me to." Little John seemed to be fixedly staring at some point beside her shoulder as he spoke.

Curious, Rhosyn glanced down and found the cause for his reticence. She had managed to tangle her legs with the blankets, leaving the entirety of their length visible. Even more, her long shirt had ridden up with her unconscious movement, a generous curve of hip on display. She quickly yanked down her clothes to keep herself decent.

Perhaps she should have felt embarrassed at the strong man having had such a view, but she was only mildly amused by his embarrassment.

"You're fine with holding me hostage and leaving me tied to your boss's bed, but a little thigh is where you draw the line?" Rhosyn teased.

"Don't drag me into it. This was all Ansel's idea." Little John folded his arms, meaty biceps threatening the seams of his shirt at the motion.

At that, Rhosyn pictured Ansel getting up before she woke and wondered if she had been in this state when he did. That thought did make her neck and chest prickle with heat, but she grit her teeth against the feeling. This situation was on him. Of course he was trying to goad her.

"Where is Ansel?" Rhosyn asked, feigning casualness as she stretched.

"Busy."

"A man of few words," she observed. "That bodes for a very long day of silent staring as I'm stuck tied to this bed."

"I can untie you, but I'll be keeping an eye on you." Little John stood and shuffled over to the head of the bed where her bonds were anchored. She waited as it took him a surprisingly long time to untie her and grimaced. Ansel hadn't been bluffing about her being well bound.

Finally free, Rhosyn sat and reached to grope around for her pants, still haphazardly tossed over her boots on the floor.

"So, what's on the agenda for today?" she asked as she pulled on her clothes and boots.

Little John looked off at the corner as she did, clearly not wanting to openly watch her dress but unwilling to turn his back. He learned quickly.

"It's not my job to entertain you, just make sure you don't escape."

"Great," Rhosyn said cheerily, "then you can just follow as I look around."

With that, she traipsed towards the door, finding it unlocked. Apparently, Ansel considered Little John enough of a guard given his leverage over her.

Stepping into the hallway, she picked a direction at random and began to walk the halls. John followed after like a large, lumbering shadow, but she paid him no mind, poking her head into open doorways as she passed.

As she suspected, nothing noteworthy jumped out at her. Ansel would have kept her locked in the room if there were anything potentially useful for her to find. Still, she started constructing a map of the building in her mind, making mental marks for windows that might make potential exits for when it eventually came time for her to escape.

It would also be useful to know the layout to relay to Chief Thorne when he conducted the inevitable raid, to upend this criminal operation.

Eventually, her search brought her down to the common room where she had fought and later listened to Ansel's tale. It was sparsely populated now though, only a few figures seated at tables bent over in quiet conversation. Two of the inhabitants were familiar.

"Olivia, Paul," she greeted, weaving through tables to where they sat.

They looked up, smiling with something that looked like relief. Perhaps they hadn't trusted that she would keep her word and cooperate as a captive until they were out of Mr. Gower's reach. The thought reached into Rhosyn's chest and twisted her heart.

She avoided grappling with those thoughts by looking at the piles of brightly colored fabric strewn across the table before them.

"What's all this?"

"Costumes," Olivia explained brightly. "I'm doing my best to make myself useful to the circus, to help Ansel."

Indeed, Olivia held a needle in her hand, poking at the eye with bright green thread that matched the cloth in her lap.

"You're sewing?" Rhosyn asked. If Olivia was any good with a needle and a thread, it wasn't due to her time in the Den. Rhosyn was only good at educating youngsters in less ladylike arts.

"I taught myself so I could pick up odd mending jobs for extra money...before the Gower's sponsored us of course." With the needle successfully threaded, Olivia turned to the garment in her lap, which turned out to be some sort of unitard onto which she was appliqueing a dizzying pattern of stars.

To Rhosyn's surprise, Paul picked up the next in the pile of garments—an obscenely fluffy layered skirt—and started using a small knife to pick apart a seam near the waist.

"You too?"

"I learned to be pretty good at undoing and redoing stitches while Olivia was teaching herself," Paul explained. Olivia shot him a look that was half annoyed, half fond at his teasing.

Rhosyn glanced around the room, a thought occurring to her. Little John had sat himself at the adjacent table, arms folded over his chest as he observed Rhosyn's conversation. She wasn't likely to get much investigating done with John hovering over her shoulder every waking moment. Maybe, the investigating could come to her.

"Why don't you teach me?" Rhosyn suggested, slipping into a chair and gesturing to the gaudy assortment of textiles. "It looks like there is plenty of work to go around."

They both blinked at her, as if she had suggested jumping off the top of the clock tower—which she had done before, although they wouldn't know that—and not helping with some mending.

"You...want to sew?" Olivia clarified.

Rhosyn shrugged. "It's not like I'd be allowed to do much else around here, and you know how hard it is for me to sit still. Besides, it's not as if I can really do much harm with a needle and thread."

Several hours later, it turned out Rhosyn had been very wrong. She could do serious damage with the most ladylike of instruments, although mostly to her own fingers. It seemed that years of calluses on her knuckles still didn't protect her from pricking her fingers and nearly bleeding all over Archer's Circus's wonderful wardrobe.

She managed to gouge the needle into her finger savagely and grimaced, using the motion to sneak a glance at where Little John still sat, watching over her. She ducked her head to hide a smile, seeing that a comrade had joined him. They bent together in conversation, John only glancing over at her every thirty seconds or so to make sure she hadn't gotten up to any mischief.

Contessa would be proud, she thought. After all, her friend had been the first one to lament how easily an embroidering lady blended in to the background, making it the perfect cover for eavesdropping—a strategy Contessa had never been able to employ because she couldn't put two stitches together without ripping out her shiny blonde hair.

Despite Rhosyn's personal lack of skill, the strategy did seem to have merit.

"You're stabbing it too hard." Olivia glanced over her shoulder. "It's muslin, it doesn't fight back you know."

"Old habits die hard," Rhosyn grumbled, staring at the plain shirt in her hand. She had been relegated to fixing ripped undergarments, where her sloppy work could be hidden under costumes. "Never mind that though. It's nice of you to help Ansel."

"We like to earn our keep if we can," Paul said.

"I was hoping to get through all of these, but I don't think we will be able to get it done by the end of the week," Olivia huffed in disappointment.

"The end of the week?" Rhosyn prodded, glancing up at John and finding him engaged in conversation still. She surreptitiously scooted around the table under the pretext of having more room to straighten out the garment in her grasp, trying to get into earshot.

"We'll be leaving for the country on Sunday," Olivia explained. "Originally, we were supposed to leave town with the circus on the train at the end of their visit, but given...current circumstances...Ansel found a way to smuggle us out with a contact earlier. He told us first thing this morning."

That drew Rhosyn's focus back to Olivia, her straining ears pausing in their efforts to overhear John and his companion. "Sunday. That's five days from now."

Olivia nodded before her eyes widened, seeming to understand what she'd just conveyed. Rhosyn only had to cooperate with Ansel and the Foxes for five days...and she only had five more days to gather all the information necessary to take them down, once Olivia and Paul were safe from the threat of being returned to the Gower's service.

Olivia opened her mouth as if to say something, but Rhosyn cut her off.

"I'm sure you'll be happy to start a new life in the country." Rhosyn kept her voice as casual as possible, trying to convince Olivia and Paul not to worry about what happened once they were out of the way.

"I am! We're planning on going to Sussex where..."

Olivia's words faded into the background of Rhosyn's thoughts as she described how she was looking forward to living somewhere where the air wasn't always heavy with factory smoke and she might have room to start a small garden.

Rhosyn also tried not to dwell on her plans for escape in five days time either. Instead, she let her senses of the room broaden as Olivia and Paul planned excitedly for the future. More Foxes had entered the safehouse as the day wore on, and conversations grew in volume as they seemed to forget Rhosyn was there.

"... Worthingtons should be the next mark."

A snippet from the table at which Little John sat grabbed her attention. She cocked her head but kept her eyes down on the needle and thread in her lap.

"His investment in the mines made out well recently. He doesn't need all that wealth," John grumbled.

"And if we do hit the Gowers again, we'll need the cash."

Rhosyn frowned at her stitches, and not just because she had managed to stab herself hard enough to get a drop of blood on her project. Her concern was twofold—not only were the Foxes planning another robbery, but they were planning to hit the Gowers house again. Try as she might, she couldn't puzzle out why they might risk returning to terrorize the same family again and again, even if they did overwork their servants.

"Ansel went to—"

A loud cheering from the far side of the room cut off Little John's companion. Rhosyn suppressed an internal groan as she looked up towards the source of the commotion.

Standing on the table was a young woman, about the same age Rhosyn had been when she left the Lions, grinning as she juggled a no fewer than seven shining objects. Rhosyn's eyes widened as she focused her gaze enough to recognize the objects as glass beer mugs. The juggler didn't seem concerned, barely looking at the flying mugs as her fingers scarcely touched the twirling handles before spinning the glasses into the air once more.

The volume of the crowd crescendoed as a spectator tossed another glass into the fray. The juggler's grin only widened as she caught it without hesitation, seaming it into her rhythm without faltering.

"Ey, knock it off, Tory," Little John shouted without menace. "I know you won't break anything, but it's not kind to our host's nerves."

Indeed, the barkeep grabbed the counter he stood behind with white knuckles, eyes wide with nervous incredulity. He had likely expected brawls when he let a gang overrun his bar—probably for a healthy cut of their scores—but very little could prepare him or Rhosyn for the sights of Archer's Circus.

The juggler stopped her rhythmic tosses, instead catching the glasses one by one and stacking them neatly in her hands. She shot a sheepish glance at the bartender and hopped down off the table as the crowd dispersed.

Unfortunately, her performance had decidedly ended Little John's conversation as his companion stood and went to speak with somebody else.

"I'm not sure I'll ever get used to the way these performers use their Talents so freely," Olivia sighed, her tone wistful.

"I don't know, you might be able to put on an impressive fire breathing show with your Talent," Rhosyn pointed out.

"Maybe." Olivia shrugged. "But even at the Gower's, I felt like I had to look over my shoulder every time I lit a fire in the hearth. I suppose it would be different if I had learned to hide my Talent in plain sight like they have, though."

Rhosyn considered as Paul and Olivia continued to discuss the Talents they had seen in the Circus—the lion tamer who could understand the creature's roars as if they were words and the magician whose tricks nobody had ever figured out, likely because he could actually make small objects pop in and out of existence.

The thoughts of a youth so similar, yet so different from her own in the gangs, where Talents were both a death sentence and a source of power, twirled in her head for the remainder of the day. While she mulled things over, she kept a sharp ear out for any gossip that drifted within ear shot, but she learned nothing more interesting than the rumor that the contortionist had been found in the sword swallower's bed—apparently both showing off their skills.

Contrary to most gang haunts, the crowds of Foxes thinned as the day wore into evening, likely headed off for a night of entertaining revelers. By the time a familiar figure wearing a top hat graced the doorway, Olivia was dozing lightly in her seat and Rhosyn was feigning heaviness in her own eyelids, seeing if Little John would take it as an opportunity to lift his watchful eye.

Ansel sighed as he entered the room, sweeping off his hat and running his hand through his hair. The stiff, pushed back style he wore during the day came undone, falling across his forehead, nearly brushing his eyes.

"You can head off, Little John." He nodded to his friend as he took in the room. "I'll watch things around here while you go to the Circus."

John nodded, pushing to his feet and stretching, several joints popping audibly as he coaxed movement back into his bones.

"He shouldn't be too tired. I went easy on him today," Rhosyn quipped.

"That doesn't mean I won't keep just as close of an eye on you tomorrow." John pointed a meaty finger at her as he tromped past. Rhosyn shot him her most winning smile in return.

"It looks like I'm the tired one today then," Ansel admitted. "And that means it's time for bed for both of us, even if you're still full of energy."

Olivia, who had woken at some point during the conversation, looked momentarily shocked by his phrasing, but Rhosyn waved off her concern.

"Mr. Blakely here is a perfect gentlemen. Aside from being a lying, cheating gangster, that is," Rhosyn assured brightly.

With that, she stood and walked towards the stairs, leaving Ansel to trail behind her. It wasn't until they were back in the room they had shared last night that Ansel spoke.

"I distinctly remember that *you* are the one who cheats. In fact, I'm pretty sure that is how we found ourselves in this predicament."

Rhosyn flopped down on the bed, preparing to take her boots off. In a roundabout sort of way, Ansel was right. If she hadn't found the playing card in his pocket, it might have taken her an embarrassingly long time to put together who the Hood was.

"I don't have many opportunities to hustle people anymore. I have to practice when I have the chance, or I might get rusty," Rhosyn explained through a yawn.

Ansel paused in undoing his cufflinks. He cocked his head. "You used to cheat at cards a lot? Not a pastime I would expect of an upstanding officer of the Royal Police."

Rhosyn's fingers stuttered over the laces of her boots, somehow knotting them tighter when she meant to untangle them. The reference to her past had tumbled out of her unbidden. A day in a gang haunt, and it slipped off her tongue like second nature—like it had only taken one day to forget that her past was behind her and she now stood firmly on the right side of the law. Or at least tried to.

"Who doesn't have a few dalliances in their youth?" Rhosyn grasped her composure back, shrugging off his question.

Ansel let out a *hmph* that didn't sound satisfied with her answer, but didn't push her further on it.

"The circus business is harder work than I expected," Rhosyn said, changing the subject. "You were gone by the time the sun rose and back after dark. It certainly keeps you busy."

"You know I do more than own a circus," Ansel pointed out. "But if you think I'm going to tell you what else I was doing today, then I'm afraid you'll be disappointed."

As he spoke, he had rolled up his sleeves and his forearms flexed as he reached up to tug at his cravat. In the dim lamplight of the room, the shadows cast by the veins there deepened, and Rhosyn had to force her gaze away, mouth traitorously dry.

"Asking about each other's day seems to be the bare minimum of polite for two people about to share a bed," Rhosyn retorted. As she did, she moved to unbutton her pants. She shouldn't be flustered by Ansel undressing after last night, but if she was, she wouldn't pass up the opportunity to disarm him in return.

As she stood to push the trousers down her thighs, she peeked out of the corner of her eye at him, and found him not looking, busy with the buttons on his shirt. She couldn't decide whether to be impressed or frustrated that a gang leader boasted such a robust sense of honor.

With a stifled sigh, Rhosyn slid into the bed, staring up at the ceiling. She tried not to listen to the rustle of fabric as Ansel continued to undress. The bed dipped as he slid into his side, and she contained a jump as bare skin brushed her shoulder. She turned her head to find that he had chosen to forgo a shirt tonight.

Quickly, she snapped her gaze back to the ceiling above her, but it was no good. Ansel's chest dominated her vision again as he leaned over her to grab the rope attached to the headboard.

Rhosyn pushed her head back into the pillow as he bound her wrist to the bedpost, as if the millimeters of distance it put between her nose and his sternum could stop her from seeing the thatch of hair dusted there and wondering if it would be soft to rub her face on. The little space the motion afforded her certainly did nothing to dampen the sweet and spicy smell of burnt sugar that clung to his skin. At this proximity, the scent permeating her senses, it struck Rhosyn as familiar—it was the aroma of toasted nuts and spun sugar at the circus. As if Ansel had spent so much time among the traveling performers, that the essence of Archer's Circus had gotten under his skin.

Ansel paused in tying his knot, glancing down at Rhosyn's face, attention ostensibly grabbed by her rigid posture.

Seeing her staring fixedly at the divot between his pecs, he chuckled, the noise rumbling from his chest so close that Rhosyn felt the vibrations.

"Sorry, I'll be quick so as not to offend your ladylike sensibilities."

Rhosyn held perfectly still as Ansel finished binding her wrist for the night. Then, he rolled back to his side and snuffed the single lamp on his side of the bed. The incomplete darkness of the lower city fell—the darkest it could get in the neighborhood where the streets never slept and the light of the tavern perpetually creeped under the door as patrons were served until the wee hours of the morning.

It was a soft sort of quiet, and the familiarity of it combined with the sugary spice still lingering on the back of Rhosyn's tongue stirred something in her.

"I'm not a lady. Never was and never will be." The words spilled out of her without permission. She paused, wondering if she should stop but finding that she didn't want to. "I'm just like you."

"A police officer like a gangster?" Ansel didn't sound derisive, but instead curious. As if he were really trying to understand Rhosyn. For some reason it hurt her chest.

"I wasn't always with the Royal Police. Before the..." Rhosyn hesitated but the words banged against her ribs, begging to be let out of where they were caged in her chest. In the quiet of the night, she was surprised Ansel couldn't hear them, even though she hadn't spoken yet. "During the Inquiries, I ran with the Lions. And not just that, I was one of their leaders."

Ansel shifted slightly, the rustling of sheets loud as a gunshot in the pregnant silence.

"That's quite a change of heart," he eventually said, but his tone didn't hold judgment.

"It didn't feel like it at the time." Rhosyn admitted—and it wasn't a lie. The decision to help Chief Thorne, when he so desperately needed officers he could trust, was a familiar one. She turned her back on her criminal past in an instant, just as she had turned away from her hopes of a simpler future when she stayed with the Lions to help Nate and Kristoff. She had joined a gang to protect those with Talents when she had none herself, and she had given up the life she had built with the Lions to protect the city in the aftermath of the Inquiries.

"It hasn't been hard...not until now," Rhosyn murmured at the ceiling. "Not until I spent time among you and the Foxes."

"And what is it now?" Ansel prompted, his voice a little more than a whisper.

"Like being homesick."

The admission hung in the air, soft and palpable. It felt like a peace offering.

Fabric rustled again, and so lightly that Rhosyn might have imagined it if she hadn't been conscious of every slight movement, knuckles brushed against the bare skin of Rhosyn's thigh. The touch was both intimate and innocent, and Rhosyn allowed it. It seemed that Ansel had accepted her offering, but didn't push for more, knowing this could only be a temporary truce. They may understand each other, but it didn't change the truth of their situation.

Hair tickled Rhosyn's nose, consciousness slowly filling her, just as air filled her lungs. But she was so comfortable, and she wasn't ready to wake yet. Pushing away awareness, she instead burrowed deeper into the solid warmth beneath her, filling her lungs with another deep sigh that tasted of spicy sweetness.

As she nuzzled her nose further into the ticklish hair, she realized that for once it was not her own rebellious curls having fallen into her face at night, but much smoother and shorter. Her eyelashes fluttered, but she forced herself to keep them closed, as the realization that she cuddled into a decidedly masculine body took hold. She didn't move as she took stock of the situation.

Somehow, she had ended up burrowed into the crook of Ansel's neck, the hair at his nape stirring with her every breath. He lay on his back, one of her legs slung across his hips, her front molded tightly to his side.

What stole her attention more than the muscular press of his side into her chest, or the way her angle positioned one of his thighs between hers, was the heavy arm laid across her own shoulders. The hand belonging to the arm came to rest on her head, fingers burrowed into her hair at the crown of her head. In response to her small movements, the fingers began to move, infinitesimally massaging into her scalp.

A breath stuttered out of Rhosyn at the tingles the touch sent down her spine. Unconsciously, she arched back into the touch, and the fingers moved again, rubbing in the tiniest of circles and pulling lightly at the hair at the nape of her neck. Her lashes fluttered as her eyes rolled back in her head.

Having Ansel play with her hair shouldn't feel absolutely sinful, but here she was one breath away from moaning.

A rustle of sheets broke the quiet of early morning as Ansel turned his head on the pillow, and a small part of Rhosyn cringed to know that he was awake and aware, not just unconsciously responding to her proximity. A much larger part of her reveled in the feel of his lips moving against the crown of her head as he murmured her name.

"Rhosyn." His voice was rough from sleep, rumbling in his chest far more than his normal smooth tone. The word was both a question and a warning—and just as delicious as the fingers that hadn't quite stopped moving in her hair.

Her only response was to nuzzle deeper into the crook of his neck. If she responded, she would have to face some semblance of reality, instead of enjoying the toe-curling feel of his nails now lightly raking against her scalp. The slight scratch sent warmth dripping down her spine to pool in her core.

She shifted her hips unconsciously at the sensation, and she discovered the delicious friction of Ansel's thigh pressed between her own. Rhosyn shifted her hips again, more purposefully this time. Now, her core was pressed firmly to him, growing so warm that she was sure he could feel the heat of it through her long shirt.

Ansel let out a strangled grunt as she circled her hips infinitesimally once more. His fingers tightened in her hair, and the response drew attention to a growing hardness against her thigh.

She moved again, this time letting her thigh move as she ground against him.

"Rhosyn." He only said the same single word as earlier, but this time it was a command—to stop or keep going, she couldn't be sure.

She shivered in response to his tone. In this haze of early morning pleasure, still laced with the sense of unreality from last night, she could think of little beyond wanting this feeling to continue—to deepen.

Rhosyn wanted to touch him.

She reached for him, only to have her shoulder jerked back as rope grew taught around her wrist. Her bonds did more than hold her back from Ansel. They snapped her back to reality, and immediately she tensed.

She wrenched herself away from his gentle grasp, rolling onto her back on the side of the bed where she was tied. Ansel blinked at her in surprise before his gaze trailed to her wrist. The openness of early awakening in his eyes shuttered at the sight. The tangible evidence of their animosity sobered them both.

While at a temporary truce, in five days Rhosyn would break free of these bonds and be his enemy once more.

Without a word, Ansel stood from the bed and pulled on his clothes with hurried efficiency. He walked out the door with boots in hand, not even bothering to put them on before leaving.

If Rhosyn's mind hadn't been reeling at their sudden sobriety, she might have tried to untie herself. As it was, Little John entered before she could make any moves towards freedom. She exhaled heavily, facing down another day captured in the Foxes's den.

Rhosyn repositioned herself in her chair for the tenth time in the last five minutes, and Olivia eyed her sympathetically.

"If I have to sit still for another hour, I'll rip my hair out." Rhosyn set down her pitiful attempt at sewing and admitted defeat.

After spending the morning and the first part of the afternoon revisiting her eavesdropping strategy from earlier to no avail, she was ready to throw in the towel. Rhosyn had never been suited for long stakeouts, preferring to face her enemies out in the open.

"I think that might be challenging, based on how thick it seems."

Rhosyn twisted in her seat to find Ansel standing at the bottom of the stairs. She wasn't entirely sure how he got there, given that she hadn't seen him come back to the Foxes's haunt after leaving this morning, even though it seemed that you had to cross through the common area to get from the main entrance to the stairs in the back.

"At least it would give me something to do besides sewing," Rhosyn griped at him as he strolled over to look over their handiwork.

He picked up one of her poorly darned undershirts and inspected it. "You might be better at it too."

Rhosyn wrinkled her nose at the jab, but didn't deny it.

"Are you sure this isn't your underhanded way of trying to put Archer's Circus out of business—to have everybody's costumes fall apart on stage until we are shut down for indecency?"

"It's not my fault you left me with nothing else to do," Rhosyn pointed out.

"And what exactly would you like to be doing?"

Rhosyn shrugged. "Punching something, probably."

"I don't think any of my men who were on the receiving end of your fists would be lining up to do it again."

Rhosyn cocked her head at him, considering. Her eyes caught on the biceps she had pillowed her head on just hours ago and her face heated. Now she really wanted to punch something.

"What about you?" she goaded.

"Me?"

"Yes. How do you feel about being on the receiving end of my fists?" She raised an eyebrow in challenge. If she couldn't work out her frustrations with Ansel on his thigh in the quiet of his bedroom, then her fists would have to do the job.

"Oh, I'm not too scared of them." Ansel shrugged. "Every time I've faced off against you, I seemed to get the upper hand."

Rhosyn bristled. "You think you won those fights? You cheated!"

"Once again, it's you who proved to be the cheater."

Rhosyn stood and her nostrils flared. In reaction to her movement, Little John rose from his table, as if he expected to have to restrain her from leaping across the table at Ansel.

"All I'm hearing is that you're afraid to fight me without all your tricks."

"Nothing is against the rules in a lower city brawl," Ansel retorted.

She bared her teeth at the words and the conflict that rose in her mind at his statement. After her time with the Lions, she knew there was no such thing as fighting dirty if it meant you could best your opponent.

The conditioning of the police force continually urged her to pull her punches. In one sentence, Ansel had prodded at the divide in her soul that became wider with every passing moment with the Foxes.

"If I stopped fighting by the rules, you wouldn't be able to get the upper hand," Rhosyn challenged.

"Why don't we test that out?"

Little John stepped closer, the look of consternation on his face echoed by Olivia and Paul. "I don't think that's a good idea, boss."

Ansel shrugged off his concern. "I'm the one who goaded her. If it's inevitable Rhosyn is going to punch something, then I'd prefer to have myself being on the receiving end of her fists than you."

Rhosyn raised her brows. "Nothing like a little sparring to combat the monotony of being held hostage." Her palms itched.

Ansel jerked his head towards the bar. "We have a storeroom we cleared out to use for training. It should do nicely."

He led the way behind the bar and Little John moved to follow. Ansel stopped him with an outstretched arm. "We'll be fine."

John opened his mouth as if to argue, but clearly thought better of it from the firmness in Ansel's tone.

An edge of curiosity broke through the simmering anticipation of a fight under Rhosyn's skin. She trailed him through a small door into a blank room. He closed it behind them as she took in the space.

A pang of something bittersweet echoed beneath Rhosyn's breastbone. The middle of the room was clear, with barrels and crates pushed haphazardly against the walls to make the most room for all manner of activities.

It looked just like the back room at the old Den where Rhosyn had trained young Lions in self-defense.

Rhosyn turned to consider Ansel as he barred the door behind him.

"I wanted some privacy," he admitted. "And if you do manage to knock me out, anything I can do to slow down the mayhem you might cause is a good thing."

She cracked her knuckles, the sound loud in the empty room. "I should probably ask you why you agreed to this, but I don't want to talk you out of it."

"I'm glad you're not asking."

Before Rhosyn could ponder the meaning of his words, he lunged.

Reflexes that remained quiet, yet awake, grabbed at her muscles, letting her sidestep his attack just in time. As he swung past her, she threw out her elbow, catching him in the flank.

He let out a pained grunt but didn't falter, swinging around and trying to take her feet out from under her with a swing of his leg. With a jump, she managed to avoid the blow to her ankles, but it threw her off balance.

Ansel pushed the advantage, coming at her with a flurry of blows. Rhosyn stumbled back for only a second before catching his punches on her forearms. The dull pain of what she knew would be bruises grounded her. At the same time, adrenaline surged in her veins.

It was a heady feeling. Like the one of drinking too much whiskey without the loss of clarity. Like the giddy sensation of Ansel's hand in her hair.

The thought of their morning encounter threw fuel on the fire in her chest. Ansel had no right to make her feel such things, yet part of her yearned for more.

With a snarl, she ducked under his next right hook and drove her shoulder up into his stomach. The momentum knocked him back.

For a moment, the pair toppled through the air, seemingly weightless. Then, Rhosyn's teeth rattled in her skull as they hit the ground.

Ansel brought his knees up as he went down, driving them into Rhosyn's stomach and trying to kick her off. Her vision swam as her breath exploded out of her, but she bore down. She wasn't much taller than him, but it was enough to allow her to pin him.

He struggled for a moment longer before giving in. With a tap on her forearm, currently braced across his throat, he signaled his defeat. For a second, Rhosyn considered taking advantage of the situation and knocking him out with a swift blow to the jaw.

He might have deserved it, for the brewing torment within her that he kept prodding into a more fervent simmer.

Instead, she backed off, sitting back on her heels.

After landing a few good blows, her tender pride at being held hostage was placated. Still, it didn't feel completely satisfied, as if she were craving some other sort of release.

"Just as fierce as I remembered," Ansel said, seemingly to himself as he sat up. The comment drew Rhosyn from her thoughts. His hand went to his ribs as he moved, likely bruised from the force of Rhosyn's ramming shoulder.

"Fierce, eh?" Rhosyn prompted.

Ansel held up his other hand to reveal a bandage around his ring finger she hadn't noticed before. "You have tried to bite me twice. Once you succeeded, and nearly took my finger off."

"Just be happy I didn't manage to get my teeth around you in the Gower's carriage too."

"Oh, I am." Ansel admitted. "I'm all for a bit of biting between friends, but that wasn't the time or place for it."

Rhosyn swallowed thickly, unsure whether Ansel's return to flirting was a sign that the tension from their early morning encounter was dissipating, or if he was trying to use it as a weapon against her.

"Why were you there that night?" Rhosyn asked to change the subject. "You had already done your job to get Olivia and Paul away."

He considered her, both still sprawled on the dusty floor, slightly sweaty and panting. It wasn't the posture of a hostage and her captor—or a police officer and a gang leader, for that matter. But something about it made such questions feel less like a game for information and more like a real conversation.

Ansel must have felt the same, because he answered, despite having no obligation to.

"Something...didn't seem right," he admitted. "When we got Olivia and Paul back to the safehouse that night, they were so tired they seemed almost ill. They've been adamant that they weren't physically mistreated, but the way they seemed positively dazed put my hair on end."

Rhosyn grit her teeth. It ached in her bones to know that young Lions had come to be in such a state—even after everything Nate had done for them. She had been there that very night and thought Paul seemed off, but it wasn't her who had been able to help him and his sister.

"I'm not sure what I expected to find," Ansel continued. "Maybe I was looking for evidence that they mistreated their staff, to explain why Olivia and Paul barely seemed to be able to talk about their time there, other than to be glad they were out. But that conversation we overheard between Mr. Gower and that other man, Hamish..."

Rhosyn pondered, remembering the cryptic words of the stolen conversation she had barely had time to process, given that she and Ansel found themselves in a tussle moments later.

"He seemed desperate to have Paul and Olivia return," she remembered.

"I still haven't been able to figure out his urgency. But I know that it doesn't feel right in my stomach. Something about the way he collects Talented servants doesn't sit right with me."

Rhosyn frowned. Mr. Gower's tone when he had demanded Paul and Olivia be returned—and seemingly to the groom of all people—was certainly sinister. It didn't give her any compelling evidence as to his intentions. Perhaps he was just a rich, pompous prick who was unused to being denied anything.

"One overheard conversation is hardly evidence of wrongdoing," she pointed out.

"I'll leave the evidence gathering to the police." Ansel inclined his head towards her. "I know when to trust my gut, and it was right."

Rhosyn grimaced. Perhaps she should be more ashamed that she had broken into the Gower's property without a warrant that night, only to come away without evidence, but more of an instinctual notion that they were up to no good. Instead of focusing on that, she asked, "You were right?"

"I've spent the few days arranging chance meetings with most of the Gower's Talented staff out in the city and casually offering the Foxes's...*ahem*...services. None of them have said anything outright against the Gowers, but they've all accepted our help."

"That's why you're planning to hit them again." Rhosyn thought out loud about her overheard conversation with Little John and his associate yesterday.

Ansel's eyebrows shot up his forehead. "And how would you have known what we've been planning?"

"Don't blame Little John." Rhosyn smiled wryly. "He thought I was too busy stabbing myself with a needle to eavesdrop."

He ran a hand tiredly through his hair. "We might call ourselves the Foxes, but I had a feeling keeping you here would be like letting a fox into the hen house. May I ask what else you overheard?"

"You may, but I don't have to answer."

"You're my hostage right now. Is it wise to deny me?" Ansel asked.

Rhosyn gestured between them. "Do you normally talk to your hostages like this? I don't think you're very good at it then."

In truth, trying to beat the sense out of each other had gone a long way to level the playing field between them. As if the fight had temporarily funneled the animosity out of them and given them the ability to speak rationally for once.

"Maybe I don't want you to be my hostage anymore," Ansel murmured, looking down at his hands, which had come to lay in his lap during the conversation.

"That doesn't seem very wise. If you let me go, I might just tell Chief Thorne about your plans to rob the Worthingtons."

Ansel glanced up through his lashes. "You know they don't need all that wealth."

"And you do?"

"Not me." Ansel shook his head. "But getting all the Talented out of the city is expensive. They need funds to help them start new lives, and getting the Gower's servants out will take a substantial bribe."

Rhosyn's interest piqued. "A bribe? Why would you ever admit that to me."

"Because..." Ansel paused, leaning back on his hands. "Because last night you gave me hope that you might understand after all. You might be an officer of the Royal Police, but what you told me makes me think it isn't because you believe in the letter of the law."

Rhosyn's voice stuck in her throat. She had no good retort to that, even as she might wish to deny it—to insist she was loyal to Chief Thorne when the police had already suffered so much corruption.

"I might understand," she eventually choked out instead.

Ansel nodded, as if he saw how difficult of a concession she had made. "To help the Talented truly be free of their sponsorships, we need to destroy the documents binding them to their sponsors. If we don't, their sponsors have the legal right to find them and force them back into service. Without that evidence, though, they have no legal hold over their Talented servants."

"Which is why you raided Contessa's office," Rhosyn said.

"Contessa? You're on a first name basis with the King's advisor?" Ansel seemed taken aback.

"She *is* married to Nathanial Woodrow." Rhosyn shot him a pointed look, hoping not to have to spell out her connection.

Realization dawned. "The Beast." He nodded.

"Don't call him that, but yes."

Ansel snorted. "I saw him at that party. He's no less a Beast now than his reputation painted him as when he was the leader of the Lions. It's what makes him such an effective bodyguard. He just has the backing of a king now."

Rhosyn frowned and tucked that line of thought away to examine later—that Nate was both the King's protector and the same headstrong fighter she had always looked up to as a brother.

"So, you got the sponsorship papers from Contessa's office?" Rhosyn prompted.

Ansel sighed heavily. "Yes and no. We got the batch that had already been completed, but after that, the next set was put in a safe. Unfortunately, many of the Gowers' current staff's papers are in that set. We tried to steal them too, but we haven't been able to crack the safe. Thus, we need the money to bribe a guard to take them for us. It will be a hefty sum."

At the mention of cracking a safe, a thought dawned on Rhosyn, accompanied by a memory. For an instant she was back on a liberation mission with Nate and Kristoff. A small girl tugged against her hand, refusing to leave and pointing a dirt smudged hand at a safe in the corner of the office they slept in, laying on the floor and locked in by the factory foreman. Even now, Rhosyn could feel the light thuds of tumblers falling into place under her fingers as she cracked the safe, the subtle clicking in her ear signaling her success as she pressed the side of her face to the cold metal. Inside she had found a delicate gold necklace—the only memento the girl had of her executed mother, taken from her by the factory's foreman.

From that day until she grew out of the Den, the girl had never taken that necklace off.

Stealing sponsorship papers so more Talented could be free wouldn't be that different.

"What if you didn't have to bribe the guards?" Rhosyn asked.

"We don't have anybody good enough at lock picking to get into that safe. And unfortunately, our magician's Talent doesn't work unless he's seen the object in question, so he can't blink the papers of the safe."

Ansel's words nearly distracted Rhosyn from what she was about to offer—against her better judgment—but she stayed with the task at hand.

"But if you did, you wouldn't have to rob the Worthingtons?"

Ansel looked at her curiously. "We'd have to stretch the circus's earnings between the Gowers' servants to give them a fresh start, but it could be done."

Rhosyn took a deep breath, stealing herself.

"I can crack the safe."

Ansel blinked once. Twice.

Silence stretched through the room, broken only by the noises from the common room outside.

"You can?"

Rhosyn released a stolen breath, somehow relieved that his question wasn't why she would do such a thing. "I'm not just the best pickpocket in London. I happen to also be the second best lockpick."

"And who would the first be?" Ansel asked.

"Wouldn't you like to know." Rhosyn's own past was hers to divulge to Ansel, even if it was ill advised. But she wasn't about to admit to Ansel that she had picked up her best safe-cracking tips from the King's closest advisor.

To his credit, Ansel didn't push her. Apparently, he was wise enough not to ask imprudent questions when somebody who was supposed to be his enemy offered their aid.

"Let's say I take you up on this. I'm not just going to let you waltz out of here and up to the palace. I have no guarantee you wouldn't just announce yourself and tell them of our plans."

"Well, that's good, because you know I'm terrible at waltzing." The quip was out of Rhosyn's mouth before she could remind herself this was a serious negotiation. Planning like this felt far too familiar. Despite being sprawled across a dusty floor, she could almost imagine she was sitting at Nate's desk, her boots up on the polished surface no matter how much he frowned, planning another liberation mission.

To her relief, Ansel chuckled, and Rhosyn found a smile toying with the corners of her mouth.

"I'm not going to let you walk out of here alone either."

"You have to let me out if I'm going to crack the safe. And I'm not doing it while Little John looks on." Rhosyn searched for the right words, wishing for Contessa's skill with a diplomatic turn of phrase. "I'm sure you'll understand that I'd appreciate discretion with the Foxes on this."

She shied away from the thought of betraying Chief Thorne in a way that had to be hidden, but she couldn't risk one of the Foxes having a loose tongue and telling somebody that an officer of the Royal Police had helped them burgle the palace. After all, once Paul and Olivia were gone, she would have to go back to strictly legal activities.

Thankfully, Ansel understood her meaning without further explanation. "Then I'll come with you."

Rhosyn hesitated. Perhaps she should worry about what Ansel would do with the knowledge of the crime she was offering to commit for him. After all, it would make good blackmail material. But his words from when he first confronted her, tied to the bed upstairs, came back to her.

Perhaps we can come to some sort of understanding.

Maybe they would after all.

"Alright. We'll do it together," she agreed.

Ansel stood and stretched out a hand to help her up as well. She took it, and he hauled her to her feet, leaving her standing nearly chest to chest with him. Maybe she should back away, but he didn't let go of her hand immediately, leaving them standing mere inches apart in the middle of the room.

Rhosyn's breath stuttered as he smiled crookedly, simultaneously wearing the charm of Mr. Blakely and the promise of mischief of the Hood.

"Well," he said, "this should be fun."

Chapter Nine

The floorboards creaked incessantly as Rhosyn paced back and forth across the small room. It was nearly annoying enough to make her stop, but she had too much energy to work out, despite her little brawl with Ansel earlier.

The past hours were the first Rhosyn had spent alone with her thoughts since being captured by the Foxes. Now that Rhosyn had offered her aid, Ansel had deemed it safe to leave her alone in his room, although he had locked the door. She supposed she should welcome the opportunity to regroup, but instead she only fretted.

After their conversation, Ansel had left again, saying he needed to make arrangements for their mission to the palace. Rhosyn knew that it would happen rather quickly, but when he said they would head out when he got back, her heart rate doubled. In just a matter of hours, she would be helping a criminal steal documents from the crown.

The thought shouldn't make her palms sweat, but still, she ended up repetitively wiping her hands on her pants. It was hardly the first time in her life that she'd be breaking the law—not even the most serious infraction in her ledger. If things went well, they wouldn't be spilling any blood.

She clung to that thought with a vice grip. By volunteering to crack the safe for Ansel, she was preventing the Foxes from robbing a family of their wealth and potentially being less scrupulous with their violence in the process. With her on the job, she could make sure the operation was as quiet and peaceful as possible. After all, wasn't saving lives and preventing crimes her job as an officer of the Royal Police?

At that thought she stopped pacing in favor of flopping back on the bed in the center of the room, her hair spreading out around her in a chaotic splash of crimson. Since joining the Royal Police, she had been able to protect her city by following the law and ensuring others did too.

The end of the Inquiries had marked a profound shift, where Rhosyn went from seeing the police and the Crown as her enemy to her allies. When Contessa's father, Chief Cook, had been leading corrupt law enforcement, breaking the law had clearly been in the name of justice, and Rhosyn had done it happily to be what the people of London needed.

When Chief Thorne took over, and the new King started taking steps to protect the Talented, the Royal Police were now on the side of righteousness, and Rhosyn had once again shifted to be what was needed—as close to a model police officer as she could be with her shadowed past. But if the law was no longer corrupt, why did she now feel like she had to break it to do the right thing?

With a groan, she dug the heels of her hands into her eyes so hard that lights exploded in her vision. Ever since meeting the Hood—Ansel—everything that had once seemed clear had become muddied.

A rustling at the window grabbed her attention. In a second, Rhosyn rolled off the bed, landing on the balls of her feet in a defensive crouch.

After days on edge, her reflexes were primed to respond quickly to any unusual sounds.

The rustling turned into scratching, and she inched towards the window, staying low so as to be out of the line of sight of anybody at the sill—an impressive feat given that Ansel's room was on the fourth floor.

A clicking and then a metallic scrape indicated that the lock had broken—forced open instead of finessed—and the window swung open on loudly protesting hinges. The muscles in Rhosyn's thighs tightened like coiled springs, prepared to leap forward and dislodge the intruder as they clambered onto the sill.

Instead, a familiar silhouette, dark against the hazy evening sky swung up effortlessly, perching in the window frame with all the ease of a sparrow in flight.

Rhosyn blinked at the maneuver as Ansel paused, seemingly spotting her defensive posture. Even Scarlett, who for some reason insisted on entering through Rhosyn's bedroom window even though she was perfectly welcome to use the door, didn't boast such gravity-defying maneuvers.

This was also Ansel's own room, which begged the question, "And you chose to risk me punching you out of a fourth story window frame instead of using the door to your own room because…?"

Ansel dropped into the room, his boots barely making a noise despite the creakiness of the old building's floors. "I wasn't particularly worried about falling. I am rarely a victim of gravity," he admitted.

Rhosyn put her hands on her hips, but he just shrugged.

"After years on a trapeze, falling from a window doesn't seem like an immediate threat."

Realization dawned. "Your Talent."

She had been so concerned with learning of the dual role of Archer's Circus as the up-and-coming Foxes that she had barely registered Ansel's admission that he had a Talent—and that he had stopped performing as an acrobat because it had become obvious.

He smiled wryly. "Don't ask me what exactly it is, because I've never really had a satisfactory answer. The closest I've come is enhanced balance, but that doesn't seem to capture it. Whenever I climb or do acrobatics though, I can almost see in advance how things are going to work out. Like..."

"Like a sixth sense," Rhosyn finished for him. It was something Nate had said about his Talent, which also seemed to defy definition, especially to someone like Rhosyn who had no Talent at all.

"It makes running over rooftops easy, and can even come in handy in a fight, but unfortunately does not give me an advantage at many other things," Ansel admitted. "For example, I forgot that I locked the window in case you decided to make an ill-advised escape attempt, and now I have a broken latch."

"Which once again prompts me to ask, what do you have against doors?"

Ansel considered her, saying after a moment, "You wanted discretion. I left this evening and none of the Foxes saw me return. If we leave and return for the palace the same way, nobody has to know that I alone wasn't responsible for stealing the sponsorship documents."

Silence stretched, as Rhosyn drew a blank on any appropriate response. She and Ansel had pushed against each other at so many junctions, but here he had gone out of his way to honor her preference for secrecy. It was an acknowledgment of the concession she was making by doing this for them, and calculated as it was, it tugged at a string under Rhosyn's sternum she hadn't known was there.

"We better get going then," she eventually said, and the moment dissipated.

Ansel nodded, stepping around her to the foot of the bed. He opened the trunk there and rustled inside for a moment before emerging with a familiar garment: a jacket with a deep hood. He pulled it on and lowered the hood over his head, before tossing a similar article to Rhosyn.

She followed suit, glad to have something to cover her hair. The garment was too broad across the shoulders, and too short at the wrists, but it would do the job.

Next, he reached into his pocket and produced a bland-looking bundle. He handed it to Rhosyn, who unrolled it curiously, only for her heart to stutter at the shine of a full set of lock picks.

"I got them especially for you," he admitted.

She chuckled as she rerolled the packet and tucked it into her boot. "You really know how to charm a woman."

When she stood, the police officer was gone, replaced by a gangster with a shadowed face and hidden lockpicks. He was the Hood, and she was his thief.

Ansel looked at her and nodded in satisfaction before stepping towards the still-open window. He hesitated when he reached it. Then he reached for his sleeve, rolling it up to reveal a hidden sheath much like the ones that Nate—and now Contessa—had always used to conceal his numerous knives.

Ansel unstrapped it hurriedly and thrust it at Rhosyn's chest, as if doing it quickly before he had a chance to change his mind. "Don't make me regret this."

"I make no promises about regret," Rhosyn said as she took the outstretched offering and began strapping it to her own forearm. "But I do promise not to stab you when your back is turned."

"I guess that's the best I could hope for." Ansel's tone was rueful, but he smiled, nonetheless.

Rhosyn found herself smiling at him too. At the feeling of the leather straps against the skin of her forearm—the familiar yet foreign weight of a blade—the sleepy Lion in her mind perked up in interest. She had grown comfortable with the weight of a baton at her hip in the past years, but this awakened something in her that she had been denying to herself that she missed.

In the dark of night, she was about to climb out a lower city window in secrecy, a hidden knife at her wrist, to steal people's freedom back from their captors. Her heart fluttered, and a strange lightness took hold at the base of her skull. Rhosyn was *excited*.

She clamped down on the realization by scowling. "Well, we better get moving. I may be better than you at picking locks, but I am not as good at climbing down a wall from the fourth story."

"Then I'll be a gentleman, and not propose we race." Without further prelude, Ansel turned back to the window and levered himself over the sill. Rhosyn darted forward, knowing he wouldn't fall but heart rate skyrocketing, nonetheless. She leaned out into the night air just in time to watch him catch a hold of a clothesline in the back alley the window faced. He swung from it, putting the excess momentum into a somersault before landing on the ground.

It was so much like the first time they met, and Rhosyn suppressed a sigh at the realization that, just like that day, she would be following at a much slower pace. She turned and lowered herself down over the sill backwards, muscles in her arms straining as her toes scrambled for purchase on the wall. She picked her way down carefully, trying not to let the fact that Ansel was staring up at her rush her movements. Given the choice between having him enjoy a rather suggestive view of her backside from below or witnessing her falling, she would take the former. As he had so annoyingly pointed out, it was nothing he hadn't seen before.

By the time Rhosyn's boots hit the packed dirt of the alleyway, she was beginning to perspire, her shirt clinging to the small of her back and curls tightening in the humidity.

"I hope you can scale a wall faster than that," Ansel said, quietly enough that she could barely make out his words over the din of the street at the front of the building. While the middle and upper city would be quieting down at this point in the night, action in the lower city was just picking up.

"We'll need to be quick if we are to make it over the back wall to the palace between rounds of the King's Guard," Ansel worried out loud.

Rhosyn paused. She should have thought about how Ansel planned to get into the palace grounds, but she had spent her time worrying about her choice to go with him instead.

There was a way to get into the palace grounds without risking getting caught climbing the wall, though. Using it would require putting even more trust in Ansel.

They had come this far.

"Lucky for you, we don't have to scale the back wall."

Ansel raised a brow.

"Follow me." It was all the further instruction she gave him before trotting off down the alley to towards the slightly better lit main streets. As she emerged, she looked both ways, taking stock of where they were, although trying not to be too obvious in plotting out the exact location of the Foxes hideout in their mind.

"Graham Street," Ansel supplied.

When she looked at him curiously, he just shrugged.

"You were going to figure it out anyways. No point in forcing you to struggle to get your bearings at this point."

Rhosyn nodded sharply, turning left and weaving deftly through the milling crowds of dirty urchins and rowdy gamblers. She walked these streets every day on her assigned beat, but tonight, it felt different. While the residents of the lower city recognized her—even trusted her, as much as they could an officer of the Royal Police after the terrifying reign of the Inquiries—Rhosyn hadn't realized how *other* the navy wool and gold buttons of her uniform made her. When she patrolled, she rarely brushed shoulders with pedestrians or had to jump out of the way of an ambling cart. Everybody gave her a respectful berth.

Now though, she weaved and dodged like the Lion's runners, whom she had trained to carry messages quickly and secretly between safehouses. Nobody spared her a glance or averted their eyes, as if afraid of being accused of causing trouble.

Tonight, she was one of them. Just another citizen going about their business—perhaps legal, perhaps not.

Rhosyn quickly steered them towards the Lion's old territory. Now it was split between a few gangs, the worst of the skirmishes over the territory in the past with the fall of the Wolves. The particular building she was looking for was currently in Rattlesnake territory, but she didn't fear them anymore.

In a matter of minutes, Rhosyn led Ansel to the front of a butcher shop. She paused outside, plotting her strategy.

"Are we in need of meat for whatever your secret plan is?" Ansel asked as she considered.

"It's not what's in the store. It's what's underneath," Rhosyn explained. She headed for a gap between buildings, planning on entering through the side door. She gestured for Ansel to follow, but paused when she realized he was no longer right behind her.

He hesitated, hovering under the darkened shop's awning. His right hand gripped his opposite forearm, a gesture Rhosyn recognized as him palming a hidden weapon through his clothes, as if considering drawing it.

"You could be leading me into a trap," he pointed out.

Rhosyn stepped back towards him, propping one had on her him. "And when would I have had time to set up a trap? You've had me watched nearly every minute, day and night."

His mouth twisted ruefully. "It's turning out that you have many skills I don't know about."

"Well, telepathy is not one of them. No hidden Talents here," Rhosyn assured.

Ansel took a single step forward. "And how will a butcher shop help us get into the palace? Unless you prefer a meat cleaver to a proper dagger."

"Do you trust me?" Rhosyn asked.

"I shouldn't."

Rhosyn shook her head. "That wasn't an answer."

Ansel sighed heavily, a sound that held more meaning and feeling than a spoken answer might have. "Lead the way."

She turned back towards the door, popping the cheap lock easily. The screech of breaking metal couldn't even be heard against the din of the tavern across the street. Rhosyn said a silent apology and made a mental note to replace it for the shop owners. This was no longer a Lions' safe house, but the shop owners were former gang members.

Once inside, she navigated to the back of the shop, where meat hung from the rafters. Careful not to bump any, she located what she was looking for.

"Help me move these." Rhosyn gestured to a few salt barrels on top of her goal.

Ansel's expression was curious, but to his credit, he did as she asked without question. However, the crease between his brows smoothed into realization as Rhosyn bent to dust off a hidden handle.

"A trapdoor? You really are a woman of many secrets."

Too many.

Rhosyn ignored that thought in favor of heaving the door open, a small puff of dust following the motion, indicating that the tunnel below had not been used in quite a long time. For the most part, they were no longer used, as the Lions had been the only ones to know of their existence for many years, and their need for them had passed.

A few trusted police officers knew of their existence as well, after the raid on the Wolves several years back. However, what most officers, not even Chief Thorne, knew, was that they were aware of a small fraction of the tunnels. Only a few people had ever fully explored the labyrinthian network over the span of many years: Nate, Kristoff, and Rhosyn herself.

"This tunnel can get us into the palace?" Ansel drew Rhosyn back from memories of using chalk to mark the walls below, spending years memorizing the best routes between the Den and various safe houses.

"Yes and no," Rhosyn said as she swept a few cobwebs from the open hatch with her hand. "It will get us onto the grounds, but not inside the palace proper. The exit is in one of the outbuildings, and we can go from there."

Nate had seen to it that most of the entrances that could be used to threaten the King had been closed off, just as the entrance in his own study had been. However, he left just one, a tiny passage not even many of the Lions had ever used, just in case he ever needed to be able to smuggle the King to safety.

"It'll be dark, but I know the way," Rhosyn said, before levering herself down feet first into the passage below.

The air was cool and stale down here, the dank smell tugging at memories in the back of her mind. She let them surface, knowing they would bring with them the muscle memory necessary to navigate the maze ahead after all these years.

A light thud marked Ansel's arrival next to her, the sound of boots hitting stone echoing in the empty passage. At that, Rhosyn reached up, stretching on the tips of her toes to grab the trap door and shut it behind them. With a *thunk* laced with a remarkable amount of finality, it fell back into place, punching them into impenetrable darkness.

With their sense of sight nearly completely gone, sounds became louder. The even cadence of Ansel's breathing, so close next to her in the tight space, lifted the hairs on the nape of Rhosyn's neck. She was going to have to guide him.

"Here, take my hand." She reached out, fumbling in the darkness. After a moment, his hand met hers. She didn't need to interlace their fingers, but she found herself doing so anyways.

"Let's go."

Rhosyn placed the hand not holding Ansel's on the wall and set off down the passageway. At first, they walked in silence. Rhosyn tried to focus on the rasp of rough-hewn stone under her palm as she used her left hand to navigate in the darkness. However, her awareness kept slipping back to her right hand and the feeling of strong, callused fingers between her own.

It wasn't the soft touch of the society men Contessa had occasionally encouraged her to dance with at social events—the kind that would draw away with polite disgust as they felt the roughness of Rhosyn's own skin. Neither was it the unwelcome grab of a lower city thug that Rhosyn had no scruples responding to with a sharp knee to the groin.

Ansel's grip was firm, but not aggressive, as he let her lead the way through the pitch black in a remarkable show of trust. For a fleeting moment, Rhosyn wished she deserved that trust and wasn't going to shatter it by arresting him the moment the temporary truce she had agreed to for Paul and Olivia was over.

If she still planned to have him arrested, that was.

That thought prompted a queasy feeling to take hold beneath her ribs. Thankfully, Ansel seemed to be unnerved by the silence and distracted her from her thoughts with a question.

"So, do the Royal Police use these tunnels?"

"They have, but not this particular one," Rhosyn hedged.

"So, you know of this one because..."

"The Lions used them." She bit the words out with a bit more defiance than necessary, as she tried to stop dancing around a truth she had already admitted.

Ansel hummed noncommittally and they walked in silence for a few more minutes. Rhosyn occupied herself by drawing up the mental map of the intertwining passages in her mind, referencing it every time she had to make a choice at a fork in the path. The only words she spoke for a while were "watch your step" at the patches of uneven ground or "mind your head" when the ceiling dipped down for short stretches. Ansel exhaled through his nose in an aborted chuckle as she was forced to duck more often than him.

It wasn't until they were a few turns away from the exit Rhosyn sought when Ansel spoke again.

"Why did you join the Royal Police?"

Rhosyn's steps nearly stuttered, but she forced herself to put one foot in front of the other at an even pace. It was something that seemed obvious in her own mind, but having it asked so plainly—and by somebody who clearly saw it as a disconnect from her path—made it seem confusing. When she had told Nate and Contessa of her wishes to join the force, they had only nodded. Their understanding of what she desired went unspoken, given that they had transitioned from leaders of the most powerful street gang in London to the King's closest advisors.

Silence stretched too long, the sound of their boots scraping against the uneven floors and a quiet dripping somewhere in the distance nearly deafening. Rhosyn thought she might not answer at all when the words tumbled out of her of her own accord.

"I've always been what people needed. For years, the young Lions needed a big sister. Then, London needed protectors it could trust."

And now, I'm not so sure what is needed.

The last part echoed unspoken in her mind.

They reached the end of the corridor they were in, a tiny space opening up where both she and Ansel could crowd behind the hidden door at the rear of the servants' quarters. In the small opening, they stood so close that Rhosyn's chest brushed Ansel's as she breathed. It was still too dark to see, but the space stirred around her as they inhaled the same air. It was both painfully intimate, and blissfully anonymous, being this close but not being able to see him after what she had just admitted.

She thought Ansel might drop the subject, but instead he asked, "So who does that make you, if you've only ever tried to be what everybody else needed? Are you a gangster or a police officer?"

Rhosyn tried to swallow, but her throat stuck. "I could ask you the same thing." Her voice was hoarse but loud in the blackness. "Are you Mr. Blakely or the Hood?"

"I have a feeling we might answer that question the same."

Neither.

"Neither." Ansel echoed her answer, although she hadn't said it out loud.

Rhosyn's heart stuttered, pain lancing through her chest at knowing her enemy and captor was the one who had been able to so succinctly cut to the core of her psyche.

"Don't we have a palace to rob?" she asked, voice scratchier than she would ever like to admit.

"Of course. Heists are hardly the best time for philosophical debates about one's identity."

And like that, Ansel diffused the tension with just one quip. Air that had been sucked out of Rhosyn's lungs rushed back in as she breathed in relief. Teasing banter sat much more comfortably with her.

Turning away, Rhosyn put her ear to the wooden panel that served as a hidden door. The movement gave her a few moments of separation from Ansel, and her mind was able to latch onto the task at hand once more. It was the middle of the night, but the servants that lived in this outbuilding would work at all hours to keep the palace running smoothly.

Greeted only by silence, Rhosyn inched the door open, thanking the powers for quiet hinges. Perhaps Nate kept them oiled, just as he kept this passage open and secret.

They stepped out into a quiet corridor. It, too, was dark, but the blackness was less thick than it had been in the passage. From one end of the hallway came the dim silver light of the moon, seeping in around a doorframe.

Rhosyn gestured towards the exit and led the way on soft feet. In a matter of moments, they emerged into the soft evening air of the palace grounds. The main building towered in the distance, a fortress of stone that would not be easily penetrated. As they crept through the shadows, towards the high stone walls, she frowned at it.

Guards would be stationed at all the doors, as well as rounding the gardens at regular intervals. She would have to shimmy open the lock of one of the windows quickly. Unfortunately, the palace would not have the cheap locks that were easily persuaded to give way with correctly applied leverage. It would be a challenge to break it quickly enough to avoid notice. At least once they were inside the offices, Rhosyn wouldn't have to worry about the patrols of the ground interrupting her work on the safe.

They reached the shadow of the walls and Rhosyn crept towards the nearest window, keeping to the side in case somebody was up working late. She bent to the lock and cursed quietly under her breath.

Ansel leaned over his shoulder, close enough that his heat seeped through his clothes onto his breath tickled her neck. "What's wrong?"

"This is going to take a while to finesse. Breaking it would make too much noise." Rhosyn explained, pulling the lock picks from her boot.

Ansel huffed. "We don't have a while. Guards round every five minutes."

Her stomach turned to stone. Who knew how long it had already been? "Then I better get started."

Ansel rested a hand on her forearm, halting her. "Look."

Rhosyn tracked where he pointed with her gaze. Several floors up was a window, swung wide open as if in invitation. She shook her head. The palace walls would not be rough hewn with uneven mortar—not easily climbed.

"I can get you up," Ansel assured.

Before she could ask how, Ansel darted away across the lawn to a blossoming tree. Rhosyn hissed, suppressing the urge to shout at him for being stupid and drawing attention. He started up the tree, and frustrated as she was, Rhosyn's eyebrows shot up at the speed with which he reached the upper branches.

The tree was well pruned by the castle gardeners, leaving no low hanging boughs for him to use as handholds, but Ansel didn't seem to need them. He scurried upwards with the swiftness of a squirrel that spent all its life among the trees.

As he reached the branches level with the open window, he stepped onto one. Rhosyn's mouth opened, but she kept herself from shouting. Still, her heart froze in her chest as he picked his way along the branch. It was too thin and too far from the open window. He couldn't possibly make it.

But Ansel didn't seem to be informed about the laws of gravity. He ran along the branch as if it were a tightrope, not even attempting to use his hands to balance himself on adjacent limbs. As the branch got thinner, he only gained speed. Just as the branch began to dip dangerously under his weight, he leaped.

The tiniest squeak of fear escaped Rhosyn's still open mouth. He soared, stretching out towards the window sill, the distance impossibly far. Before he could plummet to the ground, bones crunching against the well-groomed grass, Ansel's earlier words echoed in her mind.

I am rarely a victim of gravity.

Ansel caught the windowsill by just the tips of his fingers, but stopping his fall still seemed effortless. His feet hit the stone wall below the open window and pushed back instantly, launching him through the open window.

The whole thing had taken a matter of seconds.

The only issue was that it left Rhosyn crouched on the ground, and the guards would be coming by any minute. She certainly wouldn't be replicating his stunt—not without breaking her neck.

Her heart hammered. After she had put her trust in him, had Ansel betrayed her, leaving her to get arrested for treason? Because that was what she was doing. Committing treason against the King who had ended all her friends' suffering.

Rhosyn was jerked away from the panic clawing at her throat by a knock on her head. Her chin jerked up to see a rope, dangling from the open window Ansel had just entered.

A gust of breath escaped her lips, which were quirked by a surprised smile. She grabbed at the rope, hauling herself up. She might not be the acrobat Ansel was, but she could scale a rope easily enough. She wrapped the end around her foot, using it as a step to pull herself up towards Ansel.

Just as she crested half the distance between the ground and her entrance point, a dull crunching from below drew Rhosyn's attention. Panic gripped her chest anew, squeezing her heart in an iron grasp as she fumbled, trying to climb faster.

The quiet noise shaped into footsteps, at least two guards by the sounds of it, about to round the corner at any moment. She wouldn't be inside by the time they did, leaving her open to their watchful eyes.

In her hands the rope jerked. All of a sudden, she was rising faster, the rope being hauled in even as she climbed. Ansel was pulling her up.

She scrambled, heat stinging her palms as her skin chafed against the rope. Her toes banged against the wall as she shoved upwards.

The footsteps were nearly beneath her when Rhosyn's shoulder crested the windowsill, and she pitched forward. The momentum of her climb combined with Ansel's pulling was enough to carry her through the empty frame. With a bone-rattling thud, she tumbled head over heels into the palace. The sound of the wind being knocked out of lungs didn't only come from her, but from the firm chest she landed on.

Ansel lay on the ground, Rhosyn sprawled across his torso. They both froze, ears pricked for signs of their detection, from both inside and outside the palace. The only noise was their own ragging breathing, close enough to be sharing the same air.

When no shouting of intruders began, Rhosyn slumped forward with relief. Her forehead landed on Ansel's collarbone. A sigh rustled her hair, and one of Ansel's arms came up, a hand resting between her shoulder blades. His thumb rubbed the smallest of circles there.

Rhosyn's skin prickled with overwhelming awareness, adrenaline still rushing through her at the near miss. Now that the immediate threat had passed, all that shivering anticipation turned towards the hammering of

Ansel's heart, beating a tattoo through his clothes, so insistent she could feel it. Her own heart responded in kind.

His body was warm and solid beneath hers, and her thighs squeezed where they bracketed his narrow hips. At the motion, his abs tensed beneath hers. Rhosyn shivered at all the power and agility packed into Ansel's compact body. He had to be incredibly strong to pull her up like he did.

Ansel's hand rubbed more insistently at her back, and the movement focused the strange heat running through her body, forcing her to move. She rolled sideways, hitting the floor next to him inelegantly, but effectively separating them.

"Thank you," she murmured at the ceiling.

"It's the least I can do, considering you have to do the hard part later."

Rhosyn scrubbed at her forehead. "We should get moving. The quicker we get this over with, the less chance we get caught."

And the quicker we can go back to being on opposite sides.

She pushed to her feet and took stock of their surroundings.

The space was tight, the walls taken up by racks of worn-looking weapons and ammunition. It must be a supply room for the King's Guard, and a stack of miscellaneous supplies near the window explained how Ansel had been able to find a rope so fast. The musty smell of worn uniforms also gave Rhosyn a hint as to why the window had been left open.

"The safe is on the first floor," Ansel whispered.

Listening carefully every step of the way, they cracked open the door and exited into the hallway, once they assured themselves nobody was coming. Rhosyn didn't know the architecture of the palace perfectly, but it wasn't difficult to find stairs, as this section of the palace was a basic grid of offices and halls, stacked on top of each other.

Once they reached the ground floor, Ansel stepped around her, leading the way to the safe. It was in an office near Contessa's, but not in hers. Rhosyn was grateful not to be stealing from her friend directly, even if it still panged of betrayal in her heart.

The room Ansel led her to was nondescript, aside from the imposing safe in the corner. A standard desk and chair took up most of the space, and a large fireplace along one wall lay empty, no need for its heat in the warmth of late spring. Rhosyn approached the safe appraisingly. A brief tap to the side confirmed that the blackened metal was inches thick. The special devices some used to cut into vaults, or the acids that ate through sheets of metal, wouldn't do much good against walls this thick. Thankfully, Rhosyn was not a demolitions expert. She was a proper thief.

"Keep watch," she instructed Ansel over her shoulder, bending to her boot and picking out the tools she appraised would be the most useful.

"Don't want me stealing your secrets?" he whispered, although he had already turned towards the door.

"As if you could," she murmured under her breath, her mind already more on the task before her than the conversation.

The small door bore the crown jewel of locks for a lock pick: a Chubb lock. It wouldn't be able to be raked open, all the pins simply knocked into place. It would take finesse and subtle patience.

With that, Rhosyn got to work. She carefully selected each instrument in turn, inserting them delicately into the lock and feeling carefully for the pins' movement with a hand laid on the cool metal.

Her mind blocked out Ansel's presence, for the first time in hours forgetting the potential consequences of her actions. Where "patient" had never been a word Rhosyn would use to describe herself, she somehow managed it with the puzzle of a difficult lock before her. She had once asked Nate if it might be a Talent, but he told her he sensed no air of the supernatural around her. So, she practiced and practiced until the only person with a better knack for espionage was Contessa herself.

In the near trance that Rhosyn fell into when picking a lock, blind to all but the subtle changes in resistance under her fingers, she wasn't sure if it was five minutes or fifty before the last pin slid into place and her tools twisted easily in the keyhole.

The door fell open, revealing a thick sheaf of papers. At the sound of shuffling, Ansel left his post at the door, barely cracked to allow him to peer into the hallway.

"Are they there?" he whispered over her shoulder.

She quickly leafed through them, hissing when she gave herself a papercut in her haste.

"These look like sponsorship contracts to me," she said. Although not familiar with fancy legal documents, Rhosyn caught the words "Talented", "pardon", and "owed service" among the text. "What are the names on the documents we need?"

She bit her tongue around the word *we*, but Ansel answered before she could correct herself.

"Just take the whole stack."

"Have you ever robbed anybody before?" Rhosyn asked incredulously. "The less you take, the longer it takes people to realize something is missing—and the colder your trail will be when they try to find you."

"Well, you couldn't find me, so obviously my way works."

He grabbed for the papers in her hands, but she twisted away quickly, and his fingers closed around thin air. She narrowed her eyes at the concentrated jumble of words, seeking to find where the names of the Talented to be pardoned and employed were.

She located the names at the bottom of the page.

Name: Thomas Pemberton

Talent: Combustion

"Explosions?" Rhosyn mouthed in confusion. She couldn't fathom what service that might do to a fine family of the upper city, although maybe they didn't mean to use it at all and instead to have him be a footman. She spied Mr. Gower's signature at the bottom of the page.

Ansel peered over her shoulder, breathing down her neck impatiently. "We don't have much time."

Rhosyn ignored him in favor of flipping to the next page, also signed by Mr. Gower.

Name: Theo Hamilton

Talent: Walking through walls

Another odd Talent to pursue for a sponsorship, when there were others who could cook a perfect pie every time without a recipe. The third page was just as confusing.

Talent: Control over lightning

"Look at these Talents." She shoved the stack of papers into Ansel's hands. "And they're all for Mr. Gower."

Ansel flipped through pages, his eyebrows raising as he shuffled through faster and faster. There were dozens of documents.

"Doesn't it seem like..." she started.

"He's building an army," Ansel finished grimly. "Looking at the crimes these pardons are for, many of these are not just petty thieves, but violent criminals—murderers and rapists."

"What on earth for?" Rhosyn asked.

Ansel shook his head, and his expression was stony as her stomach felt. This, combined with the odd state of all Mr. Gower's servants, came together to paint an incomplete but sinister picture.

The silence stretched as they both considered.

That's when she heard it.

Distracted as they had been by their discovery, neither of them had noticed the growing sound of footsteps in the hallway.

Ansel's gaze snapped up, meeting hers with wide, urgent eyes.

Let's go, he mouthed silently.

Rhosyn grabbed the contracts from him and shoved them unceremoniously into the front of her jacket.

They turned toward the door, but by the time they reached it, it was too late. The footsteps were nearly right outside the door, their escape cut off. Rhosyn held her breath, lungs burning as she tried to control her hammering heart, as if it might be heard by whoever patrolled the halls at this time of night.

Right as the stomp of boots on stone—likely signaling a guard—reached its loudest, the steps stuttered. Then paused. Rhosyn's heart stopped. Where every door in the hallway they had entered through had been closed, the door to the room they occupied was ajar from Ansel's watch.

Rhosyn whipped her head back and forth. The room had no window, leaving no escape. Their only two options were to hide, or to fight their way out. For possibly the first time in her life, Rhosyn chose to hide.

She dove under the desk in the middle of the room. Ansel seemed to have a similar thought process. He darted towards the fireplace, ducking inside and reaching up into the chimney. Rhosyn grimaced as he disappeared, remembering a harrowing story of Scarlett's involving climbing through a chimney.

Ansel's toes disappeared behind the mantle just as a quiet squeak signaled the door opening.

Rhosyn counted every heavy step of boots against flagstones as the guard walked into the room. Some instinct told her to squeeze her eyes shut, as if that might make her invisible. Instead, she forced herself to keep them open, tracking the movement of his shadow as he strode across the room. Her knees brushed against her chin as she shoved herself as tightly as possible into the corner of the desk, trying to conceal every inch of herself in the shadows there.

The footsteps paused, and Rhosyn imagined the guard swinging his gaze back and forth like a lamp in the night. She thanked luck she had closed the safe after removing the papers, habit kicking in to always leave everything as she found it.

After long, breathless seconds, the guard's shadow retreated towards the door, seemingly satisfied that it had only been left open by accident. Just as his silhouette moved out of her line of sight, it happened.

A quiet sneeze from the fireplace.

Now Rhosyn did squeeze her eyes shut in despair. A metallic *shink* marked a weapon being drawn, and the guard's feet rounded the desk as he marched towards the open hearth. If he turned around and looked down, he would spot Rhosyn there, but his attention was on the fireplace, leaving his back turned to her.

He bent down to look in the hearth and Rhosyn's mind raced. With him distracted by Ansel, the route between her and the door was clear. She could make a break for it—leave Ansel to be discovered while she escaped. She could run straight to Chief Thorne and put an end to this whole thing.

The guard angled his sword ready to stab up the chimney to where Ansel hid, and Rhosyn knew that wasn't an option.

With a strangled shout, Rhosyn sprang from her hiding spot. Nate would have rolled his eyes, telling her a battle cry defeated the point of a surprise attack, but it served its purpose in bringing the guard up short before he could stab Ansel. She landed on his back, forearms coming around his throat.

He grunted at the impact, swinging his sword wildly as he tried to slash her over his shoulders. Before he could, Ansel tumbled from the chimney, so covered in soot that he looked like nothing more than a shadow. His roll from his hiding spot carried him seamlessly to his feet and he kicked the weapon from their assailant's hand.

It clattered to the ground, but the guard stayed intent on dislodging Rhosyn. She pressed down on his windpipe, trying to squeeze consciousness from him. His fingers grappled at her wrists, and her biceps screamed as she fought to keep him from pulling her loose.

With a muffled roar, he turned and lunged back, slamming Rhosyn into wall. Her skull cracked against stone, white spots dancing across her vision, but still she held tight. More often than not, brawls were won by the ability to take a hit, and Rhosyn was the best brawler of them all.

She *would* outlast this guard, who was not a scrappy boxer, but a polished fighter, much less threatening without his weapon in hand.

Rhosyn gritted her teeth as she squeezed even tighter, and his struggles began to weaken.

His knees hit the ground with a thud, and Rhosyn landed on her feet, still keeping her arms around his neck. As he lost consciousness, she lowered him to the ground, not letting his head hit the stone as she released the pressure on his neck. By the time his face lolled back to an angle where he could have seen her, his eyes were closed. He had never seen her face.

Ansel stood frozen at the guard's feet. He and Rhosyn panted as they stared at each other. He opened his mouth like he was about to say something, expression unreadable under the layer of soot on his face.

Before he could speak, distant noises drifted down the hallway. The commotion of the brief fight would not have gone unnoticed.

"Run," Rhosyn ordered.

Ansel didn't need to be told twice, and together they sprinted from the room. Their footsteps echoed as they pounded down the hall, but it hardly mattered now. The time for stealth had passed and now their priority was speed.

A few doors down on their left, moonlight streamed in through a window leaving a silvery splash on the ground.

"Here!" Ansel panted.

That was all the warning she got before he veered off, covering his head with his arms as he crashed through the glass. Rhosyn followed suit, rolling as she hit the grass outside and thankful that they were on the first floor. She sprang to her feet, grateful for the lack of injury from the fall, only to be proven wrong by a stabbing pain in her calf.

She looked down to see a shard of glass as long as her finger sticking out of the bulge of muscle there. There was no time to process the sight, as Ansel grabbed her forearm and started dragging her towards the palace outbuildings. Her thoughts turned to nothing more than a loud buzzing as her body took over, lurching her forward in stumbling, running steps beside him.

Thankfully, Ansel remembered where the passage entrance was, guiding them while Rhosyn focused on keeping moving. Shouting behind them in the distance signaled that the whole palace had been alerted to their incursion, but it was too late.

They stumbled into the servants' quarters and dove into the secret tunnel, shutting the hidden panel behind them just as the noise caused doors in the corridor to swing open in curiosity. Still, Ansel didn't stop urging Rhosyn forward.

She didn't know how far she made it, stumbling in the dark, before she tripped, tipping forward into Ansel's back. He broke her fall with a grunt, twisting and maneuvering her arm over his shoulders.

"We need to get you help," he said, hoarse voice echoing in the relative quiet. It seemed strange, given that Rhosyn's ears seemed to be ringing, pulsating in time with the hammering of her heart from lingering adrenaline.

"It's not anything I can't patch up myself," Rhosyn assured. Now that they slowed down, giving her a moment to take stock of her injuries, she knew she was right. She probably could even walk on her own if she had a moment to catch her breath, but for some reason, she was loathe to lean away from Ansel's supportive warmth. Maybe it was that the solidity of his muscles shifting under her arm grounded her after the pell-mell sprint of their escape.

Either way, she just needed to remove the glass and clean the cut. She had patched up worse scrapes on young Lions who had tumbled down the stairs or gotten in ill-advised scraps over the years.

Ansel shook his head, the movement making his hair brush Rhosyn's forearm where it draped over his neck. The touch was surprisingly soft and ticklish after the harshness of their encounter.

"It's still too far from the tunnel entrance to the Foxes' safehouse for you to limp. We'd draw attention, and that's not wise considering the guards will know within minutes that the palace was broken into."

Rhosyn grimaced. Ansel was right. Nate himself was probably already dispatching riders to the Royal Police stations throughout the city, putting the city on high alert. A man covered in soot helping a woman with glass in her leg limp down the street would draw attention, even in the mixed company of the lower city.

"Are there any exits closer to our safehouse?" Ansel asked.

Rhosyn shook her head. There was one close to her own house, but she was loathe to put the couple she rented from in the middle of things, after they had pursued a life away from crime. There was another option though.

"One path... It leads down out of the old sewer at the edge of the city. It comes out—"

"Near the circus." Ansel followed her train of thought. "It won't be hard to hide there."

"It was built to conceal people after all," Rhosyn observed dryly.

"And to do so in the best possible hiding place: in plain sight." Ansel's tone was proud.

It coaxed a chuckle out of Rhosyn, the sound chasing away some of the lingering tension from her chest. The further she limped from the palace, the more she believed they had gotten away with it, the sponsorship documents still safely tucked into the front of her shirt. With a jerk of her chin, Rhosyn directed them onto the path that would lead to the circus, and they slowly made their way through the tunnel.

However, the increasing clarity seeping through her brain gave her more of a chance to inspect her actions. She had chosen to stay and help Ansel even when she had a chance to leave the whole thing behind—to scurry back to her normal life as a police officer and try to forget this brief lapse back into crime. Yet, a string anchored beneath her ribs had yanked her forward, leaping to Ansel's rescue before she could fully consider the alternatives.

"Thank you." Ansel's voice broke the silence. Apparently, his mind had wandered down the same path.

"Yeah, well, I wouldn't have had to do anything if you hadn't sneezed," she quipped.

Ansel huffed. "It's not my fault the chimney was filthy and the ash got in my nose. It seemed like that place has never seen a chimney sweep."

"I'll remember to submit a complaint to the housekeeper when I get a chance."

Ansel chuckled, and a brief silence fell before he spoke again. "You could have run, though."

"I know." Rhosyn admitted. "Guess I just don't know how to walk away from a fight."

And that was the truth. She had never walked away from a fight that needed to be fought, even if it came back to bite her later. She hoped helping Ansel wouldn't end up being one of those occasions.

Chapter Ten

If Rhosyn could say one thing for the performers of Archer's Circus, it was that they didn't ask unnecessary questions. She and Ansel crept into the side of the circle of tents in the early hours of the morning, the sun just peaking above the horizon and casting the towering green and white striped structures in long shadows. The straw-strewn paths were nearly empty and quiet, absent of the exaggerated darkness and flickering lamp light that lent the feel of the fantastical at night, giving the whole place a sense of liminal space.

An early riser caught sight of them as they stumbled towards a tent and rushed over.

"We're going to need some bandages and something to wash up with. See if you can dig us up a change of clothes too," Ansel ordered. He had the same tone that Nate did when directing Lions or the King's Guard: with frank honesty and the insinuation that he respected his followers too much to waste their time with pleasantries. It had made people trust Nate with their lives, and now it had the same results.

Within minutes of collapsing in the tent where the Merry Men had performed before, the man reappeared with the necessary supplies.

Ansel thanked him and instructed. "Send a message to Little John. Tell him we're here and that I need to talk to him."

The man spared Rhosyn one long glance, tinged with curiosity, before backing out the entrance, letting the flap that would be tied open during the Circus's performing hours fall shut behind him.

With a sigh, Ansel sat down heavily on the edge of the stage. Now that they were alone, some of the persona that reminded her of Nate slipped away, revealing a man as tired as Rhosyn so often felt.

She sat down more gingerly next to him, extending her injured leg so as not to jostle it too much and dig the glass in farther. As it was, the shard didn't seem to be too deep. She let it be for just a second, limbs turning leaden as she finally relieved them of the burden of her weight. Her eyes fluttered shut, the sensations in her body—from the stinging in her calf to the throbbing on the back of her head that was sure to form a knot where it had collided with the wall—washed over her and carried her thoughts away in their current.

"Let me get this soot off myself, and then I'll help you with your leg." Ansel's voice interrupted her after a moment of quiet.

Rhosyn nodded, keeping her eyes shut. The air stirred, signaling that Ansel had stood, and his footsteps retreated towards the curtain separating the performing area from the backstage. After a minute, muffled splashing signaled to Rhosyn he was using the basin of water, supplied by his man, to wash up.

Finally, her eyes drifted open and she returned her awareness to what needed to be done. She crossed her injured leg over her knee, letting her see the back of her calf. Thankfully, the piece of glass that pierced the meat of the muscle still had a significant piece sticking out she could use to remove it. No need for tweezers.

She gritted her teeth, knowing there was nothing for it. Pinching the shard between her thumb and forefinger, she yanked. Her hiss of pain nearly drowned out the quiet squelch as it pulled free of her skin. She let it fall on the stage next to her, glad to be free of the twinge of sharp edges every time she moved.

Now that her pants were no longer pinned to her leg, she rolled them up to better inspect and clean the wound, shoving the cuffs all the way up to her knee. As she suspected, the wound was shallow, and most of the pain had come from having the glass still embedded in her leg.

She reached for the bandages and small glass jar the man had provided, but her hand was knocked away as familiar callused fingers beat her to it.

"Let me help you with that."

Rhosyn had been too distracted with removing the glass to hear Ansel reemerge from behind the curtains. He knelt down before her and held out a hand expectantly.

The sight made Rhosyn's heart flutter. He had changed out of his soiled shirt, the new one slightly too big and threatening to slip off his shoulder, revealing the inviting chest Rhosyn had burrowed into the morning before—how had so much happened in twenty-four hours? His hair was slightly damp around the edges, as if he had dunked his face in the basin to try to get the soot off, and now a longer strand clung to his high cheekbone.

He raised a single brow in question at Rhosyn's hesitation. The action drew attention to a black smudge he had missed on his forehead. Her fingers itched to rub it away.

Instead, she leaned back on her elbows and placed her ankle in his outstretched hand. He set to dabbing the skin around the cut, and as he did, the fingers holding her ankle rubbed back and forth soothingly. Rhosyn wasn't sure if he even knew he was doing it, but she could scarcely think of anything else as he moved on to cleaning any debris from inside the wound.

She shifted, the movement causing the papers in her shirt to crinkle. The sound provided a welcome distraction from the warmth seeping up her chest to her face. Pulling them out, Rhosyn waved them at Ansel.

"These are yours, as promised."

His eyes flicked up from his task, and the concentrated furrow between his brow deepened into a true frown.

"What do you think about what we found in those contracts?" he asked.

"It...doesn't look good," Rhosyn admitted, wrinkling her nose.

"With that number of Talented at his beck and call, with those abilities, he could do some serious damage," Ansel agreed.

Rhosyn's stomach churned. While Mr. Gower had more polish to him than the powerful gangsters who lorded over the underworld, something about this setup smelled the same as when the Wolves collected Talented for their illegal fighting rings. Mr. Gower was clearly reaching for power, but how he would go about getting it, Rhosyn couldn't be sure yet.

"What do you think we should do?" Ansel asked, interrupting her thoughts.

Rhosyn frowned. "And why would you want the opinion of an officer of the Royal Police—and your hostage at that?"

Ansel's fingers stopped moving on her ankle, tightening so the pads of his fingers dug into the soft flesh on the inner part of her foot. She suppressed a shiver.

"I thought we might have moved past that, after the night we've just shared." Ansel bit the words out, as if saying them frustrated him.

The words hit Rhosyn in the chest, and she slumped. It was a hope she had indulged in too, although guiltily. But the fact that they had each saved each other tonight—even made a good team—didn't change the truth of their situation.

"I may be a police officer, and you might be a gangster I'm trying to arrest," Rhosyn started slowly, and Ansel's frown deepened. "But maybe we don't have to be enemies. Maybe we can just be...professional rivals."

"No, I don't think so." Ansel's dismissal came so quickly that it stung as tangibly as a slap across the face.

"Why not?"

Ansel lifted his gaze from where it had been fixed on her leg, and it pinned Rhosyn with its surprising intensity. "*Professional rivals* don't think about each other the way I think about you."

Rhosyn's breath caught in her throat, but Ansel didn't seem to want her to speak anyways.

"Professional rivals don't spend a whole day so distracted they can barely function, just from waking up to the smell of your hair. They don't admire the snarl on your face when you throw a punch or the way your smile is slightly crooked. They certainly don't spend hours agonizing over what it would be like to touch you everywhere—how warm you would be, if you would snap at me like you do in a fight or if I could make you into a mewling mess. How you would *taste*."

Ansel didn't break eye contact as he slowly deconstructed Rhosyn, piece by piece, with his words. All the barriers she had put up in her mind against him, the justifications that she *couldn't* want him, caught fire as the warmth under her skin burst into flames.

Rhosyn wet her lips, reaching for the right words. This wasn't their flirty teasing, hidden in the guise of adversaries, or even during a dance at a fancy party. This was something deeper. Heavier.

"I guess we aren't professional rivals then," she said, her voice hoarse.

Ansel let out a shuddering breath, mirroring the shiver that ran up her spine when the breath tickled the inside of her ankle, still held close to his face. His gaze tracked her movement, and slowly he lowered his head. His lips were a hairsbreadth away from her skin when he paused, eyes boring into her.

It was a bid for permission—a chance for her to recognize that this would change things for them, more than sleep-addled touches, that could be blamed on circumstances. Rhosyn still grappled with what she had done in robbing the palace, knowing it was a step she couldn't take back. But this...this decision was already made.

She nodded infinitesimally, and Ansel lowered his lips to her skin. At first, it was feather light, barely a kiss as he dragged his mouth up from her foot towards her knee. Rhosyn choked down a quiet, desperate sound at the contact, surprised how affected she was by the one simple action.

Something dark flickered in Ansel's eyes at the truncated noise. He nipped at the inside of her knee, startling a squeak out of her. That pulled a chuckle out of him, the sound lower and rougher than his usual laugh. She wanted to hear it again. She wanted to muffle it with her own lips.

At that thought, Rhosyn's body moved with all the speed of a trained fighter, acting on pure instinct. She lunged forward, grasping at the front of Ansel's shirt and crashing her lips to his.

He caught her, despite the suddenness of her actions, rocking back on his knees and arms wrapping around her easily. Rhosyn was distracted from the way he crushed her to his chest by the movement of his lips and the intoxicating taste of his tongue tracing the seam of her mouth.

Rhosyn pushed back against him, catching his bottom lip between her teeth. As she tugged on it, Ansel brought a hand up to her hair and grasped it firmly at the roots. It pinned her in place, letting him take control of the kiss.

Held like that, something heady washed over Rhosyn, the racing in her mind—the constant instincts to punch, run, *do*—quieted. All she could think about was Ansel single-mindedly devouring her mouth, as if he had thought about nothing else since she first chased him across rooftops.

So loud were the sensations of Ansel pressed against her in Rhosyn's mind that she at first didn't notice the shift in light that came from the tent flap swinging open. She only came back to herself when there came a commotion, jerking back as a familiar shout broke through the haze.

Her eyes snapped open at the same time Ansel whipped around, both turning towards the disturbance. Standing at the tent entrance, pistols drawn was—

"Kristoff," she gasped, still on her knees. She staggered to her feet, unbalanced by several rapid changes in quick succession.

The barrels of his guns were trained on Ansel, but he quirked a brow, and a mischievous twinkle sparked in his eye. He ignored the handful of other circus performers hovering at the entrance, clearly unwilling to make a move that could cause him to shoot their leader.

"I came to rescue you, Rhosyn, but based on the sight that greeted me when I got here, there was no need." He bent his arms, directing his aim up and away from Ansel and resting his guns on his shoulder. "I just didn't realize what kind of kidnapping this was."

"It wasn't like that." Ansel found his voice. "Well, not at first, at least."

"It doesn't seem wise to admit to the man holding the guns that you *did* kidnap his sister for less than honorable purposes...or at least the less amusing kind of." Kristoff looked at Rhosyn with a question on his face, as if asking if he should go ahead and shoot Ansel anyways.

At his words, something between a sob and a laugh bubbled up in Rhosyn's throat, and she ended up releasing a hiccuping snort. Everybody looked at her questioningly, but a smile spread across her face.

She had been navigating protecting London and her little Lions using her own moral compass and ending up hopelessly lost. But here was Kristoff, calling her his sister and risking his life to find her. Nothing could feel that dire when faced with the sharp-shooter's crooked smile.

She darted forward and threw herself at him in a bone crushing hug. To Kristoff's credit, he managed not to shoot anybody or bang her head with his guns as he hugged her back. After a tight squeeze, he took her by the shoulders and held her back, looking at her.

"You're alright?" His gaze darted over her rumpled clothes and her bandaged leg.

She nodded. "Somehow less banged up than usual."

"That is saying absolutely nothing." Reassured that Rhosyn hadn't been mistreated, Kristoff's attention turned to Ansel, and his gaze narrowed. "I do still require an explanation."

Ansel's gaze fixed over Kristoff's shoulder, and Rhosyn followed it to the audience of circus members who had followed the commotion and now hovered, many of them seemingly unsure what to do with their hands now that violence didn't seem eminent. With a wave, Ansel dismissed them. While a few lingered for a moment, obviously curious, they did as he asked.

Rhosyn extricated herself from Kristoff, standing between the two men, who sized each other up.

"I didn't know you had a brother," Ansel remarked.

Rhosyn snorted, as nobody could mistake Kristoff for her real brother. Where he was tan and muscular with hair that always looked effortlessly mussed, she was lanky and pale with an unruly nest on the top of her head.

"He's a chosen brother," she clarified.

"Another Lion, I presume." Ansel raised a brow.

"Not just any Lion either," Kristoff answered. "And you might not have been around these streets long enough to remember, but the Lions used to be the most feared name in London. If I don't find out what you're doing with Rhosyn here soon, you'll find out why." Kristoff's tone was as casual as ever, but Rhosyn had known the sharpshooter long enough to know he didn't deal in idle threats.

"This is Ansel. He has Olivia and Paul," she interjected, hurrying to explain.

At that, Kristoff's grip tightened around his pistols, fingers drifting to the trigger. Rhosyn raised her hands, palms out.

"They're safe," she assured. "He's helping them get out of the city."

Kristoff's brow furrowed. "I thought they were joining proper society. They never struck me as the type to run away and join the circus."

Rhosyn shook her head. "It's...complicated." She looked back and forth between the two men, still looking at each other with narrowed eyes. A cord of tension ran between them, with her held taught in the middle. The thread anchored under her ribs pulled her in both directions at once—toward a past life that would never return but could not be forgotten and toward an impossible future that Rhosyn had only barely dared to dream of.

Shoving his hands in his pockets and shrugging, Ansel broke the moment, tension unraveling. "I suppose I should give you two a chance to catch up."

A breath rushed out of Rhosyn's chest, and finally, Kristoff holstered his guns. Given how quick he was on the draw, it barely made him any less dangerous, but it was clear he accepted Ansel's olive branch. Rhosyn shot Ansel a look that she hoped conveyed her gratitude.

He gave her the smallest nod and started strolling past them towards the entrance. "I am going to try to hunt down some tea. I'll be outside when you're done talking."

Kristoff kept his gaze trained on Ansel's back until it disappeared behind the fluttering tent flap. Then he turned back to Rhosyn.

"Even if he's standing guard outside, I can get you out of here right now," Kristoff said, voice low enough to not be heard through the thick canvas walls. "We can be at Nate's house in time for breakfast. You could be eating a fresh batch of Gregor's scones within the hour."

The watering of Rhosyn's mouth at the mention of Gregor's cooking did nothing to distract from the feeling of being punched in the chest. The rift inside her ached, having slowly been deepening inside her over the past days. In her subconscious, she knew she would be faced with the task of escaping from the Foxes, but that had been a problem for three days from now, when Olivia and Paul were safely out of London. Somehow, having an excuse to put it off allowed her to pretend that it was inevitable, but not immediate—not a decision she had to make, for it was not yet a reality.

But now, faced with Kristoff, who so earnestly offered to shoot his way out of this camp with her if he had to, her resolve shuddered.

"I'm not sure I can leave," she admitted, her voice smaller than she was used to.

"Is that man blackmailing you? If I need to—"

Rhosyn shook her head before Kristoff got any heroic ideas about setting things on fire, which was too often his first solution to any problem. "Ansel—all of the Foxes really—are trying to help the Talented who have been sponsored in the upper city. Something is wrong and...and I think I need to stay to help figure out what it is."

She didn't know it was true until she said it. Once the words were out of her, though, it felt like the wedge being used to crack open her chest was gone, allowing her to be a single person once more. As quickly as she could, she filled Kristoff in on what had happened since Ansel had kidnapped her at the circus, although she strategically left out the parts where she slept tied to his bed with him.

Kristoff's clear blue gaze pinned her as he cocked his head, surprisingly perceptive given how rarely he seemed to take anything seriously. "I take it you took my advice on investigating Mr. Gower, despite what the police said?"

"I think this might be another case where I need to let my instincts guide me, and those are hard to write up in a police report," Rhosyn admitted. "If I'm 'missing', then I can do these investigations off the record. I—" Rhosyn choked around the words she said next, "I'd appreciate if you didn't tell Chief Thorne you'd found me."

To his credit, Kristoff's face held no judgment. If anybody knew how to flirt with the line of what was legal and what was right, it was Kristoff.

"I have to tell Nate though," he said. "He's been going half mad since you went missing."

Rhosyn blinked, the back of her eyes suddenly stinging. "He has?"

"He nearly yelled at Joseph for not spending more resources on finding you, even though he knows the Royal Police are spread thin as it is and Joseph was doing everything he could," Kristoff said. "I've been searching for you ever since Joseph told us you didn't show up for your patrol, and Nate has joined me whenever he's not with the King. Even Contessa's had her ear to the ground, all her connections keeping an eye out."

Rhosyn's throat went tight. When the Lions had officially dissolved, it had felt oddly like losing a family, despite seeing all her friends constantly. She had felt the loss of the camaraderie that came from shared danger like a death in her heart. It was something she had never quite found in the police force, as much as she liked her new colleagues. Knowing the lengths Nate would go to filled her with the warmth of belonging once more.

"Then tell Nate and Contessa not to worry. I'll apologize for making them anxious later but for now...for now I have to figure out what the Gowers are up to."

"Is that the only reason you're staying? You and that Ansel chap seem...friendly." Kristoff's tone was playful, but she could tell his question was serious. Despite her relentless teasing of Kristoff over his affection for Gregor, he had never gotten to return the favor. There had never been any romantic liaisons in her life, and the physical relationships she allowed herself were brief and always beneath her friends' notice.

"That's new," Rhosyn admitted, kicking one foot against the ground.

"Seducing your would-be kidnapper...I must say I'm impressed." Kristoff elbowed Rhosyn playfully in the ribs.

She blushed and shoved him away. "That's hardly new for us. Didn't Contessa do the same thing?"

"Nate did *not* kidnap her. He married her."

"That's not how she saw it at the time," Rhosyn pointed out.

Kristoff chuckled. "Well, you don't seem to need my help getting Ansel on your side. But if you need my help with the other part, you know where to find me. You know I never like to miss out on a party."

"And by party, you mean all out brawl." Rhosyn's tone was dry.

"You know me too well." Kristoff smiled, but then his face smoothed into a rare serious expression. "Be careful, alright?"

"I will," Rhosyn promised. "And you be careful too."

"Never am," Kristoff quipped, making for the exit. With a jaunty wave, he stepped back out into the now bright sun of the spring morning.

Before the flap could flutter closed, Ansel ducked his head inside, eyes darting around the space before landing on her. He paused, his expression equal parts relieved and surprised.

"You stayed," he said, his tone unreadable.

A smile toyed at the edge of Rhosyn's lips. "Yeah, I guess I did."

"Well..." He seemed at a loss, but he smiled back at her, nonetheless. "I guess we better find you some breakfast."

Chapter Eleven

Rhosyn wouldn't have thought she would grow used to sharing a bed with another body in just a couple of nights. When she woke to late afternoon sun beaming in through gaps in the tent panels, though, her body instinctively stretched towards a form that wasn't there. As her fingers brushed against scratchy blankets, Rhosyn wrinkled her nose, scrunching her eyes shut.

She supposed privacy was an improvement on grinding herself sleepily on Ansel's thigh, but her body disagreed. After all, she had admitted she was staying, giving up an opportunity to leave Ansel and the Foxes behind, a sly voice in her mind reminded her. If she was already breaking the rules, what was the point in refusing to break this one? Especially when this transgression was so particularly enticing.

With a jerk, Rhosyn sat up. There was no point dwelling on things that might have been. She had slept alone, and it was likely to remain that way given that she was no longer a flight risk in Ansel's eyes.

Now, she needed to turn her attention to more important things, like the apparent army of Talented Mr. Gower had hired as household staff. The startling discovery was why she had sent Kristoff on his way, and she needed to focus on unraveling that mystery. It was how she would serve this city, even if she was betraying the Royal Police.

Rhosyn's boots lay where she had taken them off, haphazardly kicked aside as she collapsed face first onto the borrowed cot. With a groan, she shoved her feet back into them and began lacing them up with practiced fingers. Once they were on, she stood. Tilting her head side to side rewarded her with loud cracks, and she twisted her spine, adding a series of pops to the symphony as her vertebrae unlocked. Two days of forced rest had done her more good than she cared to admit, but her body still protested the previous long night. It had gotten a taste of a good night's sleep and now seemed to crave more. However, there was work to do right now.

Rhosyn poked her head out of the tent flap. The straw-strewn paths that had been relatively unpopulated this morning now carried a steady stream of people between tents, some bearing bundles, others chatting with each other easily. They seemed to be getting ready for another night of merriment and entertainment.

None paid her any attention as she stepped out fully onto the path. After Ansel had handed her off to a gruff man, who apparently ran the roasted nut stall, he had disappeared to get some sleep himself. Rhosyn had no idea where he might be or who to ask.

Instead of imposing herself on the busy performers, she meandered towards the largest tent again, where she and Ansel had sat this morning. It seemed like as good a place as any to start, and if he wasn't there, perhaps one of the Merry Men would recognize her and point her in the right direction.

The buzz of life in the city of tents bolstered her, adding more of a bounce to her previous trudge as she walked. Nobody shot her wary glances as she walked, and she felt light without the weight of a baton at her hip. To the tide of performers and staff, she could be anybody—certainly not an officer of the Royal Police or a notorious Lion. Just a woman, going to talk to a man. A man who had a tendency to tie her insides in knots.

The shade of the large central tent fell over her face as she approached, dulling the bright afternoon sun and cooling her skin. Rhosyn slipped her fingers into the gap in the closed tent flaps, which would be tied back to leave a wide entrance when the circus was open for business.

Pulling it open a few inches, she glanced inside for any signs of an occupant. A sudden *whoosh* almost had Rhosyn jerking back, before her eyes registered the blur whizzing through her vision.

Ansel swung from the trapeze over the stage, momentum slowing as his arc reached its peak. At the height of his swing, he let go, flipping easily in midair and twisting before catching the bar right as it started to descend again.

Rhosyn found herself unconsciously slipping into the tent, letting the flap close behind her. She stood transfixed with her back against the canvas, wide eyes following Ansel's dizzying dance. This next time he released the bar, he arched, head coming towards his feet as he flipped backwards, body making a perfect "c" shape in the air. The breath whooshed from Rhosyn's lungs as the trapeze swung away from him, out of his grasp. He was going to fall.

Instead, he caught an adjacent bar, weight landing on the tips of his fingers with little effort. Watching him, Rhosyn internally hit herself for ever thinking one of the Merry Men might have been the Hood. As skilled as they were, none of them held a candle to Ansel's ability...his Talent.

Now that she saw it, she didn't know how it hadn't been obvious to her from the first time she saw him flipping across lower city rooftops.

Then again, many people thought Rhosyn's lockpicking and Kristoff's sharpshooting were Talents, when they were actually born of years of practice, interspersed with countless failures.

A particularly daring swing on Ansel's part snapped Rhosyn from her thoughts. She gasped audibly as he swung on a different trapeze, this one dipping so low Rhosyn feared he would crash into the ground. Instead, his toes just brushed the wooden platform that served as a stage, before he rose into the air once more.

In the cavernous and nearly empty space, her squeak of fear echoed. Ansel's head snapped up as he reached the height of his swing, and he caught her eye—although she had no clue how he could find his bearings so easily while hurtling through space.

He let go, floating as lightly as smoke on the wind before landing on one of the platforms at the top of the arena. He turned, looking down on Rhosyn from on high and smiling.

"I didn't know I had an audience." He raised his voice to be heard easily from such a height.

Rhosyn drifted forward, stepping up on the stage so she was nearly beneath him. "And I didn't think you performed anymore...not acrobatics, at least."

Ansel shrugged, and despite his usual bravado, something in the expression seemed sheepish. "I still practice sometimes, when nobody is around. It helps clear my head."

"Hurtling through the air at breakneck speed clears your mind?" Rhosyn propped her fists on her hips.

"I'd think you of all people would understand the appeal. After all, it seemed like throwing some punches at me the other day helped you think straight."

Rhosyn shrugged but couldn't deny that he was right. Letting fists do the talking tapped into a part of Rhosyn she spent so much time pushing down, because that brawler wasn't what London needed. Right now, though, maybe it was.

Instead of saying any of that, Rhosyn cocked her head in challenge. "Are you sure you don't like perching up there because it's the only time I have to look up to talk to you?"

"Bringing my height into it? I've never heard that before," Ansel scoffed, but his tone was playful. "I'm willing to level the playing field though."

Before Rhosyn could ask what he meant, Ansel cartwheeled, propelling himself backwards off the platform. Rhosyn clapped a hand to her mouth, seeing that his hands were nowhere near the closest trapeze. Instead, Ansel caught it with his legs, knees hanging over the bar.

Absorbing the momentum of his jump, the bar swung in a spiral around the stage, circling lower and lower around Rhosyn, making her pivot where she stood in the center of the platform. As if he had planned it perfectly—which he probably had, but Rhosyn was loathe to give him the credit—the trapeze drifted to a halt right before Rhosyn.

Still hanging from his knees, Ansel folded his arms, gaze level with Rhosyn's eyeline. She propped her fists on her hips, glaring at his upside-down smirk, just inches from her nose.

"Show off," she muttered.

Ansel's smirk only grew into a grin. Then he levered off the trapeze, righting himself as he did so, to land on his feet before her.

"I guess I can't help it. I'm—" In perfect juxtaposition to the easy confidence of his showmanship, Ansel looked to the side and pushed his now unkempt hair from his face. "I'm just happy you're still here."

It was Rhosyn's turn to look down at her feet. "I am too, although I'm not sure I should be."

Ansel's gaze snapped up at that. "Why not?"

"I just..." Rhosyn grasped at words that seemed to allude her, her frustrations always better spoken with actions than breath. "Who am I anymore? I'm not really a Lion, but that part of me isn't gone. I'm not really a police officer anymore either, am I?"

"You're..." Ansel gestured at her incomprehensibly, but fervently as if it were of the upmost important that she understood his meaning. "You're Rhosyn."

Her frustration flared, and she thrust her hands into her hair. "Who even is that?" she demanded. "How am I supposed to know what I am when I've spent my whole life being whatever it was people needed most? A sister, a nursemaid, a lockpick, a thief... I became these things because that's what Nate and Kristoff—my family—needed, and the Lions needed somebody to care for them. Then I became an officer of the Royal Police because Contessa and Nate needed somebody they could trust. Now...I fear this city needs something else, and I will become whatever it requires of me. I just wish I knew what was really *me*."

The tirade poured out of her, unbidden. By the time Rhosyn finished, she was breathing heavily, as if the words had ripped free of her chest with great effort. The heat of embarrassment at such an emotional outburst began to compete with the burning of tears behind her eyes, until she met Ansel's gaze.

His face held compassion but no pity. And deep in the pools of his emerald eyes, she found what she hadn't even realized what she was searching for—understanding. After all, hadn't Rhosyn known that both the Hood and Mr. Blakely were masks Ansel wore? Parts of him, but not the whole truth of the man beneath?

A breath shuddered out of her, goosebumps dancing over her skin at the thought that Ansel was looking at Rhosyn and truly seeing her and not just the role she filled. In that moment, she saw him too.

He took an intentional step, the sparse distance between them shrinking to nothing.

"I can tell you one thing you are," Ansel said. His breath puffed across her face, warm and sweet.

Rhosyn's eyes drifted to his lips, and for the first time since they met, Rhosyn didn't fight the way her body pulled her to him.

"What's that?" she prompted, nerves drawn so taut that she could barely follow the thread of the conversation but needing to know what he would say regardless.

"You're everything I want."

The words were spoken nearly against Rhosyn's lips, and she closed the rest of the distance between them so quickly, he barely finished his thought. Close as they had been, Rhosyn dove into the kiss with such force that it knocked him back a step. He took it in stride, arms wrapping around her back and crushing her nearer still.

Her hands braced on his shoulders, fingertips digging into his shirt, slightly damp with the sweat of his earlier exertion. Rhosyn wanted to taste it. She groaned, and it gave Ansel room to deepen the kiss, tilting her head and delving into her mouth with a singular focus.

It was far from gentle and sweet, but neither was it the rapid, selfish kiss of a man seeking a vessel for his own pleasure. No...this was the kiss of a man who wanted to devour her piece by piece. To learn exactly what took her apart, from the way she whimpered when his tongue slid against her own to the way her legs began to shake when he nipped at her bottom lip.

Ansel's hands traveled up and into her hair, pulling free what remained of the haphazard braid she had slept in. His blunt nails raked against her scalp with none of the shyness of his previous morning explorations, and she whined unconsciously.

Fisting the roots of her hair, Ansel pulled her head back, gently but insistently. Her eyes fluttered open to stare sightlessly at the striped canvas of the ceiling as Ansel's lips traveled down the column of her throat. His mouth was so hot against her skin, she imagined it would burn marks into her pale skin. She almost hoped it would.

Not one to let Ansel have all the fun, Rhosyn pushed her pelvis forward, grinding into the growing hardness against her hip. The choked grunt that rewarded her actions pulled a mischievous smile from her. She dragged her hands down his chest, nails catching on Ansel's shirt as her fingers traced a path to his belt. Before she had struggled with it for more than a few moments, one of Ansel's hands flew to her wrist to stop her.

"No." His tone was firm.

Rhosyn began to pull away in stinging confusion, but his hand in her hair pinned her firmly where she was.

"No," he repeated, softer this time. "You just said you have spent your life doing things for other people. I don't want this to be about that. I just want you to feel."

Rhosyn stilled, one of her fingers still stroking the notched leather of his belt. She itched to push him back, rip off his belt and drop to her knees, just to show him she could give as good as she got. And he would let her. If that was what she truly wanted, Ansel would let her control this encounter and take her pleasure from him.

Instead, she paused, a shiver running up her spine at what he proposed. *Just feeling.* She was no stranger to sex, but even in her brief encounters, she had found herself drawn into being what her partners desired—normally the untamed spitfire that treated everything, even pleasure, like a competition.

But with Ansel...the proposition was as terrifying as it was delicious. And Rhosyn wasn't one to scare easily. Slowly she nodded.

She was rewarded by the movement of Ansel's lips curving into a smile against the hollow of her throat. "Good girl."

A shudder trailed down Rhosyn's body in the wake of Ansel's hands, trailing over her flanks towards her hips. She let her own hands fall to her sides, clenching into fists as she endeavored to do as Ansel asked, and just feel what he was doing to her.

So slowly that Rhosyn thought she might scream, Ansel inched her shirt up, sliding his warm, rough palms against the planes of her stomach. She sucked in a sharp breath, wanting to pull away from the all-consuming heat that ran through her, while also craving more.

Ansel continued to lift her shirt until he pulled it off over her head and let his fingers trail back down from her shoulders to her clavicles.

"You even have freckles here," he murmured as he traced over the swell of the top of her breast.

"Comes with the territory." Rhosyn intended to joke, but the breathless rasp of her voice detracted from the effect. Any further teasing gave way to a gasp as Ansel's lips replaced his fingers on her sternum.

He dragged his mouth sideways, tongue darting out to taste her skin until his mouth latched around the peak of her breast. Her mind fixated on the exquisite pleasure so adamantly that she barely even noticed his hands drifting lower to the button of her pants.

He switched his attention to her other breast, and she couldn't help herself. She plunged her fingers into his hair, pulling him closer at the same time she arched towards him, not sure what she was chasing except *more*.

He pulled back, looking up at her with already glassy eyes, lips red and wet in a way that almost undid Rhosyn right there.

"You really can't stay still unless I tie you to a bed, can you?" Ansel asked. His tone was teasing, but with the hoarseness in his voice, Rhosyn couldn't help but picture what it would be like to be tied in his bed again, this time in a completely different context.

Already flushed, a fresh wave of redness rushed down from Rhosyn's face to her chest. Ansel's gaze flickered over her, taking in her visceral reaction to his words. His eyes darkened as he looked up at her through his lashes, pressing an open-mouthed kiss to her sternum.

"Maybe some other time," he murmured.

Rhosyn refused to wonder if they would have a chance for *some other time*. Not when her mind was occupied being melted by the heated expression on his face.

"For now, reach up and grab the bar."

Momentarily confused, Rhosyn glanced up to find the trapeze Ansel had descended on so gracefully dangling over her head.

"I'm not much of an acrobat," she huffed.

"I know, but it'll give you something to do with your hands," Ansel murmured into her skin. "Be good for me and grab the bar."

When he put it like that, Rhosyn was of no mind to disobey. Her arms stretched above her, fingers wrapping around the solid wood of the handle, the grain against her palm grounding her. She didn't have to go on her tiptoes to reach, but only just, the position leaving her fully stretched out and vulnerable.

"Perfect," Ansel murmured, so low it might have been more for his own benefit than Rhosyn's. Then, he proceeded to systematically drive her towards the brink of insanity, alternating dragging his teeth over her nipples before soothing over them with the flat of his tongue.

Rhosyn's chin fell forward onto her chest and she whimpered. The wooden bar dug into her palms as she gripped it tighter, a throbbing starting in her core that she was helpless to do anything to relieve.

Seeming to sense her growing desperation, Ansel smirked against her skin before falling to his knees. He pressed a kiss to her lower belly as he undid her pants and dragged them down her thighs, soothing some of the feeling that she was going to vibrate out of her skin, which Rhosyn tried desperately to contain.

When he finally tossed her trousers over his shoulders and let his gaze rest on the apex of her thighs, a low curse escaped Ansel. "Your hair is even red here."

"What color did you think it would be?" Rhosyn tried to retort, the bite completely drowned out by the urge to beg him to finally touch her there.

"Honestly?" Ansel pressed a kiss to her hip bone. "I tried not to think about it. Because I knew when I started imagining what it would be like to have you, I wouldn't be able to stop. And up until yesterday, I never thought I'd get the chance to see you like this at all."

Rhosyn's breath stuttered as he drew his nose across the crease of her thigh. "But you hoped?" The question came out more desperate than Rhosyn wanted, but she had to know.

"Oh, how I hoped."

The warmth that suffused her chest at his answer only registered for a moment before she arched her back in pleasure at the kiss Ansel planted directly over her sex. She tried to spread her legs to give him more access, but Ansel had other ideas. A broad hand grabbed her thigh, pulling it over his shoulder and leaving her completely open to him.

She squeaked in a most undignified manner, suddenly glad to have the bar for support as she balanced on one leg. Ansel chuckled against her heated flesh before returning to his task.

His tongue parted her in one long stroke, and suddenly it was all she could do to stay upright. He repeated the motion, finding a cadence that made her squirm. She tried to pull him closer to her with the knee draped over his shoulder.

When he sucked at the most sensitive part of her, Rhosyn's standing leg gave out completely, leaving her nearly hanging from the trapeze above her. Ansel didn't relent, throwing her other leg over his shoulder as well, leaving her supported only by her arms and his hands on her ass, spreading her open as his mouth did unspeakable things to her.

The peak of her pleasure was at the tips of her fingers, beginning to spark through her limbs. Desperately, she bucked forward, trying to grind herself against his face and finding she had no leverage as the trapeze she hung from wobbled.

Ansel pulled back, and Rhosyn whined high in her throat as the pleasure that had been about to crest over her dissipated.

"What did I say about just feeling?" he scolded, turning his head to nip the sensitive skin of her inner thigh.

With concerted effort, Rhosyn relaxed her hips, letting herself settle in his hands again. She was rewarded with a satisfied hum and a soft kiss to her inner thigh. Then, he began working her up anew, and Rhosyn fought every instinct to buck against him and chase her own pleasure. She squeezed her eyes shut, and her fingers grasped the trapeze bar so tightly it creaked, as if it might splinter in her hands.

Ansel worked her higher and higher until Rhosyn feared she might float away. Finally, Ansel sucked her flesh into his mouth once more, and she came undone with a voiceless shout. One of her hands let go of the bar to fist his hair, just to ground her to the man who had brought her such pleasure as she shuddered uncontrollably.

Unable to hold herself up with one arm as the pleasure started to ebb from her, leaving her boneless, she began to slide down. Ansel helped her, cushioning her descent until she straddled his lap where he kneeled on the floor, cradled to his chest.

She panted there, the spicy sweetness of him mixing with the heady rush of pleasure in an indelible mix in her mind. Mindlessly, she nuzzled into the "v" of skin visible on his chest, the rough fabric against her cheeks reminding her that he still had all his clothes on.

Now that Rhosyn was boneless with pleasure, she assumed Ansel's request for her to *just feel* was fulfilled. She wanted to do much more than feel right now.

No sooner had her fingers slid under the collar of Ansel's shirt, ready to feel the solid warmth she knew hid beneath, than a loud cough sounded from the door. Before Rhosyn had even registered they were no longer alone, Ansel dove forward, covering Rhosyn's exposed form with his own, substantially more modest body. Rhosyn buried her face in his shoulder with a squeak, half embarrassment and half-surprise.

"Sorry, Boss... I—" Little John's deep rumble sounded by the door along with some shuffling as if attempting to make a hasty retreat and stumbling over his own feet.

"You've already interrupted, John," Ansel growled, his back hunched over Rhosyn protectively as she tried to cram herself into as small a ball as possible, to stay hidden beneath him. "Just spit it out."

"I've made the arrangements you asked for and have all the volunteers gathered. They'll meet you in the office." John spat the words out as if it were a race before a swish of canvas and retreating footsteps indicated they had fled.

With a sigh, Ansel dropped his head to Rhosyn's collarbone. It was a position of such abject defeat that Rhosyn couldn't help but chuckle. The motion jostled Ansel's forehead where it rested on her chest, and he began to laugh as well. Maybe it was the fizzling pleasure still running through her veins making Rhosyn feel light, or the shock of suddenly being discovered, but in a matter of moments, she had descended into full on cackles.

To his credit, Ansel joined her in her mirth, lifting his head and laughing along. His eyes crinkled at the corner as he smiled sheepishly.

"We should...probably talk."

Rhosyn nodded in agreement. The heat of the moment had dissipated, and as humorous as the situation had suddenly become, reality was sleeping back in. She had chosen to join Ansel in uncovering Mr. Gower's plots, but there was no guarantee of where they would stand once the issue was resolved. And there were still sponsored Talented to help to their freedom.

Bracing her hands on Ansel's shoulders, she pushed him back lightly, and he went easily. His hands patted the floor around him until he located her clothing. She sat up and began pulling them on, trying to make herself look as unruffled as possible, although she knew it was a lost cause. Her disarrayed hair and crimson flush spoke volumes—not to mention that Little John would clearly know what had been happening between them.

Still, Rhosyn stood and arranged herself as best she could, but she couldn't help the flutter that ran through her as Ansel wiped his still-glistening mouth with the back of his hand.

She cleared her throat. "What are these arrangements Little John mentioned?"

Ansel ran his hands through his own hair, pushing it back out of his face, although the single silver strand fell forward defiantly again. He glared at where it hung between his eyes in frustration, the expression so endearing that Rhosyn felt herself smiling despite her efforts to be serious.

"Archer's Circus was lucky enough to get a fortuitous invitation during our trip to the palace," Ansel explained. "I thought accepting might give us a chance to get more information about Mr. Gower."

Rhosyn lifted an eyebrow. "Do tell."

"It seems the King enjoyed our performance at his ball—so much so that he wants the circus to provide some entertainment for an excursion to his country estate that he is planning with some members of society. I had some of the Foxes do some digging, and it appears that Mr. Gower is on the invite list."

"Do socialites really have nothing to do but throw parties and attend balls? What about their supposed business?" Rhosyn mused.

"Parties are where their daughters find wealthy marriages and influential men find women with dowries to support them. That *is* their business," Ansel pointed out.

Rhosyn frowned. It was such a strange way to think of things, but she supposed Ansel was right. "I suppose the Circus is going to another party then."

"We are. And you're coming with."

Chapter Twelve

The glass chilled Rhosyn's nose as she all but smashed her face against it, watching the countryside roll by. She had never known there was so much green so near the incessant grays and browns of London. In the clearer air of the country, the leaves seemed even brighter than those on the sparse trees outside the manors in the upper city, where the smokey air from the nearby factories made everything muted.

A dry chuckle from the bench across from Rhosyn made her pull back.

"One would think you'd never seen a tree before." He teased.

"One tree? Yes," Rhosyn conceded. "This many in the same place? No."

Ansel tilted his head. "You've really never been out of the city before."

Rhosyn shook her head, looking away towards the window to avoid the feeling in Ansel's eyes as he observed her. They still hadn't talked about what had happened between them in the Merry Men's tent, and Rhosyn was loathe to bring it up. After all, what was there to say? It couldn't possibly mean more than a simple physical release. Not when Ansel would leave with the circus and Rhosyn would go back to the police after Mr. Gower's plans were uncovered.

"I never had the chance to travel," Rhosyn admitted. "When I was with the Lions, none of us had much time to do much but stay alive and keep the young ones fed."

Of course, after the Lions had dissolved, life had been different. Nate had taken Contessa to a cottage by the ocean, and even Kristoff and Gregor had managed to steal away for a holiday. But Rhosyn had entered training for the police as fast as she could and never taken more than one consecutive day off since. Not until her time with the Foxes.

"But you wanted to?" Ansel asked, drawing her from her thoughts.

She turned back to him. "Yes," Rhosyn admitted.

"Where did you want to go?"

It wasn't a question Rhosyn had expected, so much so that it surprised the truth out of her without a second thought. "The ocean."

"Really? The consummate city girl has a taste for exploring?" Ansel's brows rose, and a smile toyed with the edges of his lips.

Rhosyn sighed. "My father. He was a sailor on transatlantic steam ships. I barely remember him, but the images I do have of him are always headed off to another adventure. All the time away from London was probably what let him hide his Talent for so long. I've always wanted to see where he was running off to for all those years."

Rhosyn swallowed, looking down at her hands in her lap, unconsciously popping her knuckles. The sound was loud in the quiet carriage at the end of her speech. She had once admitted to Contessa that her dream had been to follow in her father's footsteps. At one point, when she was barely more than a child, she had inquired about jobs on one of the steam ships down at the port. Rhosyn had even gone so far as to gather up her meager belongings, to leave the perils of London and the lower city behind.

Then Nate and Kristoff had come to check on the overcrowded Den, looking hopeless and harrowed by the monumental task they had set for themselves, and Rhosyn knew she couldn't go. They were her family, and she owed them her life after they had broken her out of the textile factory she lived in after her parents' deaths. So, she stayed. Only Contessa had ever heard that she dreamed of something else for her life at one point. It wouldn't be fair to lay that responsibility at the feet of the men who had loved her like a sister for so many years.

"You know," Ansel said with purposeful casualness, "I've thought about taking the circus to America for a tour before. Talents are so much more widely accepted over there, after all."

Rhosyn blinked. The way Ansel said it almost sounded like an invitation—like a chance for a new life where her mixed past wouldn't have to constantly be locked in eternal battle for her future. But that would be impossible.

Rhosyn hummed noncommittally and turned her attention back to the countryside rolling by outside the window. In the absence of conversation, the rattling wheels of the carts traveling with them permeated the enclosed space. Alongside the modest carriage carrying Ansel and Rhosyn, Archer's Circus had sent several wagons of performers, whose equipment could be easily packed up and transported without the train. They had been on the road for an hour now and should be just over halfway to the estate where the King's gathering was to be held.

"We only have a little while until we get there." Ansel broke the silence to echo her thoughts. "We should finish getting you into your disguise, just in case."

Rhosyn turned towards the bundle at her side, containing the remainder of the accessories for her ensemble. She already wore a deep purple dress with sleeves more flowy than were strictly fashionable, but that gave her the appearance of drifting through water when she walked.

A muffled jingle came from the bag as she opened it, and she raised her eyebrows.

Ansel shrugged. "It's not like I haven't hidden somebody in plain sight by dressing them up as a circus performer before. When people are used to seeing you in a Royal Police uniform, they will barely notice you at all bedecked as an eccentric fortune teller."

"Hopefully, most of the people at this gathering will only ever have seen me in passing, on one of the few occasions Contessa and Nate took me to a party." Rhosyn pulled out a long navy scarf embroidered with silver moons and stars.

"For your hair," Ansel explained. "It's...rather distinctive. I thought it would be best to cover it up."

Rhosyn sighed, but he was right. She piled her curls on top of her head and began winding the fabric around it. The reason she and Ansel had decided on a fortune teller for her disguise was so she could mingle easily through the party, giving her better chances to eavesdrop on any important conversations Mr. Gower might have. It wouldn't do for him to spot her from across the room based on the top of her head.

She fumbled as she reached the end of the length of fabric, fingers struggling to tie the short ends into a knot at the base of her skull.

"Here, let me." Ansel shifted across the carriage, sliding onto the same bench as Rhosyn.

She turned her back to him, to give him a better angle to help. His warm hands came up to cover hers and she let them fall back into her own lap. His nimble fingers made quick work of the knot, but his touch lingered. The pad of one callused finger ran down the nape of her neck, so lightly she questioned if it was intentional.

A shudder washed over her. Ansel snatched his hand away, as if Rhosyn's response shocked him out of a trance.

"Sorry, rough hands." He cleared his throat.

Rhosyn turned on the seat, so her back was no longer to him, busying herself with the bag once more. "Between the trapeze bars and the knives, I'm surprised your skin hasn't turned to stone."

"I'd think the calluses are more from the knives at this point," Ansel admitted. "I almost completely stopped doing acrobatics for many years, when I was afraid my Talent would be too obvious. Not to mention, I'm not actually Talented with knives, so building that skill required a lot more practice...and a lot more accidentally slicing myself. I count myself lucky I still have all my fingers."

As Ansel spoke, Rhosyn fished a handful of silvery bangles out of the bag, explaining the earlier jangling. She slid them on and let them settle on her wrists, where they threw sparkling lights all over the carriage every time she moved her hands.

The bracelets jingled like tiny bells as she dug around in the bottom of the sack for the last few items. As she fished out a pencil of kohl and a small pot of rouge, she raised her brows curiously at Ansel.

"It'll make your face less familiar," he explained.

"It will just make it clear how much I don't know what I'm doing with this." Rhosyn frowned at the objects in her hand. The only times she had ever gone anywhere where her appearance might matter, Julia had helped her with her hair, only applying the most minimal amount of powder to her nose. Otherwise, whenever Rhosyn looked in the mirror, the lack of freckles made her feel like a ghost.

"I can help you." Ansel gestured for her to hand him the makeup.

Rhosyn's brows rose even higher. "You're going to help me with my makeup?"

"I run a circus. You don't live with this many clowns and not know how to paint up your face." Leaning in close, Ansel motioned for her to close her eyes.

When she did, he began smudging the kohl sticks on her eyelids, fingers sure despite the jostling of the carriage. With her vision gone, Rhosyn's ears pricked, zeroing in on the sound of Ansel's breath so close to her own.

A finger pressed into her top lip and her eyes snapped open, to find Ansel's gaze fixed on her mouth. He pushed at it again, smearing the rouge on it. As he moved towards the bottom lip, the pressure forced Rhosyn's mouth open slightly. Her breath caught, and Ansel's gaze flicked up to her eyes.

The glimmer she saw there made her bold. Quickly, she flicked her tongue against the tip of his finger where it rested against her lip. His gaze darkened.

"Be good," he purred.

Something in Rhosyn's core melted at the words. Where so often she rose to every challenge presented to her with bared teeth and flying fists, something about the way Ansel said it made her pliant. She ached for more, and the way Ansel looked at her told her he did too.

Rhosyn sat perfectly still as he finished applying the tint to her lips before pulling back to admire his work. "Dramatic and eccentric. Nobody will suspect a straight-laced police officer under that get up."

"I'm not sure I ever would have called myself straight-laced, even when I wasn't running with a gang of thieves," Rhosyn countered, her voice only slightly hoarse from Ansel's recent touch. She cleared her throat and shook herself free of his spell as he retreated to the far side of the carriage.

"Good, because you're going to have to be creative and have a little fun with your fortune teller ruse," Ansel said. "In fact, why don't you do a little bit of a practice run on me."

He dug in his coat pocket and produced a small packet, which he held out to Rhosyn. Seeing what it was, she stared at him quizzically.

"Playing cards? Shouldn't I be reading tarot cards or something a little more...mystical?"

"Do you know anything about tarot cards?" Ansel countered.

Rhosyn shook her head.

"In my years of hiding Talented in the circus, I've learned that it's best to stick to what people know. That way their ruse isn't completely a lie. Besides, I'm pretty sure you already know a few card tricks that could convince people you can read their minds." Ansel's look was pointed.

Rhosyn grabbed the deck from his outstretched hand with narrowed eyes. "Alright then."

She pulled them from their paper packaging and began shuffling. They were clearly new cards, snapping energetically as they jumped in her hands. She bent them in a rippling bridge, using the motion as a distraction as she palmed one card, surreptitiously glancing at it.

Keeping the one card in her hand, she restacked the deck and held it out to Ansel to cut. He did, and as she restacked it, the card in her palm found its way to the top of the deck.

"Draw your card," Rhosyn instructed, adding a dramatic timbre to her voice.

He did, the ghost of a smile playing over his lips before he schooled his features again.

"Now, think hard on your card, and I will tell you what it is and what it means." Rhosyn closed her eyes, breathing in deeply with a look of upmost focus on her face.

"You are holding...the three of spades."

Ansel huffed in amusement, and Rhosyn smiled slightly, although she kept her eyes closed.

"This card carries great weight. You have an important trial before you, and the fates of many others lie in your hands," Rhosyn intoned with as mystic of a tone as she could manage.

"That's hardly hard to figure out," Ansel snorted.

Rhosyn opened her eyes to glare at him. "Isn't that the trick of this sort of thing anyways? Be just vague enough and base your predictions off what you already know of somebody? Unless you have somebody with a Talent to actually predict the future..."

"That I do not. I'd think that would be much too powerful a Talent," Ansel admitted.

"I have a friend who can predict danger but nothing specific."

"Even if all those who tell fortunes at Archer's Circus are using tricks, you definitely used some slight of hand to make me pick the three of spades," he pointed out.

"It's not like you didn't know I knew my way around a deck of cards." Rhosyn shrugged one shoulder, smiling crookedly.

Ansel reached out and snatched the deck from her fingers. "Well, since you used that to swindle me out of a bet, I think I should have a chance to even the playing field."

"What did you have in mind?" Rhosyn's curiosity piqued. She watched his deft fingers manipulate the cards, and although his shuffling wasn't as elaborate as hers, the nimbleness of his fingers still held her attention. Realizing she was staring, she snapped her gaze back up to his.

"You draw a card," Ansel purposed. "If I guess the correct card, you have to answer a question."

"What kind of question?"

"Any question I want. And you have to answer honestly."

Rhosyn swallowed, her eyes drifting back the deck, which he now held out to her. It was a dangerous proposition.

And Rhosyn loved danger.

She reached out and slid the top card off the deck. Flipping it towards her, the perfect face of the Queen of Hearts stared back. Rhosyn glanced up to find Ansel smirking at her knowingly, and she grimaced. She wasn't the only one with tricks up her sleeve.

"You're holding the Queen of Hearts," he said.

"Yes," Rhosyn admitted, "But you already knew that."

"Now to figure out what to ask." Ansel leaned back in his seat and folded his arms.

Rhosyn wrinkled her nose. "You don't just want to know my favorite color? Or maybe my favorite food?"

"You might tell me that without a wager. I need to use this on something you wouldn't answer otherwise."

It was Rhosyn's turn to fold her arms. "Bold of you to assume I'd tell you my favorite color."

"Even more reason to make this question count." Ansel narrowed his eyes. "Would you rather be a Lion or an officer of the Royal Police?"

Rhosyn sat back in her seat as if she had been slapped. To answer Ansel's question would be to dive off the knife's edge that her life was currently balanced on. She had been picking her way through every situation on tip toes, precariously balanced between upholding the law and thwarting it based on what the situation required.

In the secret tunnels, Ansel had asked her what she truly was. But which one did she *want* to be?

"Both."

Neither.

She wanted all of it, yet something beyond what either position had offered. Something, that Ansel seemed to offer more with every moment they spent together, yet Rhosyn remained terrified to grasp onto it.

"That's not an answer," Ansel argued.

Rhosyn opened her mouth to respond that it was the most honest answer she had when the carriage jolted to a stop, cutting her off. After a moment, the door to the carriage swung open, late afternoon light spilling into the darkened space.

Rhosyn squinted past the coachman, who pulled down the stairs on the carriage, towards a sprawling estate.

They had arrived.

Wearing the face of somebody else was simultaneously stifling and liberating. Rhosyn drifted around the party, shrouded in an air of mystery. She stole glances at guests under hooded, heavily kohled eyes and talked with her hands so that the bangles on her wrists glittered in the lantern light.

The persona of Archer's Circus's newest fortune teller sat heavily on her like a mask, allowing her to be less self-conscious than she had been on accompanying the Woodrows to parties in the past. Still, the evening of putting on airs gave her new appreciation for the exhaustion she found in the crinkles of Ansel's eyes, and the slump of his shoulders when he shed the personas of the dashing Mr. Blakely or the devil-may-care Hood.

At the thought, Rhosyn's gaze darted across the milling crowds scattered across the lawn to where Ansel stood. He was currently engaged in conversation with several posturing gentleman, who had paused in front of one of the many performers stationed around the garden.

Rhosyn recognized the girl who juggled the glasses at the Foxes hideout, now fully made up and in top form as she tossed flaming clubs in the air. The men gaped as the performer spun, tossing the clubs behind her back for a few passes before turning back around and grinning.

As if Ansel sensed Rhosyn looking in his direction, he glanced up from the partygoers he was entertaining, his gaze catching hers. The silken sheen of his top hat and his glittering eyes reflected the flames from the juggler beside him, giving him the appearance of incandescence.

Rhosyn tore her gaze away in favor of focusing on the knot of people approaching her. The group was mostly composed of young women who giggled and whispered behind their hands. It was several minutes before the ladies drifted away, all pleased with promises of marrying for love. Rhosyn hoped the fortunes she gave them would come to pass, fabricated as they had been.

Unengaged again, she glanced over to where Ansel had been, to find him gone. A furrow formed between her brows as she scanned the crowd for him. While the gathering had been underway for almost an hour and the revelry was gathering steam, neither of them had encountered Mr. Gower yet.

The gleam of Ansel's top hat finally caught her attention, his silhouette almost completely hidden in a tight knot of people. The man standing next to him explained the eagerness of the crowd in that area. The King.

Hovering just over King Byron's shoulder was a scarred and scowling face that Rhosyn knew almost better than her own. Internally, Rhosyn cursed. She had known there was a chance Nate would be serving as the King's bodyguard this evening, but she had hoped it would be another of the King's Guard in rotation, so she could avoid being recognized and having Nate accidentally ruin her cover.

Maybe if she could catch him alone, she could explain the situation to him and get Nate to play along. Rhosyn spun on her heel, dress swirling in a rippling pool around her, and walked towards the servants' entrance at the edge of the garden.

She slipped past white gloved footmen carrying silver trays of food and drink into the staging area. Some of the servants shot her odd looks, but she strode past with confidence, and nobody stopped her. Once she was hidden from view of the main garden by a dense wall of hedges, she paused, evaluating her next move.

One of the servants could pass Nate a message asking him to meet her away from the main party. Before she could grab one of them to ask a favor, an eddy in the flow of activity in the staging area caught her attention.

Off to one side, three men stood bent in close conversation. Rhosyn recognized with a start the impressive silver mustache of Mr. Gower. From the redness of his face and the sharp gesticulations of his hands as he talked, Rhosyn could guess he was arguing with the two other men. She was unsure what he might have to argue with his servants about, as the other two men were clearly his staff—not dressed nearly as finely.

Rhosyn drifted closer as subtly as she could manage, straining to hear their words, although the ambient buzz of party made picking out a single conversation nearly impossible. As she approached, it became apparent that Mr. Gower and one of the men were in disagreement with the third.

Mr. Gower snapped something at his companion, and the conversation stalled for a moment. Then, the man who appeared to be on Mr. Gower's side said something, and the third man stiffened, standing as straight as a board. Mr. Gower said something next, but the stiffened man barely reacted at all, only blinking slowly.

Something about the blank expression on his face trickled cold down Rhosyn's spine. It reminded her of something she had seen before.

It reminded of her of Paul's listless appearance when she had seen him at the Gower's house.

Mr. Gower and the second man each said a few more words before turning around and striding purposefully back towards the party. Rhosyn moved to follow them, sure that whatever was happening with Mr. Gower's servants was untoward and likely held the answers to what he was trying to accomplish with such a dangerous group of Talented. Her gaze clung to the third man, though, who remained oddly inanimate.

Before Rhosyn could follow Mr. Gower and the second man to the main garden, the third man turned on his heel and marched from the side garden, motions as mechanical as a tin soldier. He strode quickly in the direction of the manor house, and Rhosyn frowned.

Something about the oddity of his behavior called to her instincts. She hovered for a split second of indecision before trailing him in the direction of the house. Ansel was still at the party, where he could keep an eye on Mr. Gower.

On light feet, Rhosyn followed the servant out of the side garden towards the manor. She held her wrists with her opposite hands to keep her bangles from jangling and giving her away. The servant ducked in a side door, and she waited for a moment before following suit.

She thanked luck for hinges kept well-oiled by the royal housekeepers as it shut silently behind her. The quiet in the empty hallway lay heavily after the liveliness of the party. Rhosyn took short steps, afraid even the quiet swish of her skirts would alert the man to her pursuit, but he didn't react.

In fact, he seemed blind to all around him, marching with purpose towards his unknown destination. He led Rhosyn up a flight of stairs, out of what appeared to be the servants' quarters and into the manor proper.

The halls here were richly appointed, paintings in gilded frames decorating every wall and elegant furniture upholstered in brocades and velvets. The man clearly wasn't here to steal, for he easily would have been able to pocket a fortune, unattended as they were. He instead made a beeline for the stairs.

Up on the second floor, they passed several closed doors that Rhosyn assumed concealed bedrooms, until the man opened one and strode inside. There was nothing marking this door as distinct from the others, and Rhosyn might have thought it was chosen at random if not for the purposefulness of his stride.

Rhosyn stopped outside the closed door, weighing her options. Looking up and down the hallway for anybody who might be watching, Rhosyn found the place deserted, everybody apparently at the party. She leaned forward and pressed her ear to the door. Only a faint shuffling greeted her, the absence of voices indicating he had not come up here for a surreptitious rendezvous.

In a rustle of skirts, Rhosyn fell down onto her belly so she could peer through the slight gap under the door. She squinted, as she tried to concentrate her vision through the narrow slit. As the man's silhouette came into focus, her stomach dropped.

In his hands was the long, thin length of a repeating rifle. A metallic click told Rhosyn he was loading it.

The time for secrecy was at an end.

She sprang to her feet and grabbed the door handle, only to curse when it didn't turn. He had locked the door behind him. Bending over to get a better look at the lock, she was momentarily distracted by a distant cheering from the party.

Something told her she didn't have much time. Rhosyn didn't know what the man planned to do with the rifle, but she doubted he was using it as a back scratcher. With a grimace, she took a step back. Then she drew her knee up into her chest and kicked out, foot hitting the door firmly, just above the handle. The blow rattled her teeth, and a shock ran from the sole of her foot up to the top of her head, the slippers she wore not offering nearly as much protection as her usual boots.

Still, it was enough for the lock to give way, and the door crashed inwards.

The sight that greeted her left her with no time to think about the jolt echoing through her. Seemingly unperturbed by the interruption, the man stood in the window, back to her with the rifle raised. He stared down the sights through the open window, which offered a clear view of the garden where the party was being held.

At the near end of the garden was a small platform, erected by Ansel for some of his performers, and standing on it, with his arms raised as if in speech, was King Byron.

The safety on the gun clicked, the sound echoing as time stretched. Rhosyn bounded across the room in three long strides. The man's finger was already tightening on the trigger by the time she reached him, giving her only enough time to crash into him. She grabbed him around the chest, forcing his arm up as the gun fired.

The volume of the shot shattered through her, leaving both her and the gunman momentarily frozen. The ringing in her ears quickly gave way to screams from the party. Over the gunman's shoulder, she spotted Nate hustling King Byron off the stage, both seemingly uninjured.

Before she could process anything else, the man lurched back into her, trying to throw her off. The motion loosened her grip just enough for him to spin in her grasp. He tried to lower the gun to point it at her, but the close quarters gave him very little room to maneuver. Rhosyn grabbed the rifle, keeping the barrel pointed at the ceiling and trying to wrest it from his grip.

He was deceptively strong and tugged back. Rhosyn grit her teeth and held on with all her might, knowing that her chances for survival were infinitesimal if he controlled the weapon. She kicked out savagely, foot catching him in the shin.

He grunted in pain, and she gained the advantage. As she tried to get a better grip on the gun, her finger slipped onto the trigger.

A blast echoed through the room as the gun discharged, so loud and so close that Rhosyn's vision swam. Stunned, she staggered back, letting go of the gun.

A heavy object plummeted past her, missing her by inches as she stumbled away. The gunman wasn't so fortunate, a heavy light fixture dropping from the ceiling, knocked loose by the accidental shot.

One of the wrought metal arms caught him square in the forehead, and he crumpled like a marionette whose strings had been cut. Rhosyn took the opportunity to lunge across the destroyed light fixture to where he lay on the floor. She pinned him to the ground and wrenched the rifle from his slack fingers as he blinked dazedly.

In the few seconds of relative calm, shouts drifted in through the open window.

"—tried to kill the King!"

"On the third floor!"

Slamming doors and pounding footsteps accompanied the voices.

Rhosyn's attention was drawn away from the commotion by gunman's expression going from dazed, to confused, and finally settling on horrified.

"What happened?" he gasped.

"What do you mean what happened?" Rhosyn snarled. "You tried to assassinate King Byron. Did Gower put you up to this?"

His eyes widened so far that white showed all the way around his irises. "He wanted me to do something... I told him I wouldn't," the man sputtered. "But then the groom, Hamish—the one with the unnerving eyes—he said something to me. I...I don't remember."

Rhosyn froze. Mr. Gower's groom. Something began to click into place in her mind, only to be blocked by shouting from the hall.

"Down there! That's where the shot came from."

Panic overtook the man's expression. "No...no! I'll hang."

Before Rhosyn could do anything, the man shifted beneath her. She moved to press her weight into him so he couldn't escape, but he didn't try to push her off. She had the odd feeling of sinking and blinked incredulously as the servant beneath her appeared to sink into the floor as if being submerged in water.

In a second, he was gone. Rhosyn patted the floor where he had been in disbelief before an image flitted through her head: Sponsorship papers for a Talented who could walk through walls.

She shot to her feet, ready to dash out into the hallway and try to cut the would-be assassin off downstairs. Before she took one step, several King's Guard and Royal Police piled through the door, shouting.

There she stood, alone in the very spot the shot had come from, holding the weapon that had been used in an assassination attempt on the King.

"There she is. Arrest her!"

Chapter Thirteen

R hosyn's brain tumbled to a halt, like a carriage meeting an unfortunate end in the street races that crashed through the lower city. In the smoldering wreckage of her plan, her mind fixated on one thing: The widened eyes of Royal Police, taking in the person who had attempted to take the life of their country's leader.

The scarf that had been tied around her head fluttered to the ground at her feet, having come loose in the mayhem. Even without her hair showing, she would have been recognizable to those who had crossed paths with her at the station for years.

Fletcher and Davies stood to one side of the bunch, expression morphing from open in shock to contorted in fury as the moment stretched.

"I... It wasn't—I didn't..." Rhosyn searched for words to deny the appearance of the situation.

But it wouldn't change what was about to happen. They would arrest her as the real killer ran away. After she had disappeared from the Royal Police with no explanation—and was clearly no longer a hostage—they wouldn't be quick to believe any of her explanations.

The shock that held the room in temporary suspension was shattered by a ripple that ran through the assembled guards and officers. A tall figure pushed its way towards the front of the crowd.

Rhosyn swallowed as she caught sight of shaggy auburn hair. Then, Nate stood before her. A long moment stretched, where she was sure everybody assembled could hear the pounding of her heart. Nate's good eye widened slightly before his face became unreadable, his mouth set in a hard, straight line.

"You are under arrest for attempting to assassinate King Byron."

Rhosyn's ears rang, and her knees trembled. Even Nate—the closest thing she had to a family—believed the worst of her right now. She expected the rage of betrayal to burn like fire in her veins, but instead an icy cold washed over her. She nearly crumpled where she stood, but a flicker of Nate's eyes caught her attention.

He glanced back and forth between her face and the rifle still clutched to her chest. He took one slow step forward. Surely he didn't think she would shoot him?

No. Nate could have had her disarmed and on the ground by now, and never shied away from jumping into danger to protect his family or his King.

He was dutiful and proud of his position, and he wouldn't refuse to arrest her in front of all these onlookers. But he would give her a chance to escape. Rhosyn's fingers tightened on the gun. Nate's chin dipped in the tiniest of acknowledgements.

Before she could second guess herself, Rhosyn angled the gun forward slightly and pulled the trigger at the same time. Plaster exploded everywhere as the bullet hit right at the base of a second chandelier. People shouted as the chain holding the light fixture detached, but Rhosyn didn't stay to watch it plummet to the floor between her and her would-be captors, momentarily blocking them from view.

She dropped the gun, knowing she was unwilling to actually shoot anybody to escape, and spun towards the window. Not breaking her stride, she jumped up onto the sill and twisted in midair, catching the overhang above the opening with her fingers.

If she descended, she would be throwing herself into the path of more guards. The roof was her best chance to make a getaway, and she only had a few seconds head start. Wishing for Ansel's agility and thanking the royalty's gaudy architecture for its ample handholds, she scrambled up the last story to the roof.

As soon as her feet hit the slate tiles, she took off, dashing up the steep slope of the gable. The garden where the party had been was in the back of the manor, but her best chance of escape from the property would be through the gates at the front, left open for all the comings and goings of guests.

She reached the towering peak of the roof and crested to the other side. Instead of running down hill, she fell to one hip, sliding down feet first. The tiles rucked her skirts up and skinned her legs, leaving a stinging in their wake, but Rhosyn didn't stop. She let gravity build her momentum, gaining speed—and hopefully distance on her pursuers.

At the end of the steep slope was a small flat section of roof over the front entrance. She tumbled onto it, descent halted with enough force to knock a grunt from her. A few stumbling steps took her to the very edge, when her eyes lit on exactly what she was hoping for: carriages.

She had never driven one before, but there was no better teacher than necessity.

Her gaze lit on a sleek navy coach with gold accents, hitched to a pair of brown horses whose muscles rippled under shining coats. They would do quite nicely—not that she had time to shop for options.

Already, shouts of pursuit were echoing from the side of the house as people on the ground ran around the manor to stop her. Rhosyn crouched before springing forward. Her heart flew up into her throat as she fell for one extended second. Then, she landed in a crouch on the top of the carriage.

Before she had a chance to catch the breath the impact knocked out of her, the carriage lurched, sending her sprawling, and nearly knocking her off. A sharp whinny told her that her sudden appearance had scared the horses. They took off, and she rolled, not having a good grip, only managing to keep herself from tumbling to the ground by grabbing the edge of the roof before she toppled over it.

The vehicle bumped as it picked up speed, the horses seemingly only spurred on further by the yelling behind them, as Rhosyn's pursuers commandeered carriages of their own. The clatter of wheels over the cobblestone drive echoed through her skull as she crawled over the roof towards the driver's seat, remaining flat on her belly lest the bumping knock her loose.

Wind whipped at her unbound hair and stung her eyes as she dragged herself on her elbows, until she at last tipped over the front edge and collapsed onto the driver's bench.

Her fingers scrambled for the reins, but even as they closed around the worn leather, her heart sank. Any hopes of driving the carriage were a lost cause. She had never handled a horse before, and the shock combined with shouts from behind of "Halt in the name of the crown!" seemed to have whipped them into a frenzy. The horses would gallop until they deemed it appropriate to stop, and Rhosyn was at their mercy.

By now, they had already charged down the long drive leading to the manor and careened through the front gates of the property. The horses followed the road through a sharp bend. Rhosyn's nails bit into the reins so hard they would leave marks in the supple leather, as the carriage rocked precariously at the suddenness of the turn.

As it righted itself, falling back onto four wheels after skittering on two for a moment, Rhosyn chanced a glance over her shoulder. She had gained considerable distance from her pursuers thanks to the horses' reckless speed, but she was likely to end up thrown from the carriage with a broken neck if this went on much longer.

Dust rose from the pounding of hooves on the country lane, stinging Rhosyn's eyes and burning her throat as she fought to think. The rattling wheels drowned out her thoughts, and she gritted her teeth so hard she thought they might crack in an effort to focus.

Her gaze caught on a dense wood off to one side of an upcoming turn in the road. It could provide good cover.

Especially if her pursuers thought she had continued down the road.

The bend approached quickly, as did her opportunity to decide: jump voluntarily from a hurtling carriage or wait until she was either thrown from it or captured and thrown in jail.

Rhosyn always liked to play the odds.

The horses thundered around the corner. As soon as they rounded the bend, hiding the carriage from view for mere seconds, she jumped.

She threw her arms up over her head and tucked herself into a ball as best she could. The ground hit her with all the force of a steam engine, and the world twirled sickeningly as she tumbled through brambles into the ditch. The sharp scratch of thorns against her skin cut through the haze of disorientation as she rolled into the thicket of the forest, and the clattering wheels of her stolen carriage moved away. Hopefully her pursuers thought she continued with it.

As she reached the bottom of the downhill slope away from the road, she threw her hands out, but the trees approached too fast. Her forehead smacked against the base of one, bark cutting into the skin of her temple.

The brown and green of the trees around her swirled together as she tried to grapple onto consciousness, only for it to slip through her fingers like smoke. The last thought before darkness took her was that she hoped Ansel found her before the Royal Police.

Cool fingers stroked her temples. Rhosyn's eyelashes fluttered in pleasure, the touch soothing enough to counteract the mild throbbing on her forehead. The knot there was not nearly as bad as it could have been for running headfirst into a tree, mostly stinging from the abrasion left by the bark.

At the memory of tumbling into a forested ditch, Rhosyn's eyes snapped open. Instead of the dappled light of trees at night, or the dingy gray of a prison cell, her gaze focused on concerned green eyes.

"Ansel," she sighed, her voice a breathy croak.

"Rhosyn." Ansel's voice was hardly any better.

Movement beneath her drew attention to the firm thighs cradling her head, flexing as Ansel bent over his lap where she rested. Rhosyn had been knocked out more times than she cared to admit, and all those occasions would have been vastly improved by waking like this. Her instincts pushed her to rise and get back in the fight as soon as possible, but Ansel's gentle touch pulled her even more insistently to stay right where she was.

Although she wasn't entirely sure where here was.

"What..."

"We're back at the safehouse in the lower city," Ansel explained. His fingers drifted to her hair as he spoke, twisting a ringlet around his finger absently. "After the commotion died down and I put together what had happened, the performers and I started combing the area for you. Once we found you in the ditch, we snuck you into our carriage. We figured you were the least likely to be found out here."

"You found me," Rhosyn echoed. Ansel had known she would be wanted for trying to assassinate the king—a treason punishable by death—and he had hidden her among the Foxes anyways. He and his people would be seen as accomplices if she were caught, likely suffering the same punishment, but he had recounted the events like it hadn't been a choice. As if he hadn't even considered that it might have been an opportune time to sever their unlikely alliance.

"You could die for helping me," she croaked, the hoarseness in her voice no longer just from disuse. "Why would a gang leader risk himself for one crooked cop?"

Ansel's hands drifted down to cup her cheeks, so gentle that Rhosyn thought she might shatter. "I would think it was obvious."

Rhosyn stared up at him, a bubble of something warm forming in her chest as she waited for him to continue.

"I love you. Isn't it awful?" He chuckled dryly, with no small amount of affection, as though he couldn't conceive of how they had possibly ended up in this situation.

Rhosyn's breath caught, and she had a moment where she understood how Ansel must feel on the trapeze, right before letting go and trusting his fate to gravity. "The worst part is, I love you too."

All of this consternation about whether she was a Lion or an officer of the Royal Police faded to the background with the admission that she was a woman who had fallen in love under the most inconvenient circumstances.

"What are we going to do about it?" Ansel asked, seemingly half to himself.

A simple question held so much weight. With the disaster at the King's party and the horrible revelation that Mr. Gower appeared to be using his Talented servants to try to kill the King, the world outside this room held nothing but chaos for Rhosyn and Ansel.

"It certainly is problematic, given that my life is pretty much ruined and I'm well on my way to bringing you down with me," Rhosyn said.

Ansel smiled softly down at her. "Love is hardly ever convenient, but something tells me it's worth it, despite the trouble it causes."

Rhosyn's heart fluttered up into her throat. "Well then, I guess we'll just do what people in love do."

Before Ansel could ask her what she meant, Rhosyn surged upwards, crushing her lips to his. In an instant, his arms went around her shoulders, supporting her as she draped across his lap, holding her to him with a heady mix of firmness and gentleness.

Her lips moved over his, searching and insistent, but he did not yield to the franticness of her kiss. Instead, one hand came to hold her jaw, tilting her head to give him better access to her mouth. With her at his mercy, Ansel deepened the kiss, slowing the pace as his tongue slid against hers with single-minded focus.

Rhosyn whimpered, and Ansel drew back. Her lips chased his, but his hand at her jaw held her firmly in place.

"We shouldn't. Your head…" The rasp in Ansel's voice sent tingles all the way down to Rhosyn's toes.

"Is fine." Rhosyn insisted. She took advantage of their momentary pause to sit up all the way and throw one leg over Ansel's hips, so she straddled him. "Once we leave this room, there will be no escaping reality. But for now, I'm a woman in bed with a man who just told me he loves me. If this is all we will ever have, let me have this. *Please*."

Ansel let out a groan, the rumbling of his chest vibrating against Rhosyn's nipples. She squirmed, increasing the friction so they grew hard, begging for more attention.

"If you say 'please' like that one more time, you won't be leaving this room until you are mine in every way."

"Show me," Rhosyn breathed.

Ansel obliged, diving forwards to nip and suck at her neck. The heat of his mouth drew a shiver from her. She squirmed, working to ruck up her skirts, still wearing the fortune teller dress. Hands grabbed her wrists, rough skin against her sensitive skin halting her.

"You asked me to show you, and that means I give you everything." His thumb drew small circles around the inside of her wrist, her pulse hammering against his touch. "Which also means you have to be patient."

Rhosyn's breath caught in her throat. The strange shimmering warmth that Rhosyn had felt before when he told her to *be good* washed through her again. Slowly, she nodded. Ansel smiled, the brightness of the adoration in his gaze doing nothing to detract from the feral edge of desire seeping into his posture.

Carefully, he unlaced her bodice, each drag of his fingers across the fabric tortuous as she waited for him to reach skin. When he finally pushed it off her shoulders, leaving her bare from the waist up, her hands flew to his shoulders. Her fingers dug into the firm muscle there, needing to hold on, as if she might fly away from the intensity of his gaze on her alone.

"Perfect," he murmured, before lowering to press an open mouth kiss to the valley between her breasts.

Rhosyn tipped her head back, eyes staring unfocused at the dingy wood ceiling. The single word echoed through her. Here with Ansel, she was not a Lion, a police officer, a brawler, or a thief. She was Rhosyn, and all she had to do to be perfect was just *be*. She wanted—needed—to watch Ansel come undone. Not because he expected anything of her in this moment, but because if she didn't give this man beneath her, who had given her so much, all the pleasure as she was capable of, she would regret it forever.

In one motion, she slid off Ansel's lap, landing on the floor between his thighs in a puddle of skirts.

"Rhosyn—"

"*Please.*"

"Anything."

A fine tremor ran through Rhosyn's fingers as she undid his trousers, pulling them open and finally pulling Ansel's hard length free. As her fist closed around him, the guttural groan that ran through him sent heat rolling down her spine and into her core. While her gaze remained fixed on her hand around him, his fingers in her peripheral vision clenched the edge of the bed so hard they turned white.

Rhosyn's tongue darted out to lick her lips and glanced up at him through her lashes. He wore a thoroughly wrecked expression, even though she had just started touching him. His eyes went wide as she leaned forward, wrapping her lips around his head.

"*Fuck.*"

Rhosyn was drunk on his reactions, the twitch of his manhood against her tongue and the strangled grunt of pleasure as she took as much of him into her mouth as she could. She began to slide up and down, but her gaze remained fixed on his face. Her eyes desperately catalogued every twitch of his jaw and the way his teeth dug into his lower lip as he tried to contain his desperate noises. Her rhythm faltered as she stared.

One of Ansel's hands came to hold her jaw, guiding her gently as his hips twitched.

"You're incredible like this," he growled. "I can't decide whether I like you better when you're throwing punches at me or when you're on your knees with your lips stretched around my cock."

Rhosyn whimpered around him, the noise unadulterated desperation.

"Maybe that's why I love you. Because I don't have to choose."

And I don't have to choose either, Rhosyn echoed in her mind, her mouth too busy to speak the words out loud.

Ansel pulled her off his length, and Rhosyn stared up at him with her mouth still hanging open. She only had a moment to admire him, his flushed face and the way his hair had fallen into his eyes, the silver piece gleaming in the lamplight, before he gathered her up into his arms and swung her onto the bed.

Her back landed on the mattress with enough force to make the ancient springs creak, but Ansel paid no mind, already prowling up her body. He shucked off his pants completely along the way, sitting up above her to pull his shirt off as well. Rhosyn took the cue to shimmy the dress the rest of the way down her hips, until their clothes lay in a discarded heap at the foot of the bed.

Once they were both completely bare, Ansel fell to his forearms, elbows bracketing her head. He circled his pelvis against hers, dipping into the considerable moisture that had gathered there, but not entering her yet.

Rhosyn bucked her hips, but one of his hands fell to her waist, pinning her down.

"Patience, love." He breathed the words into her neck before nipping at her collarbone.

Ansel sat back on his heels, pulling Rhosyn's hips into his lap. As he lined himself up at her entrance, a breathy moan escaped her, just the feeling of his tip stretching her open enough to drive her to the brink of madness she had been flirting with for so long.

The noise snapped his gaze to her face, and he pinned her there with it. Holding her eyes, he slowly pushed forward, sliding himself inside her inch by glorious inch. The tortuously slow drag made her eyelids flutter, but she dared not look away from the intensity of his expression. The expression that told him he saw *her*, not the mask of whatever role she was wearing, in this moment and all others.

Just as she saw him.

His hips met hers, and his mouth fell open in pleasure.

"So good. You take me so well," he panted.

Rhosyn hardly had time to register the zing of pleasure his words sent through her before he rolled his hips. At this angle, with her hips raised, his pelvis ground against her most sensitive spot and she gasped.

He repeated the action, grinding against her before withdrawing. He repeated the motion again and again, picking up speed until every thrust punched a breathy moan from her. As his hips pistoned into her, Ansel fell forward, bracing one hand on the wall above the headboard. The other gathered her wrists, bearing down on them with his weight and pinning her hands to the pillow above her head.

She rolled her hips against his, her world narrowing to the rising heat radiating out from her core, threatening to liquefy her into a pool of pleasure. But Ansel slowed, denying her the last bit of friction that would send her spiraling in pleasure.

She whimpered, and Ansel planted a kiss in the hollow just behind her ear. "Just a little more, Rhosyn."

The sound of her name on his lips, dripping with adoration and desperation, was all she needed to dive deeper into the well of pleasure he was driving her into. She tunneled further and further into the roiling inferno of her impending release as his hips snapped against hers relentlessly.

Rhosyn tossed her head side to side, as if it could help her contain the intensity of the moment. But at that instant, Ansel picked up his pace, his own control snapping as he chased his release.

The tension within Rhosyn shattered, so hard it bordered between pleasure and pain as she cried out her release. Her back arched and fireworks danced behind her eyes. She convulsed around Ansel, making it almost impossible for him to withdraw as he stuttered through a few more thrusts before spending himself inside her with a broken groan.

"Rhosyn."

They both drew in long, shuddering breaths as Ansel's forehead came to rest on her collarbone. He released her wrists from his grasp, and she moved her hands to his head, where she gently carded her fingers through his hair. The thin sheen of sweat covering both of them glimmered ethereally in the flickering lantern light. It combined with the deep quiet of early morning, amplified by the rushing of blood finally calming in Rhosyn's ears, to give the moment an otherworldly effect. As if the world beyond this room didn't exist, and they were held in the perfect bubble of this moment.

When it popped, the direness of their situation would sink back in. But for now, Rhosyn let Ansel bundle her into his arms as he rolled off her onto his side. For now, there was nothing besides his fingers in her hair and whispered praises between the kisses he pressed to the top of her head.

Chapter Fourteen

The smell of bacon roused Rhosyn from her doze. Her stomach growled before she even had a chance to open her eyes, prompting a low chuckle from somewhere across the room. She cracked one eye open to find Ansel standing at the foot of the bed wearing a bemused expression.

In his hands was the source of the smell: a plate of breakfast and a cup of tea. It looked almost as delicious as he did in that moment, his hair mussed from bed and his shirt open at the neck, exposing one shoulder.

Rhosyn opened both eyes to appreciate the sight and reached her arms over her head in a long stretch that drew attention to several sore spots in her body, both from her enjoyable night with Ansel and the much less enjoyable chase before that.

"Breakfast in bed? You're giving me the real princess treatment," she remarked as she sat up.

"I knew you must be hungry, but I figured we should let as few people know you're here as possible. There is a substantial reward for your capture, and people can't let slip a secret they don't know," Ansel explained, passing off the plate before setting the teacup on the rickety side table.

"Ah, so not a princess. Just a wanted criminal." Rhosyn grimaced, any illusions of domesticity in Ansel's breakfast delivery thoroughly shattered.

"Speaking of, we need to discuss why you're a wanted criminal. I'm assuming you didn't actually try to shoot the king?"

Rhosyn shook her head, mouth already full of bacon and a hefty slice of toast.

"Then, what actually did happen?"

"I was following one of Mr. Gower's men who was acting strange." Rhosyn explained the odd argument she witnessed in the garden, and how she had jumped in to thwart the assassination. She furrowed her brow when she began to recount how she had been the one left at the scene of the crime with a weapon. "It was so strange, though. Like he didn't even remember how he had gotten there."

Ansel's face grew pale. "So, Mr. Gower wants to use the Talented he's sponsored to get rid of the King."

Rhosyn grimaced even as she nodded in agreement. The cadre of Talented with violent abilities, combined with the assassination attempt at the party, painted a clear picture of what Mr. Gower wanted. "It's bold, considering that King Byron is wildly popular among the Talented after ending the Inquiries. It would be hard to convince them to take violent action against him."

Ansel's mouth formed a hard line, the look in his eyes causing the breakfast in Rhosyn's stomach to turn leaden.

"I had Little John look through the sponsorship papers we stole from the palace, and Rhosyn...one of the Talented he sponsored almost two years ago had powers of extreme persuasion, even to the point of being able to control somebody's actions."

Bile rose in Rhosyn's throat. "The groom."

Ansel nodded grimly. "His name is Hamish. It would explain what we overheard that night in the stables. Why they thought Olivia and Paul might come back of their own accord."

"And why they hardly seem to remember their time there. When the groom persuades them, it seems to put them nearly in a trance to force them to obey." Rhosyn's throat burned, and she put aside the plate of breakfast, food suddenly unappealing. All those Talented thinking they were getting a chance at a better life, only to be turned into thralls and set to a violent purpose.

"If Mr. Gower was willing to go to such lengths to oust the King, he won't give up after one failed attempt," Ansel pointed out. "He needs to be stopped. If a Talented assassinates another king, and one who was their best hope of equality, it would start the Inquiries all over again. Fear of the Talented hasn't abated, especially among the rich and powerful, and this would stir things up again."

Ansel's words picked up in pace as he spoke, signaling to Rhosyn that under the surface of his analytical approach stirred the beginnings of panic. It was panic she recognized all too well in the young Lions who started to show Talents, afraid that it would end with them at the end of a noose. A fear that she had felt responsible for protecting them from, as she had been lucky enough to have no Talent to hide.

"Mr. Gower *will* be stopped," Rhosyn promised. "But we can't do it just the two of us."

Ansel grimaced. "Do we have a choice? With you neatly framed for the attempt, I don't think many people would believe us."

She cracked her knuckles one by one as she thought. "I didn't escape the estate without a little bit of help. I know somebody who would give us the benefit of the doubt."

Rhosyn had never wished more that Nate had not bricked up the secret passage into his office. The darkness was thick tonight, wind blowing the smog from the factories back into the upper city so that it blocked out the light of the stars. Still, Rhosyn wished for Scarlett's powers to thicken the shadows even further as she and Ansel crept over rooftops.

Ansel had donned the outfit of the Hood, face and hair covered, with a wrist bow strapped to his forearm. Rhosyn hoped he wouldn't have to use it.

He had leant her a spare hood too, and together they stole like shadows up through the middle city. Below them on the streets, Royal Police prowled between pools of flickering lamplight, out in force after Rhosyn's perceived betrayal.

She paused on the edge of one roof, waiting for a pair of officers to pass by on the street below, before jumping the gap to the next building, Rhosyn tried not to wonder if she knew the officers—if she had worked with them before, and what they might be saying about her now. Ansel's shoulder brushed hers as he crouched beside her, and the warmth of his touch dulled the chill of those thoughts.

It took the pair longer than it might have to make their way to the upper city, as careful as they were to not be spotted. Once they reached the affluent neighborhoods where the manors were too far apart to travel directly from roof to roof, they picked their way between shadowy hedges in back gardens, heading for a familiar house.

Rhosyn dropped to her belly next to a familiar hedge and dragged herself by her elbows through a narrow gap below the thick shrubbery that served as a natural wall. She cursed quietly as brambles snagged on her hood, nearly ripping it free.

When she emerged from the leaves, the familiar sound of tinkling water in a fountain drifted through the air. She pushed to her feet, waiting for Ansel to follow. However, no rustling signaled that he was following her through the shrub. She frowned with concern, only to start when a dark shadow flew overhead.

Ansel landed neatly before her on the balls of his feet, as if he hadn't just flipped easily over a hedge that stood as high as she did.

"Showoff," she muttered under her breath as she turned towards the house. As always, the back garden was a veritable Eden, flowers all at full bloom, dripping with the verdant life that Gregor coaxed from them so lovingly.

Rhosyn hadn't been here in too long, but she didn't have time to admire the roses.

As she had known they would be, the back door on the ground floor was locked. She didn't want to draw attention by knocking, in case they had company over, so they would have to climb. Rhosyn gestured to a window on the second floor, indicating to Ansel that it would be their point of entrance.

As picky as Nate was about security, he had a habit of leaving the entrance to the rose room unlocked so Scarlett could come and go as she pleased, without the apparent indignity of using the front door. Ansel started up the wall first, the agility from his Talent offering him incredible speed. Rhosyn's toes had barely left the ground by the time he pushed at the glass, swinging it open easily as she had hoped.

Rhosyn continued climbing as Ansel disappeared inside the house. Just as her fingertips reached the sill, a crash and a shout echoed from inside. Lightning shot up Rhosyn's spine and she flung herself over the ledge, tumbling into the bedroom.

Nate stood on the far side of the bed, knives drawn and a snarl on his face. Ansel had his wrist bow raised, pointed squarely at Nate. One bolt already quivered in the wall just over Nate's ear, the glass shade of a decorative sconce that had been there shattered on the ground.

"Stop!" Rhosyn shouted, throwing up her hands.

Nate froze, his gaze darting to her for a split second and then back to the threat before him. In one movement, Rhosyn stepped between them and ripped her hood back so Nate could see her face.

"It's me," she said. For half a second, everybody was still and Rhosyn stood frozen at the sight of the assassination again. Nate's eyes flickered gold in the lamplight, and her heart stuttered at the reminder of how truly dangerous he could be, even though she had never before been on the receiving end of his blade.

"We're here to ask for help." Rhosyn raised her hands to communicate that they came in peace, giving Nate a chance to feel her intentions.

Nate moved so fast Rhosyn couldn't react. His knives clattered to the floor and he crossed the room in two strides, before his arms came around her with enough force to knock the wind out of her. Still, he squeezed relentlessly, lifting her feet off the ground.

Rhosyn's arms wrapped around his shoulders, and for a moment, she was just a girl again, desperately holding onto one of the only people who had been able to make her feel safe in a city torn apart by hate.

She made a sound that was half chuckle half sob. "Nate, you're going to break my ribs if you keep on like this."

He put her on her feet and promptly punched her in the shoulder, not hard enough to hurt, but still enough to mean business. "Don't ever scare me like that again."

Rhosyn rubbed her shoulder and grimaced. "I would rather not have done it the first time."

Nate looked over her shoulder to where Ansel stood just behind her, weapon lowered, watching the reunion.

"You're lucky your friend missed, or I might have hurt him before you stopped me," Nate grumbled as he gestured to the bolt in the wall.

"I didn't miss," Ansel retorted, pulling his hood back now as well. "It's called a warning shot."

The two eyed each other appraisingly, each puffing out their chests and squaring their shoulders. Rhosyn resisted scolding them for their posturing by reminding them that she had beat both of them in a fist fight at one point or another.

"Nate, this is Ansel Blakely," she gestured between them. "You can trust him."

"I take it you're the one the Royal Police have taken to calling the Hood." Nate folded his arms across his chest.

"I do have that dubious honor," Ansel admitted. He opened his mouth as if to say more when a swishing sound came from the doorway.

"Rhosyn!" Contessa crashed into the room, still managing to have her skirts drift around her elegantly as she threw herself at Rhosyn. She hugged her around the waist tightly but briefly before holding her at arm's length to inspect her.

A slight glassiness in her eyes and pallor in her complexion took Rhosyn off guard, as Contessa's polished exterior rarely showed a scratch. Especially now that Rhosyn didn't have the chance to knock her guard down by training her in self-defense.

"Sorry to stop by unannounced." Rhosyn smiled ruefully.

Contessa's lips pulled up at the corners slightly. Behind her, the rest of the tension in Nate's posture relaxed. If Contessa's Talent wasn't signaling any danger, then he would be convinced that Ansel wasn't planning any betrayal.

Contessa's eyes darted to Ansel.

He sketched a small bow. "Ansel Blakely. I do apologize for the light fixture."

With a frown, Contessa stared at the broken glass on the floor. "No apology necessary. Everything in this room is hideous. I'm just sorry I wasn't the one who got to smash it. But we'll be redecorating soon enough anyways."

Rhosyn caught Nate's eye over his wife's shoulder and snorted. The gaudy wallpaper of the rose room was a running joke, but no matter how many times it came up, they had never gotten around to changing the décor in Contessa's old bedroom.

"We've been saying that for years," Nate pointed out.

Contessa hummed noncommittally before turning back to Rhosyn and Ansel. "Come downstairs and I'll have Gregor make some tea. Although, I assume you're here for more than a polite visit."

Rhosyn's gaze flicked to Nate. "I have an explanation...and some information."

The four cups of tea on Nate's desk were empty by the time Rhosyn finished her tale. Nate's knives were unsheathed and spread across the desk, glimmering almost as lethal as his golden eyes in the lamplight. The metallic *shink* of a whetstone being drawn across a blade punctuated the heavy silence. Rhosyn wasn't even sure Nate realized he had begun sharpening his knives, just falling into the habit as Rhosyn informed him of Mr. Gower's treachery.

Even worse, though, was the complete absence of color in Contessa's already pale complexion. Her gray eyes were as cold as ice, reminding Rhosyn the woman could be even more intimidating than her husband in the right circumstances. The twisting of Contessa's hands in her lap, knuckles white against the blue fabric of her dress, gave away her distress, though.

Nate set his knife down and put one hand in Contessa's lap, interlacing his fingers with hers so she let go of the now wrinkled silk of her skirt.

"They'll try again," Nate broke the heavy silence. "Especially since he can use you as a scapegoat." He nodded at Rhosyn.

She nodded in agreement. "You need to keep the King safe at all costs."

"The sponsorships were supposed to help the Talented. Instead, Mr. Gower is using them to try to start the Inquiries all over again. To turn people against the Talented." Contessa's voice cut through the stillness of the night like a blade, so sharp Rhosyn nearly flinched.

Her heart squeezed at the anger in Contessa's words—how much it must hurt to have her life's work turned against her, when she had put her own father in jail to put a stop to the persecution of the Talented.

Before Rhosyn could offer any words of comfort, Nate squeezed his wife's hand. "We'll arrest Mr. Gower."

Contessa shook her head. "He'll be out of jail in no time without hard proof. You know that better than anybody." She fixed Nate with a pointed look and he ducked his head, acknowledging that she had married him in the first place to get a hold of hard evidence necessary to send a known gangster to jail.

"The only proof we have is the testimony of a person already wanted for the attempted assassination and documents that were stolen from the palace by a gangster. Even then, the sponsorship contracts are circumstantial at best," Contessa explained.

"We have to prove he was behind the attempt at the party to clear Rhosyn's name," Ansel chimed in.

Rhosyn twitched in surprise, as he had been silent through her whole story, letting her tell it uninterrupted. She glanced at him to find his gaze fixed on her.

"And what do you have to gain from all of this?" Nate asked, fixing Ansel with a deep stare, sharp enough to look into Ansel's soul. Knowing Nate, he probably was.

Ansel raised his chin. "I've spent my life trying to give the Talented a better life too, albeit in a different way than you. This is my fight as well."

Nate's eyes narrowed. "And clearing Rhosyn's name?"

Rhosyn cleared her throat and glared at Nate, clearly trying to intimate that now was not the time for such discussions. His eyes darted over to her, and she detected the slightest hint of amusement in them before they landed on Ansel once again.

She supposed this was his payback for the way she ruthlessly teased him about Contessa when they were first married.

"Rhosyn should have the chance for the life she wants too," Ansel said firmly.

Crimson climbed up Rhosyn's neck to her face, and she looked down at her hands. Somehow, she felt more exposed than if Ansel had admitted to their truly debauched activities on a trapeze a few days earlier. But this statement went farther than skin deep, flaying her open more thoroughly than something that would just result in incessant teasing from Nate and Contessa. Rhosyn had fallen for her kidnapper, and the feelings were reciprocated.

"Then we will bring to justice the people really responsible for the plot against our king." The voice was Contessa's, proud and firm. Rhosyn glanced up at her friend, finding some warmth returned to her steely gaze.

If anybody understood falling in love with somebody you didn't intend to, it was Contessa.

"What we need is to catch Mr. Gower and his Talented in the act, so there is no way he can wiggle out of the charges," Contessa mused, her brain whirring almost visibly as she turned her mind to planning.

"If we set up a prime opportunity for the King to be assassinated, we might be able to entrap Mr. Gower into trying again." Ansel nodded along.

Nate frowned. "I'm not sure it would make me a good bodyguard if we used the king as bait in a setup."

Contessa shook her head. "We won't use him as bait. The king needs to go into hiding. Get out of the line of fire until we know the threat on his life has passed. We need to come up with a way to sneak him out of London."

"I think we might have a way," Rhosyn interjected. She looked over at Ansel, and understanding dawned across his face.

If he could dress Talented up as acrobats and clowns and smuggle them out on his circus train, then he could certainly sneak out a king.

"Archer's Circus," he chimed in. "We've been offering Talented safe passage out of the city with our performers for years. Our train is scheduled to leave the day after tomorrow. We may just have picked up another act while we were in town."

Nate's unscarred brow raised in curiosity at the admission, but there was no time to get into the hidden history of Archer's Circus—not when Contessa's eyes were already narrowing in renewed calculations.

"Then the King will take the train to his country estate where he will stay until Mr. Gower is arrested. Who knows how long he will have to rule from there, so I'll have to accompany him," Contessa thought out loud.

"And I'll be going to guard him," Nate added.

"No." Contessa's voice was firm, causing her husband's gaze to snap to her. "You'll be needed here to make it seem like the King never left and apprehend anybody who participates in the next assassination attempt."

Nate scowled—an expression known to send grown men running away with their tails between their legs—but Contessa stared him down coolly.

"I won't leave you unprotected," Nate growled. "Not when you've been ill recently."

"I'm not ill." Contessa looked down at her lap.

"But—"

"You can tell I'm not lying," Contessa snapped.

Rhosyn looked at her friend more closely, seeing her pallor and the circles under her eyes in a new light. Guilt began to gnaw at her belly for not noticing how drawn she appeared and for laying these concerns at Contessa's feet when she already shouldered too many troubles. Maybe she and Ansel could solve this problem without bringing Contessa into it.

"I can tell you're not telling me everything though," Nate argued, standing and squaring on his wife, completely ignoring the others in the room. "You barely gave me any information on what the doctor said last week."

"I wanted to wait to tell you until you weren't so busy worrying about what happened with Rhosyn," Contessa said softly.

"Tell me what? If you need treatment, I want to know as soon as possible. We can go anywhere you need for the best—"

"We're having a baby."

The room froze as Contessa stared up through her lashes at her husband. Nobody breathed at all. The thuds of Nate's boots against the floor echoed loudly as he stumbled back a few steps, before sitting down heavily on the top of the desk.

"You're...pregnant?"

"We've been trying so long. I just wanted to be sure before I told you," Contessa's voice had softened to something full of hesitant joy.

Rhosyn looked over to Nate, his scowling face blooming into an expression softer than it had any right to be, with the fearsome scar bisecting his face. It was the way he looked at Contessa when they were first married, every time he didn't think anybody was looking—back when he didn't think there was any way she might love him.

Warmth bloomed in Rhosyn's chest—a delicate tendril of hope springing forth amid the darkness of recent events.

"I guess we do really have to redecorate the rose room," Nate mumbled, shell shocked. "We're going to need a nursery."

Contessa stood slowly and took a few steps forward, to stand between his knees. Nate's hands drifted to her waist and pulled her closer. He buried her face in her hair and breathed in shakily, paying no heed to the delicate mass of braids that must have taken hours to weave together.

"You're definitely not going anywhere without me," Nate declared into Contessa's hair.

At that, she stepped back, not far enough to force him to let go of her waist, but enough that he had to lift his head and meet her gaze.

"No. This is exactly why we have to do this." Contessa's tone brooked no argument. "I want our baby to know that we always do what must be done. They are likely going to be Talented, with the two of us as their parents. I do not want them born into a world where they have to fear their Talent, like we did. If we fail to catch the Gowers, that is exactly what might happen."

"I won't let you go alone," Nate said, his voice the closest to pleading it had ever been.

Rhosyn sprang to her feet. "She won't be alone."

In a few strides, she had crossed the room and slung her arm around Contessa's shoulder. The shorter woman smiled up at her fondly.

"You know I would walk over broken glass for both of you, and my future niece or nephew," Rhosyn added.

"You have also done much stupider things for much less important reasons," Nate pointed out, but his gaze softened.

"Even more proof that I won't hesitate to do what needs to be done."

"I'll be there too," Ansel volunteered, joining them all in standing, stepping up at Rhosyn's shoulder.

"And you think you have what it takes to protect my wife? And my sister?" Nate looked at Ansel appraisingly.

Before he answered, Ansel leaned forwards and picked up one of Nate's knives off the desk before him. He tossed it in his palm a few times as if testing its weight. Then, his wrist whipped forward faster than Rhosyn could blink.

A thud punctuated the air as the tip embedded itself into the wall above the shelf that served as a bar. Pinned to the knife was the cork of a bottle of whiskey, neatly removed by Ansel's throw.

Nate's eyebrows rose in admiration, a feat rarely achieved by anybody when it came to knife handling. "You certainly know your way around a blade."

"That's settled then," Contessa said, with finality in her tone. "I'll have plenty of protection."

Rhosyn clapped her hands and rubbed them together. "Let's go catch a king killer."

Chapter Fifteen

Steam drifted through the early morning air in thick blankets, turning all the busy figures in the train-yard into hazy silhouettes. Rhosyn lifted another crate, this one labeled "Fire Whips", onto the Archer's Circus train.

Her hair was hidden under a woolen cap to conceal the color, but the hazy dawn made it seem unnecessary, even the garish green and yellow on the train cars appearing dull and muted. Her eyes darted down several cars to where Ansel stood, directing traffic as the circus loaded up their supplies for a supposed tour. The confident clip of his voice and sureness in his gestures as he pointed to where things should go painted him as in his element, but Rhosyn could just make out the outlines of weapons through his sleeves. She had even watched him shove a small pistol into the waistband of his pants before they left the safehouse this morning.

They had to be prepared for anything.

Two figures emerged from the mist and approached Rhosyn. The shorter of the two peeked up from under a hat, revealing Contessa's determined face. The taller silhouette paused just behind her, and Rhosyn couldn't help staring at the king's face for just a moment.

Dressed in a worn, striped shirt and gray trousers, a cap pulled low over mussed hair, it was hard to believe he wasn't just another lower city worker. Still, Rhosyn's throat stuck with nerves as she went to speak.

"Grab that crate and take it to Ansel over there. He'll tell you where to put it." If the King took offense to being ordered around, he didn't show it, doing as Rhosyn ordered. Apparently, Contessa had prepared him for the situation well, and he understood how important it was for him to get on the train undetected.

The pair disappeared into the mist, and the circus performers made quick work of loading the remaining crates and barrels in an organized dance, speaking of how used to being on the road they were. Before the sun had risen a few more degrees, Ansel was at her elbow, jerking his head to tell her it was time to get moving.

As he stepped up into the rearmost car and offered a hand to help her in after him, she opened her mouth to admit she had never been on a train before. Instead, she snapped her mouth shut as he helped her into the passenger car. This was too important a moment to admit to her inexperience.

Still, he saw her hesitation and interlaced their fingers, even when she was inside, his thumb rubbing a soothing circle on her skin.

"Nate will catch Mr. Gower," he assured, voice soft enough to not be heard over the hustle and bustle of all the performers finding a place to wait out the journey. "Mr. Gower already accepted an invitation to go to the palace today to discuss his sponsorships and to bring his Talented servants with him. Once he has his entire Talented army at the palace, he won't be able to resist taking another crack at the king...or the decoy who will be stationed in his study at least."

Rhosyn nodded, but a lump still rose in her throat. "So many things could go wrong."

"And he's got the best possible team for thinking on his feet." Ansel's arm dragged up to her shoulder, warm against her skin that had been chilled by the morning air. "From what I heard of your friend Scarlett, I wouldn't bet against her in any situation. She'll be keeping a close eye on the situation from the shadows, especially given that her husband volunteered to be the decoy."

Ansel pulled Rhosyn further into the train car, toward the cabin Contessa and the king had disappeared into. "By this time tomorrow, it will all be over, and you'll be free to live your life."

Rhosyn tugged his arm, stopping them in the hallway, now sparsely populated as people had hurried to find their place on the train. Slowly, the steam engine rumbled to life, and they started to trundle down the tracks. The train whistle blew, and Rhosyn paused what she was going to say until she could be heard, the locomotive picking up speed beneath her.

"What is the life I'll be going back to?" Rhosyn asked.

"Well, you don't have to go back to the exact same life you had, if you don't want to." Ansel hesitated. "You have some...new opportunities now. Archer's Circus is always looking for more security and I—I would like to have you around."

Rhosyn swallowed. It was such a momentously huge decision—to leave behind the life she had built to follow this thief, who had plucked her heart out of her chest as easily as she picked purses from pockets. But maybe it didn't have to be. Maybe, for once she could make a decision based on her heart, instead of just volunteering herself to solve the biggest problem she could find.

She opened and closed her mouth, trying to find the words to say this to Ansel. Before she could speak, an echoing *thud* ran through the train car. Rhosyn threw her hand out to catch herself on the wall as it rocked side to side, nearly throwing her off balance. Ansel frowned as the lamps hanging from the ceiling swayed in response.

Contessa's head poked out of the compartment she had disappeared into with the King. "Did we hit something?"

"It sounded more like something hit us," Ansel said.

Rhosyn moved to ask what would hit a train, but he held up his hand to silence her, looking up at the ceiling. They all froze, when over the rattle of iron on rails came the tromping of footsteps on the roof.

Rhosyn's heart leapt into her throat. Contessa's eyes widened.

"Stay in there, and bar the door," Ansel ordered Contessa.

Then, he marched off down the hallway. Rhosyn wasted no time in hurrying after him, towards the door between cars. When he reached it, he slid it open and stepped onto the narrow metal platform between the two bobbing compartments. Rhosyn tried not to look down as she joined him, but the blur of rails flying by, just inches below her feet, made bile rise in her throat. She had enough fear about being thrown from a carriage, it hardly bore thinking about what would happen if she fell from a train.

With little hesitation, Ansel turned to the short ladder leading to the top of the car and began to climb. As his fingers reached the top rung, Rhosyn looked up and gulped. She might not have the advantage of his Talent for balance, or years of experience on a trapeze, but she would not let him face whatever was up there alone.

She scrambled up the ladder, knuckles white as she gripped each rung with all her might, following Ansel as quickly as possible. When she crested the edge to crouch on the swaying roof of the train, any fear of the climb was overshadowed by the sight that greeted her.

Four men in dark clothes crouched at the far end of the car. The silver of knives and pistols glinted in their hands, and while three of them were unfamiliar, the face of one stood stark in her mind.

The man she had stopped from killing the king, who had sunk through the floor as if it were water.

"They're Mr. Gower's men," she hissed, barely audible over rumble of the steam engine. "Our plan."

Somehow, they had been found out. Nate, Scarlett, and Benedict were waiting for an assassination attempt at the palace, but the real danger was here, on the train that was supposed to be their safe getaway.

Rhosyn didn't have time to wonder how Mr. Gower had discovered their deception, as the man in the rear of the pack stood and pointed towards her and Ansel.

"Get rid of them first, then find the King."

When he spoke, his voice had an odd echoing quality. Rhosyn found herself blinking in a moment of stunned stupor, when it hit her. It was similar to the effect of Paul's voice when he lulled somebody to sleep, but the tone underneath was different.

Hamish, the groom with the power of persuasion. These other Talented were under his thrall as they stood and began prowling towards her and Ansel.

"Don't hurt them if you can help it!" Rhosyn shouted to be heard over the train whistle, sounding again as they trundled towards the edge of the city. "They aren't in control of their actions."

Ansel stood as well, and knives slid into his hands. Rhosyn dipped her hands into her pockets and slipped on the pair of brass knuckles, which Nate had handed her with a heavy look before she set out.

Then, Ansel charged. She was hot on his heels, dashing across the roof of the train towards the attackers. Before Ansel clashed with the first one, he jumped, flipping over his head and landing on the far side as if gravity were just a suggestion. Before his opponent could get his bearings and turn, Ansel kicked out at the back of his leg, forcing him down to his knee.

As much as Rhosyn's heart jumped into her throat, she didn't have time to worry about Ansel, her own assailant facing off against her.

He swung first, broad and wide against her, as so many did when faced with a willowy woman. She ducked under his meaty arm before driving her shoulder up into his diaphragm. He stumbled back, lifting one hand palm out.

For a moment, Rhosyn was impressed with herself for forcing her opponent to surrender in one hit, until a ball of light started forming in the palm of his hand.

Name: Thomas Pemberton

Power: Combustion

The sponsorship paper flashed through Rhosyn's mind for a split second before she threw herself sideways to avoid the blast. A strangled yelp escaped her as the force of the explosion clipped her right shoulder, sending her spinning out of the way. Her feet slipped on the roof, slick with droplets of condensed steam. She scrambled for a foothold, but it was too late. She landed hard on her side, and the gentle slope of the roof sent her sliding towards the edge.

The world whirred by in a sickening mix of steel and smoke as she scrabbled for purchase on the hard surface with her fingernails. Her grasp caught on the edge of the roof as she reached it, but her momentum was too great to stop.

Her body swung over the edge, and for a sickening moment, the rails flew by beneath her dangling feet. Then, her weight caught with a jerk as she managed to hang on, body colliding with the side wall of the train car with enough force to make her eyes water. Her toes scraped against the surface, trying to get enough purchase to adjust her grip and climb back up.

Every sensation in her body screamed for attention, from the howling of wind in her ears to the sharp pinch in her shoulders as she tried to haul herself up. She tried not to think about the certain death, splattered on the cobblestones, if she were to lose her grip.

She had just managed to get enough traction to start inching up the wall when a shadow darkened her vision. She craned her neck upwards to find her opponent standing above her, looking down at where she dangled precariously on the edge of life and death.

Bile rose in her throat as he opened his palm, pointing his arm straight down at her.

He was going to blast her off the side of this train. She wasn't going to be able to protect Contessa like she promised Nate. And she wasn't going to be able to tell Ansel that she wanted more than anything to see the world with him and his circus.

Light began to coalesce in her attacker's palm, but a new bolt of fire shot through Rhosyn.

Their plan had gone to utter hell, but when had that ever stopped Rhosyn before? Chaos was where she thrived, and she could cause a little of her own.

Gritting her teeth, she peeled the fingers of her left hand free of their death grip, so she dangled by just her right. The train shook, nearly knocking her free, but she gritted her teeth as she dug her free hand into the inside of her jacket.

Praying that some of Ansel's skill had rubbed off on her, her fingers wrapped around the smooth handle of a knife. In the same motion that she drew it out, she threw it forward, aimed squarely between her attacker's eyes. The pommel struck him in the forehead, and he stumbled back. As he fell, his arm shot up, and his explosive burst shot straight into the sky, shimmering like a silver firework.

Rhosyn struggled to climb back up, but before she could get a hold of the lip of the roof once more, Ansel's worried face appeared above her. He grabbed her by the elbows, hauling her back onto the roof. As she tumbled over the edge, she landed on her knees, one of his arms wrapped firmly around her to keep her from toppling off once again. Adrenaline from her brush with death left her shaky, but ready for another brawl.

Her eyes darted around the roof, finding three thugs lying unconscious. One was conspicuously missing.

"The groom," she shouted, just as her eyes caught on a silhouette running towards the front of the train. His form was obscured by the steam billowing from the engine and wafting in thick clouds towards the back, and he disappeared into the thickening haze.

Without hesitation, Ansel hauled her to her feet and they took off after him. When they reached the end of the car, he didn't break his stride before leaping over the gap onto the next one. Rhosyn refused to falter as she followed, her mind offering her an image of how she did the same chasing the Hood over rooftops during their first encounter weeks ago.

She didn't waver then, and she wouldn't now.

Before they were halfway across the second car, Ansel skittered to a stop in front of her so suddenly she nearly crashed into his back. She was about to shout at him when she saw why.

The front of the train passed under a bridge, and as it did, several figures jumped off it, landing on the roof before them and cutting them off. Heavy thuds sounded behind Rhosyn, and she spun, finding at least half a dozen more adversaries there as well.

They were surrounded by Mr. Gower's army of Talented, and all Rhosyn had was her fists and a few spare knives.

She backed up a few steps, until her shoulders hit Ansel's. Standing back-to-back with him, she raised her fists. The thugs started closing in like a noose, and Rhosyn's heart hammered in her chest.

"Think we can take them?" Ansel asked over her shoulder.

Despite it all, fondness tugged like a string below Rhosyn's ribcage. If she was going to go down, then she wanted it to be fighting side by side with Ansel.

"You kidding?" she quipped back. "If I were you, I would be worried that there weren't enough for both of us."

"I'll be sure to leave plenty for you," Ansel promised. He shifted his weight against her back, ready to leap into action.

Rhosyn bared her teeth, a growl building in her throat, when a screech of horses and clatter of wheels drew her attention. An open-topped phaeton crashed along the street running parallel to the train tracks, and Rhosyn started as she recognized the man in the driver's seat.

She hardly had time to register Benedict's reckless driving before two figures jumped from the back of the speeding vehicle. A cloud of shadow fell over the train as wings of darkness formed around the figures, helping them sail onto the train.

Nate landed in a crouch beside her, the Beast in action. As knives sprang into his hands and he snarled, the thugs around them couldn't help but back up a few steps.

Scarlett stepped out of the dissolving shadows, the darkness clinging to her like morning dew. Her expression was no less feral than Nate's as black daggers of pure night formed in her hands, turning her into the dark shadow only referred to in feared whispers.

The hope that had sputtered in her chest flared again.

"Well, now there definitely aren't enough for all of us," Rhosyn mused dryly.

Scarlett leaped into action first, Rhosyn only a beat behind her. The satisfying thud of knuckles against flesh overtook her mind as she took on her first opponent. She struck his cheek first, before he landed a kick to her shin. The sharpness of the pain shooting up her leg honed her senses, and she threw a vicious uppercut. He crumpled like a sack of potatoes, but she spun to find her next enemy before he hit the ground.

Her gaze caught on Nate, currently warding off three enemies. Rhosyn's vision swam as one of them seemed to waver in and out of existence, as if the light around him bent out of his way. Lightning danced at the fingers of a second, while the third loomed large enough to eat Scarlett for breakfast.

Rhosyn darted forward to come to her aid, but Nate caught her eye and shook his head.

"Follow that one!" he shouted, jerking his head towards the front of the train. "Contessa—" he shouted before he was cut off by a bolt of electricity that forced him to dodge out of the way.

Rhosyn didn't wait to be told twice. She darted through the mayhem, following the shadow of the man who continued running towards the front of the train. She couldn't quite make out who it was, but her gut told her it was the groom. With the Talent of persuasion pulling all of these Talented into his thrall, Hamish was sure to be the leader of this whole operation.

Rhosyn pumped her arms, feet pounding against the metal roof as she gained ground on him. Up closer to the engine as they were, the smoke grew thicker, burning her eyes and nose as she panted for breath.

She could barely make out the groom's silhouette, forced to squint against the billowing haze and the roar of the engine in her ears. Then, he dropped down and disappeared, and Rhosyn skittered to a stop at the edge of a car.

He had gone inside the train.

Rhosyn hurried down the ladder, fear of falling far outweighed by the fear of what would happen if the groom made it to Contessa and the king before she did. She burst inside to find that the chaos in the train was nearly as dense as the pandemonium outside.

Some of Mr. Gower's Talented army had managed to get into the cars, but the circus performers seemed to share Ansel's fighting spirit. One armed man was cowering on his knees, arms over his head and two men pummeled him with juggling batons. Rhosyn tore her eyes away from the spectacle to search for the groom, only to find him slipping through the door at the far end of the hall, back towards where the king was.

Rhosyn pushed through the mayhem, ducking around a clown armed with a pie, which he enthusiastically smashed into the face of another of Mr. Gower's thugs. She crashed through the car, following the groom into the next. In this one, one of the Talented assassins had been backed into a corner by a snarling lion, while the lion tamer stood next to him with folded arms in satisfaction.

She gained on the groom, but he was still half a car in front of her when he slipped through the door to the train car containing Contessa and the king. Rhosyn shoved through as fast as she could, lungs burning and heart hammering.

The door slammed open as she shouldered through it, only to find the hallway...empty.

Rhosyn froze, head whipping back and forth to locate the missing groom.

A hand landed on the back of her neck, and her shoulders hunched up.

"Stop."

The word rung through the air with crushing weight and settled into Rhosyn's limbs like lead. She struggled, but it was as if the connection between her brain and body had been cut, leaving her dangling like an abandoned marionette.

A rough chuckle sounded behind her, grating against her skin like stone.

"Usually it takes me weeks of building influence over somebody to be able to command them with my Talent so thoroughly. But if somebody lets their guard down enough to let me touch them, skin to skin, well..." Hamish chuckled again, Rhosyn's current helplessness clearly illustrating his meaning. "It's how I got one of the King's Guard to tell me where he had gone when I suspected a trap."

"Why are you doing this?" Rhosyn growled, seemingly still capable of speaking, despite being otherwise immobilized.

"Why shouldn't I?" he spat. "King Byron is like any other powerful man, willing to step on the rest of us to maintain control."

"You don't have to do this," Rhosyn insisted, voice taking on a pleading edge. "Whatever Mr. Gower has told you, it doesn't have to be this way. King Byron ended the Inquiries... You're safe now."

"I'll never be safe while my Talent makes me useful," Hamish growled, but his voice broke on the last word. "Mr. Gower...he has my son somewhere. I don't know where, but if I fail, he'll hurt him."

Rhosyn's heart sank. Another parent and child separated by a Talent. As much as her heart stuttered in sympathy though, she fought against his mental hold. If he succeeded, the Inquiries would start anew, and many more children would be ripped from their parents.

"I can help you," Rhosyn insisted. Her fingers started to wiggle, as if her paralysis eased, but then his grip tightened at the nape of her neck once more. She went rigid.

"Oh, you will. You're going to kill King Byron for me. You were already blamed for the last attempt, and I can't very well get my son back if I'm in jail."

His words doused Rhosyn in cold like ice. She tried to shout, but her voice seemed taken from her now too.

"Go on," he urged. "Knock on the compartment door. Your friend will recognize you and let you in. Then one slice with one of your knives, and it'll all be over."

His grasp on her nape loosened, but the claws that gripped her mind only dug in further. Rhosyn's feet took one step forward, then another. It was the sensation of being in a dream, her unconscious mind taking charge and leading her down a perilous path while her conscious self screamed helplessly from the sidelines. But there would be no waking from this dream. Not until the King's blood stained her already dirty hands.

Her arm raised, knuckles poised to knock on the entrance to the compartment holding Contessa and King Byron.

A crash interrupted her actions. She managed to turn her head to see Ansel crash into the car from the same direction she had come, although she couldn't move away from her position. Ansel froze in the doorway, panting heavily as his gaze darted over the scene in front of him, rapidly cataloging the situation.

"Ah, the infamous Hood, I presume. You've caused too many problems already," Hamish mused. "I suppose I can knock out two birds with one stone here. Kill him first."

Horror rose in Rhosyn's throat, a palpable thing making her unable to draw breath. Still, her hands slid into her sleeves, the knives within settling on her palms with the weight of finality. Rhosyn might not be the knife fighter Nate was, but she had brawled with Ansel enough times to know that in a fair fight, his odds were slim. If he were holding back for fear of hurting her... Rhosyn could only hope help came in time.

Ansel raised his hands, but Rhosyn advanced on him as if pulled forward by a string. With her eyes, she begged him to arm himself—to grab his blades before she was forced to drive her own into his flesh.

She raised her arm, and in the instant before it came down, silver flashed in his hand. He grabbed his knife just in time to catch her blow on the hilt of his weapon. In a flurry, Rhosyn disengaged. Rhosyn swung again and again, but Ansel only dodged, making no attacks of his own.

Her mouth was not under her control enough to form words, but she managed to squeeze out a choked sob. She hoped it conveyed all that her voice couldn't say right now.

Fight back. Please. I'd rather die here than have to watch myself kill you.

When she raised her arm next, Ansel took his shot. A blade *thunked* into the wall behind her. As her arm swung forward, she was jerked back, Ansel's knife pinning her to the wall by her sleeve—just as he had the first time they'd met.

Another *thunk*, and her other arm was pinned.

"Break free! Kill him!" the groom shouted, his voice clawing into her mind as she started to struggle against her restraints.

Ansel rounded on him, advancing when a ripping split the air as Rhosyn's sleeve gave way. To her horror, she brought the blade in her hand to her own throat.

"Stop," the groom commanded Ansel. Hamish's voice was his own, with no Talent behind it, but he didn't need it. Ansel froze as Rhosyn's movement caught his eye.

"If you attack me, I'll have her kill herself," the groom announced triumphantly.

Ansel's gaze met hers, his deep emerald gaze pleading. Her hand trembled, against her throat, the tip of the knife scratching the delicate skin there. A warm rivulet of blood trickled down to pool in the hollow of her collarbone. The sensation did something to cut through the odd haze of her mind.

"Rhosyn."

Ansel had said her name many times before. To get her attention. In frustration when she challenged him. At the peak of his pleasure.

But this was different. This was both a prayer and a plea. Full of love and a promise that Rhosyn didn't want: that he wouldn't hurt her even to save himself.

It struck something within her, the blow forming cracks in the stone grasp around her mind. She squirmed physically, her muscles twitching in response to her commands, although not yet fully responding.

"End this," the groom growled.

His orders pulled at her muscles, but Rhosyn knew now she could break free. She had to.

An image flew to her mind unbidden. The last assassin's eyes clearing of their odd haze as the chandelier knocked him squarely in the forehead. A blow to the head had freed him of the grip of the groom's Talent.

If Rhosyn knew how to do anything, it was take a hit.

With an almighty roar, she lunged forward, ripping her sleeve free and leaping at Ansel. The groom still compelled her to fight him, but she used the foothold of control she had to lead with her head.

Her forehead connected with Ansel's with a resounding crack. They both stumbled back, Rhosyn hitting the wall behind her and sliding to the ground. The groom screamed at her to get up. To kill Ansel.

But Rhosyn didn't move.

Her mind was free.

Her vision swam and her limbs flailed uncoordinatedly as she tried to recover from the blow to her head. Her vision cleared and she looked up, only for her heart to stutter once again.

The groom had drawn a pistol from his coat, and she now stared down the barrel of it.

"I'll have to do this the hard way then," he growled.

Rhosyn stiffened as a bang split the air, but no pain bloomed in her chest. Instead, the groom's face smoothed in shock. He wavered where he stood, crimson blooming across his chest.

He looked down at the spreading stain, but no horror crossed his expression. Instead, his eyes filled with something like relief.

"It's over then."

That was all he said before he toppled sideways, dead before he hit the ground. Behind him sat Ansel, back propped against the wall as he held a small pistol in a shaking hand. Rhosyn met his gaze over a bloody and already horrendously purple nose.

The gun fell from his hand, and Rhosyn was on him before it clattered to the ground. Blood dripped over his lips, streaming from a crooked nose, clearly broken by Rhosyn's inelegant attack. But his eyes were full of life, and his arms were warm and solid as he wrapped her in them.

She sat there in his embrace, and she wasn't sure if the shaking in her limbs was from the rumbling of the train or the trembling relief running through her body.

"You saved me," she murmured into his chest.

He nuzzled into her hair, smearing blood all over it, but she didn't care. "You did that yourself. You fought tooth and nail, like you always do. And you won."

They inhaled each other's presence in silence for a moment, only for it to be broken by the creak of a door sliding open.

Rhosyn raised her head to find Contessa, standing in the doorway, a look of utmost relief on her face. If Contessa's Talent told her it was safe to come out, then the fight must be over.

Contessa nodded at the question in Rhosyn's eyes. "We're safe now."

Chapter Sixteen

Rhosyn stared down the line of her friends and family, pride blooming in her chest. To her right stood Contessa, resplendent in silver silk, although when she looked closely, she could see it wasn't nipped in as close at the waist as usual. Nate hovered off her shoulder, unable to look away from his wife, even as King Byron stood before his throne, thanking them for serving King and Country.

Rhosyn snuck a glance to her left, looking past Ansel to Scarlett and Benedict. She nearly chuckled at the pair they made, Benedict's charming smile a perfect contrast to Scarlett's perpetual scowling at all the pomp, made even fiercer by the knot of scar tissue on the side of her head where one of her ears should be.

Ansel's shoulder bumped against hers, and he shot her an amused glance as if saying to her, "You only get inducted into the Royal Order once."

Rhosyn returned her attention to the King's words, but as he thanked each of them for their fearless actions to foil the plot against the crown, her mind kept drifting to Ansel's warmth at her side.

The week following the fight on the train had been a whirlwind, but Ansel stood by her through it all. Despite the bandage on his nose and the dark circles of bruises under his eyes, he sat with her through Mr.

Gower's trial, squeezing her hand before she took the stand to testify against him.

Although Rhosyn had put many criminals behind bars in her life, no guilty verdict had given her as much satisfaction as Mr. Gower's. As they dragged him away, he hissed and spat that King Byron had ruined this city by allowing the Talented to run free—that he should be removed from power for ending the Inquiries.

As the Royal Police hauled him past the box where Contessa sat, he had momentarily pulled free to spit in her face.

"You're no better than your father," he snarled, turning purple under his impressive mustache.

Everybody surrounding Contessa froze at that, and Nate nearly leaped out of the box and strangled Mr. Gower where he stood. But Contessa had stayed him with a hand on his wrist. Instead, Contessa stood and stalked to the front of the box, somehow towering over him despite her slight stature, as always, her poise making her larger than life.

"I am *not* my father, and I know this because I am willing to change course when something I've done is being used for evil. My father let the Inquiries, which were meant to protect his people, warp London into a place of hatred and fear. You tried to abuse the Talented through their sponsorships, but I won't let the work I've done in protection of the city be twisted into something violent and hateful. I *will* stand up for what is right, and I won't let you abuse the Talented of this city any longer."

She watched with ice in her gaze as he was dragged off to prison, where he would await execution for high treason. Anybody who heard of the display at the trial would think twice before challenging the king's advisor and bodyguard.

A search of Mr. Gower's study had also uncovered his co-conspirators, and although more trials would come, the evidence would allow King Byron to rip out the dissent against his support for the Talented by the roots. At last, the future of the Talented in London seemed bright. The King had even pardoned all the Talented Mr. Gower had sponsored for their involvement in the assassination, knowing they hadn't acted of their own free will. When the groom died, it was as if they had woken up from a trance, and they all immediately dropped their weapons and surrendered.

Scarlett had used her network of whispers to track down the groom's son at a hidden house in the country and bring him back to the city. Rhosyn sat in Nate's old office next to Contessa as she drew up papers for him to be adopted to a couple who wanted nothing more than to raise a child.

Her eyes were glassy as she stamped the paper with the King's seal.

"I hope this is the last orphan of Talented parents."

Rhosyn squeezed her friend's hand and sat with her late into the night.

In the past week, Rhosyn had also not returned to her rented room, staying in Ansel's bed with him at the Foxes' safe house. They didn't need to hide anymore, given that King Byron had personally exonerated them of any crimes, given their involvement in saving him. Still, she didn't feel like she could go back to her old room and her old life like nothing had changed.

Not to mention, knowing that time in bed meant being wrapped in Ansel's arms helped her get more sleep than she ever had in the past.

Now, she puffed out her chest proudly as King Byron pinned a medal to her jacket, smiling at her kindly before moving on to do the same to

Ansel. She had come a long way from a rough and tumble Lion to having bestowed upon her the highest personal honor that royalty could award.

The audience behind them roared, and as the six of them turned to smile at the crowd, Ansel slipped his hand in hers. He didn't let go even as they walked down into the audience to receive their congratulations.

So many people shook Rhosyn's hand and patted her on the back that she stopped recognizing faces or remembering names until a familiar voice drew her from the haze of celebration.

"Officer Walsh." Joseph stuck out a hand.

Hesitantly, Rhosyn took it, but his smile was warm as he clasped it back.

"You don't have to look at me like I'm going to discipline you. I'm proud," he admitted.

"You are?" Rhosyn asked. She may have saved the King's life, but she certainly hadn't been following protocol when she did it.

He smiled, something softer and less tired in his gaze than it had been the last time she had been in his office. Rhosyn briefly wondered if it had something to do with the way Benedict's sister, Lottie, had been hanging on his elbow during the ceremony.

"You know, when I inherited the Royal Police, they may have followed the law, but they certainly weren't good. Even though something isn't perfect, and may never be, doesn't mean it isn't worth fighting to make it better. And you always fight to make things better," Joseph smiled wryly, "even if you tend to break a few rules along the way."

"Well, thank you," Rhosyn struggled for words. "I didn't think you'd want me back on the force after the things I did."

"I would always want to have somebody like you in my corner, but I think you would be whether you wear a uniform or not," Joseph admitted. "The question is, do you want to come back to the Royal Police? It would seem to me you might be looking for a...change in pace."

A smile crept across Rhosyn's face as she turned to look at Ansel—he was eyeing her curiously. Mischief twinkled in his eyes as her smile grew into an unrestrained grin.

"I've always wanted to run away and join the circus."

Epilogue

Even after more than a year, the sparkling lights of Archer's Circus still dazzled Rhosyn. Every time they stopped in a new town, she felt like one of the visitors drinking in the spectacle for the first time. The sweet warmth of roasted nuts and spun sugar made even the air seem magical. At night, the flickering lamplight gave the whole place an enchanted quality, as if magic and adventure might lurk around any corner.

And at Archer's Circus, it did.

Tonight's performance, though, was particularly electrifying. They were back in London after touring most of Europe, and Rhosyn had convinced Ansel to celebrate the occasion by performing with his Merry Men.

He hadn't had time to perform before, when he was so busy running the business side of the circus and leading a secret Talented smuggling train. Now, though, with Rhosyn helping him, he had some time to spare for acrobatics.

Although, they still managed to find trouble—legal and otherwise—in almost every city they visited.

Rhosyn peeked out from her post backstage to the box where their most honored guests sat. She smiled at the sight of Contessa and Nate, baby Eliza, who was named after Contessa's mother, perched happily on Nate's lap. The child watched with wide eyes as the colorful acrobats flew and arced through the air, gravity having loosened its hold in the confines of this tent.

Even Scarlett was wide eyed with wonder, leaning into Benedict, who wrapped an arm around her obligingly. Kristoff and Gregor sat in the back of the box, but based on the way Gregor blushed after Kristoff whispered something in his ear, they were paying far less attention.

The sight of them all warmed her heart. She loved being on the road with Ansel, and each homecoming was sweeter knowing she had a family to come back to.

Rhosyn ripped her eyes away from her friends in the box, and she turned her attention to the performers on stage. As always, the Merry Men were consummate performers, but her gaze fixed itself on Ansel as he flipped and twisted through the air.

Her eyes tracked him through every improbable maneuver until at last he landed on the stage and the audience exploded in wild cheers. He bowed several times at their appreciation before ducking behind the curtain to the backstage area.

Rhosyn jumped on him in a heartbeat, never able to contain herself after watching him perform—something that had played no small role in Ansel's eagerness to appear regularly with the Merry Men once more.

He caught her easily as she jumped into his arms, and the rest of the acrobats groaned and chuckled good-naturedly.

She kissed him soundly, not discouraged in the slightest by the thin sheen of sweat coating his skin, but he pulled away in favor of nipping her earlobe.

"What have I told you about being patient?" he murmured, his voice taking on the deep, teasing timbre that made her shiver.

"You know I'm not very good at being patient," she quipped, but he just smiled and kissed her again before putting her down.

"Then it's a good thing I have all the time in the world to work on that."

As always, Rhosyn couldn't wait.

Not ready to leave the world of The Talented Fairy Tales? Get a FREE short story featuring Gregor and Kristoff's first meeting when you sign up for S.C. Grayson's author newsletter using the QR code below!

Also by S.C. Grayson

THE TALENTED FAIRY TALES

Beauty and the Blade

Little Red Shadow

The Hood and his Thief

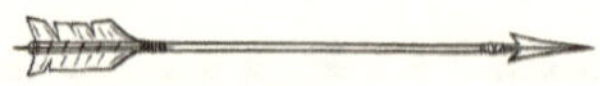

THE BALLAN DESERT TRILOGY

Blood of the Sands

Crown of the Dunes

Heart of the Desert

Acknowledgements

Staring at the book that marks the completion of my first full series is surreal, and I know I wouldn't be here without an incredible amount of support. First, a huge thank you to the group of authors that has become my cheering section. I wouldn't be where I am without the help of each and every Discordant Owl. A special shout out goes to Lily, for being the author bestie I never knew I needed.

I would be remiss not to acknowledge my amazing family. Without their support in every aspect of my life, I wouldn't have even put my first words on paper, let alone be completing my first series. I also want to offer all the thanks in the world to my husband, Rhys, who is always the first to tell me to *"Do the thing"* whenever I'm facing down a goal that scares me.

And most importantly, thank you to my readers, who have stuck by me through book one and encouraged me to continue the journey of The Talented Fairy Tales. This one is for you.

About the author

S.C. Grayson writes fantasy and paranormal romance filled with dangerous magic, slow-burn tension, and heroines who refuse to stay in their place. She is the author of several gaslamp fairytale retellings, as well as *The Ballan Desert*, an epic fantasy romance series set among nomadic clans in a brutal magical desert. Across her worlds, she delights in complicated loyalties, immersive world building, and romances built on emotional connections that still bring the heat.

When she is not sitting in a local coffee shop writing and drinking an iced americano, Grayson is a professor and nurse researcher, focusing her efforts on breast cancer genetics. She lives in Chicago with her loving husband and their two cats, who enjoy contributing to her work by walking across her keyboard at inopportune moments (the cats, not the husband).

www.scgrayson.com